AN HEIRESS'S GUIDE TO DEATH AND DIAMONDS

KRISTEN BIRD

Storm

ALSO BY KRISTEN BIRD

Dakota Green

A Beauty Queen's Guide to Murder and Mayhem

A Bride's Guide to Happiness and Homicide

The Night She Went Missing

I Love It When You Lie

Watch It Burn

For Sadie, the artist.
Draw us a beautiful world.

PART I

You are invited to
the Class of 2015 Reunion Party
at the Rose Palace *

Friday, October 24, 2025 at 7:30 p.m.
following the homecoming game
at the Aubergine High School field

Come cheer on Aubergine's Fighting Farmers as they take on
Mount Cedar's Tigers!

* Hosted by Savilla Finch

ONE

Less than an hour before one of my former classmates dropped dead on the dance floor, I was counting down the minutes until I could leave my ten-year high school reunion.

Taylor Swift's "Bad Blood" sounded through the speakers in the Primrose Ballroom at the Rose Palace as I took another sip of my carbonated water with lime. The singer wasn't Swift though; it was Jemma Jenkins, in between off-off-Broadway productions. She'd been hired this evening as the lead for the live band at the Aubergine High School Reunion.

Former beauty pageant contestant Jemma Jenkins was impressive up there, belting out the decade-old song while my classmates danced and colorful lights flashed in time to the beat, transforming the stately ballroom into something that looked more like a school gym. I had the sense of worlds colliding: twenty-eight-year-old me merging with my eighteen-year-old self.

For the décor, my best friend Lacy had leaned into the rose motif of the estate as well as the Halloween season. A strange combo, but she'd delivered—and on a budget. I'd been surprised that Savilla Finch, now the official owner of the sprawling Rose

Palace, knew the word "budget," but the end result was gourds and pumpkins at every table and giant paper-mache marigolds, roses, and tulips hanging from the vaulted ceiling until they hovered nine feet off the ground. Branches and autumn leaves lined the stage, and swaths of dark green tulle were interspersed with white lights, creating the effect of a field of wildflowers filled with fireflies.

Seventy-two of us had graduated ten years ago, and I would estimate, based on the ratio of people on the dance floor to the number of spiked punch bowls, about fifty of us had returned for the reunion party at the Rose Palace.

"Wine?" A man's voice spoke beside me, and I looked up from where I was seated to see Joe Larson.

Joe was the guy who'd dropped out of college after one semester—or been kicked out, it was unclear—and he made a living by doing odd jobs around town. He'd been a security guard at the pageant this summer, though that hadn't prevented a dead body from turning up, and he was catering the shindig tonight. After the centennial pageant had been put on hiatus, Aunt DeeDee, former queen and long-time coordinator, had flailed, wondering what to do with her life for all of a week before deciding to give her time to helping young Aubergine entrepreneurs. As one of her projects, she'd taken security guard Joe under her wing, and she was teaching him the ropes of small business ownership.

"Aren't you supposed to be in the kitchen?" I asked, looking around for Aunt DeeDee. *He'd better not be shirking his duties and making her do all the grunt work.*

"Nice to see you too," he said, with a tight grin. "The bartender called in sick last minute, so after working in the kitchen all day with your aunt, I'm on duty." He extended the tray of drinks he was holding. "Wine? Or the featured drink? It's called an Aubergine Thresher. One part vodka, one part gin, two parts grape soda, and a sprig of rhubarb."

"That sounds disgusting."

Joe shrugged as if it wasn't his decision and kept the tray steady in front of me. I relented and selected the red wine.

I held up the plastic cup. "No crystal goblet?"

"Not tonight, I'm afraid." Joe leaned forward, conspiratorially. "Brett's footing half the bill for this party, and he's cheap, that son of a bitch. Wouldn't even spring for name-brand Fanta."

Joe wasn't wrong to call him that, but I couldn't tell if he meant it as a term of endearment or condemnation. His eyes trailed to Brett Brinkley, the man of the hour who was laughing and flirting and dancing like a man who'd fulfilled his senior class prediction of Mr. Most Likely to Succeed. There was something in Joe's expression that I couldn't quite read. Bitterness? Envy? Disdain? Brett had become a household name after winning a reality dating show, and I did recall hearing someone say at a graduation party ages ago that Joe wanted to be an actor. Perhaps he was jealous of our former classmate's success.

He raised an eyebrow before continuing to circulate.

I leaned forward, perching my chin on the base of my palm. One hour, that's what I'd promised Lacy. Then, I could flee the ballroom and meet Charlie after his shift. I only had three days in town, hardly enough time to see the people I loved, attend Mr. Finch's will reading, and figure out what I would do after finishing vet school. This reunion was the lowest priority on my list.

My watch's second hand was barely moving—forty-one minutes to go. I looked around the room and noticed a sign hanging above the stage. It read *Let's Hear You Scream, Class of 2015* and featured a caricature of our school's farmer mascot. Decades ago the mascot had been an actual eggplant—the crop from which Aubergine once got its name—so, all things considered, an agricultural icon holding a pitchfork was a move in the less phallic direction.

Surveying my half-drunk peers on the dance floor was a good distraction at first, but it made me realize that, even after ten years, I still cared what the people here tonight thought about me. I could almost hear former Homecoming Queen Becky Jones asking me what I was doing now and me responding, *Sometimes I get to express a dog's anal gland.*

A few yards in front of me was Lacy, rocking out with her high school sweetheart while a professional camera crew captured them from various angles. I'd heard that Brett was trying to sell a new show about life with the woman he'd wooed in front of a national audience—but that's not what the cameras were currently filming.

Lacy's boyfriend Anton stood at the edge of the dance floor watching her dance far too close to Brett Brinkley.

After a minute or two, the upbeat song ended, and Lacy, glistening, came over with a drink and a handful of gummy bears that she'd swiped from the abundant snack table laden with candy corn, Mike & Ikes, cherry sours, and M&Ms of every kind. Catered canapés and crudités were also circling the room, but we both preferred the cheap, sugary stuff. She pasted on a smile that didn't quite reach her eyes and offered the handful to me. I picked out the yellow and green bears and popped them in my mouth.

A new song began to play, one I vaguely recognized. Cheers went up around the room, and people started lifting hands in Brett's direction, singing along.

"What song is this?" I shouted into Lacy's ear.

"'The One That Got Away,'" Lacy called back, eyebrows knit in concern. "Brett recorded it. Remember?"

I listened for a few more seconds, and the melody started to come back to me. I even recalled having a lively discussion one time with Lacy about whether or not the popular song was about her. I certainly hoped not. "Is this the one that goes, 'She was the hottie who made me wanna be naughty?'"

"That's the OG version. I heard he had to change the lyrics to get more radio play. Apparently his manager thought the line might be too sexist, and that he should go for a more brooding, wholesome kind of love song. Listen." Lacy pointed a finger in the air, and instead of the lyrics I'd just quoted, Brett's voice crooned, "She was the mind who made me wanna find... myself."

"Great rhyme," I said, with a hint of sarcasm.

"Did you see his girlfriend?" Lacy asked as she nodded toward the other side of the dance floor.

I followed the direction of her eyes to where Savilla, wearing a belted, one-shoulder, deep purple midi dress and matching ankle boots, stood speaking to a fashionably dressed woman in tight black pants, a fuzzy gray jacket, and stilettos. Even I, who considered most of pop culture a mindless wasteland, had recognized her immediately when I'd arrived tonight. At the door, Savilla had introduced the two of us, and we'd all exchanged a few sentences of pleasantries before I'd excused myself to find my table and begin the countdown.

I hadn't needed the introduction because Brett's girlfriend was Presley Lombardi, the contestant who'd won his heart on *Small Town, Big Romance* two years ago. I still remembered the ridiculous teaser that was played and replayed and quoted all over town the summer before it had aired:

You've loved and hated *The Bachelor*. You've binged every season of *Love Is Blind*. Coming this August, you'll fall in love all over again with *Small Town, Big Romance*, a new reality show that will test whether opposites really do attract and whether or not you can put a price on love.

Before the show aired, Presley had already run with the New York elite, but she'd become ultra-famous after the show when a sex tape of the two of them, everything laid bare, had been released online.

Since then, Presley had started her own fragrance line, performed cameos in a few films, opened a New York restaurant in her name, and somehow put up with Brett Brinkley, which was likely more doable because the two of them seemed to lead separate lives, him living on the West Coast and pursuing his acting career while she mostly stayed on the opposite side of the country. Unfortunately, I knew this last part because I'd seen a tabloid headline about them having separate residences and questioning whether a breakup was imminent. Not that I actually cared.

Anton approached from the left. I gestured toward him as I said to Lacy, "I think some guy is looking for you."

I sensed Lacy stiffen slightly as Anton placed a kiss on her cheek and his arm curved around the small of her back. They were cute together, her polished persona parallel to his rugged Texan vibe, but her reluctant smile concerned me. Lacy was nervous about something.

"I saw you on the dance floor," he called above the music. "Aren't you supposed to be working this thing?"

Anton sounded so much like me that I sometimes teased Lacy about him being me in male form. No wonder they worked well together—although, right now, I couldn't tell if he was annoyed or simply curious.

Lacy shrugged off his question. "My job is to make sure everyone has a good time. That includes me."

"Just be careful, Lace," Anton said. He tilted his head toward Brett Brinkley and frowned. "Especially around that guy. He looked like he was ready to lean into your neck and take a bite."

"I know how to handle a man who bites," Lacy said with a side eye, and Anton laughed, whatever tension I'd imagined between them broken momentarily.

But then a new song started, this one Ed Sheeran's "Thinking Out Loud," and Brett came and stole Lacy away for a slow dance. Immediately, the crackle in the air was back, and Anton excused himself, stalking toward the bar.

I watched people pretending to have—or perhaps actually having—a good time while I debated whether or not I could break the promise I'd made to be social. I checked my phone. Screw it. Twenty-four minutes to go, and I was calling it. I was going home, putting on my sweatpants and an old T-shirt, and eating brownie batter until Charlie arrived to have his way with me.

I took one last swig from my cup of wine, but as I turned to go, Jemma Jenkins abruptly stopped singing and knocked over her microphone. I spun around to see her pointing at Brett in the middle of the ballroom. Lacy was right behind him, receding into the darkness at the edge of the dance floor.

The room went silent except for the sound of the speaker system trying to recalibrate itself for a handful of seconds that, to my ears at least, lasted an eternity. A shadowed figure ran to the back and spoke to the sound guy, who fixed the problem. Just as the feedback ended, the sound of coughing began.

Brett Brinkley was grabbing—no, clawing—at his throat as if an invisible string had been tied around his neck. He was emitting a new noise, a kind of gurgling that quickly became a violent spewing. He hunched forward and fell to the center of the dance floor, where the crowd had parted around him.

Suddenly, it was as if a spotlight had been pointed straight on his sprawling figure.

Behind the bar Joe Larson dropped the bottle he'd been holding, and glass broke across the diamond designs on the marble. He hurried toward Brett, propping him up enough to attempt the Heimlich maneuver, thrusting into his abdomen in steady pulses.

When that didn't work, Joe dropped Brett on the ground

and started yelling, "Is there a doctor? Does anyone know CPR?"

Out of the class of 2015, there wasn't a single medical professional in the room—except me, but this wasn't a horse with a hernia. Seconds passed, and no one else stepped forward. It had to be me.

"Call 911," I told Lacy as I rushed to the center of the dance floor and fell to my knees. I sprang into action as Presley Lombardi came closer to the now-unconscious man's side.

I quickly checked for a pulse, and once satisfied he was still alive, I opened Brett's jaw and stuck my fingers inside, too focused on the job to be disgusted by the scent of alcohol and the wetness coating my hand. I checked the airway to clear it, but from what I could tell, nothing was blocking his throat.

I put my left hand on top of my right in the center of his chest and squared my shoulders over his body. As I began to press down to the disco beat of "Stayin' Alive," Brett's chest popped, and even though I knew to possibly expect this, the sensation of breaking bones and cartilage in his rib cage wasn't a pleasant one.

After thirty compressions, I tilted back his head, pinched his nose, and breathed deeply into his mouth. From this angle I could see tiny capillaries that had burst along his neck. He had red indentations from clawing at his own throat, and I swear that it looked like he'd been strangling himself.

I didn't have time to consider the reasons because, for now, I could only focus on trying to save him.

I continued this way for four rounds, but my arms were already tiring.

"Can anyone help?" I called out.

Within seconds, a woman I recognized as having been one of the two camera operators was on the floor ready to switch off with me, dropping a fuzzy boom mic as she knelt down.

"I can do it," she said, her hands shaking as she extended them.

"Get in place, and you can take over after this set. Got it?"

The camerawoman nodded and I counted off the compressions.

Time warped as we worked, glacially slow yet dizzyingly fast. My arms burned as she and I traded places, Brett's ribs resisting beneath our hands while Lacy's voice trembled into the phone. The sounds and sights blurred together, near and far all at once.

When the medics arrived, they moved us aside and worked with practiced efficiency—oxygen, defibrillator, preparation to intubate.

After several minutes the head medic checked his watch and bit his lip, finally shaking his head. Fifteen minutes had passed since Brett's last breath. We'd failed.

Brett Brinkley—former high school golden boy, one-hit wonder, reality TV star—lay dead on the dance floor at our ten-year reunion. The party was over in more ways than one.

TWO

I stared at my phone, willing Charlie to respond to my texts and calls.

Emergency at the Rose Palace.

Need you immediately.

But the screen remained dark. Maybe he was already on his way, hurrying here to perform his duty as sheriff, but that didn't stop me from begging him to appear.

The reunion's festive atmosphere had faded with Brett's last breath. Gone were the pulsing lights and pounding music. They'd been replaced by the harsh glare of chandeliers and hushed whispers. My shocked classmates huddled in clusters, their faces blurring together as they speculated about what had just happened, about how someone who'd been dancing only minutes before now lay dead on the ballroom floor.

Living, Brett's entire aura had exuded the relaxed confidence of the wealthy, which was far from his actual lower-middle-class upbringing. His mom had been a teller at the local bank and his dad had worked for the coal mines. It was an inside-outside job, meaning that he'd rarely had to descend into the earth, and he'd earned only nominal pay.

Brett Brinkley had escaped Aubergine and made it big, slipping easily into his new persona. Even when I'd given him CPR, I'd noticed that he must've spent money on personal trainers, what with his chiseled pecs and his firm biceps bursting from the sleeves of his designer shirt. His neck and jaw were thick, and while to me he was still completely unattractive, I could see why he'd drawn the eyes of television viewers two years earlier.

I was thinking that it's an awful, harrowing experience, watching someone die, particularly when you were the one trying to save them, when I felt a hand on my shoulder. I looked up to see Jemma standing there, her stage makeup garish in the overhead light.

"This place is, for real, cursed. Has to be," Jemma said with arms crossed in front of her. Even though we hadn't spoken in months—not since I'd beat her out for the title of Rose Palace Queen—aside from sending a few texts and memes, she acted as if we were old friends picking up on a recent chat.

The camerawoman who'd helped me with CPR was nearby and overheard Jemma's musings. Her expression seemed just as lost as I felt, which meant she was likely grateful for the distraction of conversation, even if it was with strangers.

"Is this place cursed?" The woman's eyes were wide and her throat scratchy. "Because Presley totally believes in those things." She glanced in the direction of Brett's girlfriend, who sat at a table on the other side of the ballroom, tears streaming from her eyes, her cheeks splotchy from crying. Joe Larson sat across from Presley Lombardi, watching her intensely. "For the last episode of their new series, she and Brett visited a psychic." The woman let out a shuddering breath. "The lady told Presley that 'hard times lay ahead.'" She put the last few words in air quotes. "I had no idea that meant..." She couldn't finish the words as she started crying.

To me, the prediction sounded more like it had come from a fortune cookie than a fortune teller, but I wasn't about to correct her.

"I'm Dakota Green," I said, not putting out my hand. It seemed pointless to introduce myself in the traditional way after we'd both knelt side by side, trying and failing to save a man's life.

"Mina Davis," the camerawoman responded.

"Mina, thanks for helping... earlier... out there." There wasn't a good way to communicate the magnitude of what we'd attempted and failed to do. I motioned to the dance floor, and her eyes once again filled with tears that she wiped with the back of her arm. The second person in the camera crew came to her side.

"This is Lee Frank," Mina said by way of introduction. The man was a couple of decades older and had the deep frown lines to prove it.

Lee gave us a slight nod, but the sour expression he wore didn't change as he tugged at Mina's sleeve. "There's something you should see."

"Right now?" She glanced from Jemma to me as if she'd much rather stay there with us.

He nodded, that same solemn look on his face.

"All right, but if I need to answer any questions from the medics, the police, the"—she stumbled on the final word—"the coroner, I'll be nearby." She motioned to the corner of the ballroom as Lee yanked her away, knuckles white. I didn't like that at all.

"He seems delightful," Jemma said drily. She turned in the direction of Brett's body, now covered by a sheet. "God, what are the odds? Two men dead at The Rose, only a handful of months apart."

"And we were here for both," I mumbled, my stomach flipping.

This past summer I'd helped solve the murder of the owner of the Rose Palace, Mr. Frederick Finch. The man who I'd also discovered was my biological father. At least this tragedy seemed less complicated, unless… A creeping uncertainty nagged at me. Something about the way Brett's body had looked up close wouldn't let me call this a straightforward death.

People were assembled into cliques just like we'd been in high school, except now it was the exhausted moms who'd left infants and toddlers at home, the guys who'd already had more than enough to drink, the singles who'd been magnetically drawn to one another, and the couples who were offering each other comforting embraces.

I spotted Lacy, her head burrowed into Anton's shoulder as she cried. I wanted to go to her, but my legs were heavy and my mind cloudy. Thankfully, at that moment Charlie stepped into the ballroom, and I got to my feet and started toward him as if propelled by a motor.

He met me in the middle, and as the familiar scent of his aftershave hit me—cedar and citrus—my throat clenched with unshed tears.

"I'm so glad you're here," I whispered.

"Me too." His eyes traveled over me, checking for damage. He wasn't planning to move or speak until he was sure I was okay.

His hazel eyes said all that and more, reminding me of when he'd first asked me out after the pageant had ended this past summer.

He'd dropped by the stables, where I'd been picking out Bella's hooves in her stall. Kitty, his gray and black speckled Great Dane, was by his side. I distinctly remember wanting to cuddle that dog—and maybe the owner too.

"Look what we found backstage in the Primrose Ballroom,"

Charlie had said, waving an enormous check in front of me. "They must've been planning to present it at the end of the pageant"—Charlie's voice had lowered to a whisper as if the animals were too sensitive to hear the final few words—"before you revealed Mr. Finch's murderer."

I'd kept a hand on Bella's mane, trying to appear easygoing, playful. "You know I can't cash that, right?"

"You mean you don't need to take this six-foot-long check to the bank?" Charlie's face had crumpled in feigned disappointment. "I thought they had a huge vault for useless, massive checks."

I'd tried to maintain a straight face, but despite myself, I'd chuckled. I liked the sarcastic sheriff, and based on the way Bella was eyeing him, I thought she might like him too. Horses know the good ones.

"Actually," Charlie had said, setting the cardboard against the stall. "Kitty and I came by to ask you something."

That *something* had been about a date, and I'd been surprised. Based on Charlie's personality shifts during the pageant investigation, I'd had no idea he was actually interested. At the Rose Palace, he'd gone from playful to purposeful, charming to chiding, blithe to brooding in zero to sixty. I was still learning to anticipate the shifts, though mostly these days I got the sexy, funny man rather than the intense, suspicious sheriff.

All that to say, our romance had been brief and mostly long-distance thus far, but regardless of his persona in any given moment, I always felt safe with Charlie.

"Savilla called me on my cell while Lacy was on the phone with 911," Charlie explained, answering the question I hadn't yet asked.

For reasons I couldn't explain, at the mention of Lacy's name I had the sudden urge to shield her from him, even though he'd said nothing to warrant my defensiveness. That was ridiculous though. Charlie hadn't seen Lacy and Brett dancing, the way they'd moved in sync, the way Brett had leered at her. He had no idea that Lacy had been close to him right before he died.

"Before I examine the body, is there anything I should know?"

"Such as?"

"Savilla said you did CPR, right?"

"Right," I answered. "And one of the people on Brett's camera crew helped me. When my arms got tired, she stepped in." I gestured toward Mina, who was in the corner of the ballroom as promised, looking down at a camera screen with Lee. "Nothing worked. Brett couldn't breathe... he..." How to describe what he'd looked like as he'd died? How he'd gasped for air that wouldn't come. The stillness of his features as he stopped struggling.

"Did you see anything suspicious?" Charlie asked, one eyebrow lifted.

I thought of Anton's warning about Brett, heavy with meaning; of Lacy shrinking away from Brett as he began to struggle for breath. But I wasn't going to throw either of them into the spotlight of an investigation without first talking to my oldest and closest friend about what had happened.

"No. I just... I saw, or I heard, Brett coughing, or gasping. I think he choked on something."

"Sounds pretty open and shut," Charlie said, studying my face. He could see that I wasn't saying something.

"Yep," I said, because I wanted this to be true.

He kept his eyes on me for a moment longer, but then one of his officers approached. Her badge read *Deputy*, and I recognized her as the woman Charlie had been chatting with at the Spoonful Diner before I'd left for vet school. We'd only been dating a month at that point, and he hadn't even introduced me.

"Did you need something?" Charlie had asked me, as I

approached their table. I'd walked away without answering, debating whether I would answer a call from the sheriff ever again.

Of course, I'd relented and given him a chance to explain himself. Later that night over a piece of pie I'd refused to share, Charlie had explained that she was his former police partner, now back as his deputy. I'd tried not to seem jealous, but it was hard when his second-in-command looked like Snow White and smelled like strawberries and vanilla. Harder still knowing they spent more time together than Charlie and I ever could.

Today, she wore a uniform, her hair was pulled back in a tight bun, and she didn't have on any makeup, but she was just as stunning. I hated that I noticed.

"The medics called the time of death," the deputy said to Charlie, ignoring my presence entirely as she leaned close enough that even I caught a whiff of her minty breath. "I told them to move the body backstage since it's the closest place out of the sight of the guests."

"Got it," Charlie responded, surveying the ballroom. As he took in the clusters of people and the décor, I could see an invisible veil fall across his features.

The deputy somehow leaned even closer to Charlie, her eyes landing on his in a way that said she knew him well and trusted him without reservation. "I'm not certain that this was an accident," she said in a low voice.

I watched him turn to her, saw some unspoken message pass between them.

"Understood," Charlie said, and then he turned and followed her through the ballroom and backstage without even a glance behind to reassure me that everything would eventually be okay.

THREE

A man lay dead, and here I was obsessing over my boyfriend... or whatever he was to me. I forced my gaze to sweep the room, to focus on what was in front of me instead of the chaos in my head. Somewhere in this crowd of former classmates was a person who might've wanted Brett Brinkley dead.

Joe Larson was now back behind the bar, serving up shots of bourbon, which was probably a good idea after the attendees had watched one of their own perish right in front of them.

Presley Lombardi was on her phone, speaking in hushed tones to someone on the other end of the line, occasionally hiccupping soft sobs.

The cameraman, Lee Frank, was slouching near the stage, seemingly confused as to what to do now that their camera subject was gone, and Mina was sitting behind him, a pinched expression on her face as she continued to stare at the camera screen.

Savilla was directing a server to place trays of hors d'oeuvres on long tables in the back.

Our former class president held hands with a few others

and seemed to be finishing a prayer circle. This was Valerie Hurt, née Warren, who had returned home with a husband a few years ago to take a position as a third-grade teacher at the elementary school in town.

She was very pregnant with their first child and very proud of the fact, rubbing her belly as—the prayer circle now disbanded—she walked over with her husband, whom I'd never actually met.

She sank her off-kilter frame down into one of the covered chairs, and her husband followed behind her, grabbing another chair and placing her swollen feet on the seat. He did all of this without a word, and for his efforts she gave him a scowl.

"My husband, Will." Valerie motioned at him by way of introduction.

"Will Hurt?" I repeated.

She nodded as if this was an absolutely normal name, as if anyone who met him wasn't thinking, *This Will Hurt.*

Valerie patted the seat next to her, and I felt compelled to sit. "How are you?"

"Um... not great," I answered.

Valerie shot me a pitying look. "I'm so glad that I have a chance to chat with you, especially after all this." She peered into my eyes as if she was about to confess to murder.

I had the urge to stand and call for Charlie, but I would wait. I inched forward, anticipating her next words.

"Well, it's just... I haven't seen you at church in forever," Valerie finished.

I sat back. That was not what I'd expected.

Valerie put out the hand that wasn't on her stomach to grip my forearm. "I know you may have struggled to return since your mother passed, God bless her, but you're still on the membership roll and can come back anytime."

I had no idea how I'd gotten on the membership roll in the first place, but I could guess that it had something to do with

Aunt DeeDee. Regardless, "struggling" wasn't exactly the issue. I no longer lived here, and even if I did, I preferred my Sundays spent in the hills that surrounded our town rather than sitting in hard pews beneath a popcorn ceiling.

"The Lord always welcomes his little lost sheep," Valerie reassured me. She smiled in a way that made me feel both accepted and also broken, but perhaps that's exactly what Valerie intended.

"I live in New York," I said. "I'm in vet school and just in town for the weekend."

I left out the real reason why I'd chosen this exact weekend to come home because I didn't want to explain that I was actually the illegitimate daughter of Frederick Finch and his will reading was tomorrow. As far as I knew, Savilla was still in the dark about our biological connection, though I was beginning to wonder if Mr. Finch somehow knew that I was his daughter. Otherwise, I had no idea why I'd been summoned by the lawyer. Regardless, I certainly didn't need any judgment from Valerie.

"Are you really?" Valerie's eyes lit. "Maybe you can come to our career day at the end of the school year. You could talk about all creatures of our God and King." She released my arm and I noticed red marks from where her fingers had pressed into my flesh. "We'd also love to see you at our knitting circle—or maybe our book club? We read Amish romance fiction, which is quite inspiring, and once a year we have a conference where we..."

Before Valerie could give a rundown of the entire church calendar, she remembered something else. "Oh, and we have an excellent singles group! They go into Roanoke once a month to meet up with the other singles at churches in the area."

"Oh, I'm not... single," I corrected involuntarily, before practically hitting myself for the admission.

"Oh?" Valerie was waiting.

"I'm dating Charlie Strong," I admitted, reminding myself that this fact wasn't actually a secret even though I wasn't sure where exactly we stood at the moment. "You know, the sheriff we elected earlier this year?"

"Okay, then." Valerie eyed me, a new look of respect creeping into her expression. "That's a different story. You two could join our Sunday school class for young marrieds."

I didn't have the heart to tell Valerie that not only had Charlie and I not yet defined our relationship, we'd also already surely broken whatever rules she had in place for a dating couple. We'd slept together every chance we'd had, which with the long distance was probably about a couple dozen times by now. Ninety percent of those encounters had been amazing, which Lacy said was outstanding odds for a new relationship. In fact, when I'd reluctantly offered the estimated number, Lacy had screamed, *You sweet little slut, you better hang on to him*, a detail which I also would not share with Valerie.

"I'll talk to Charlie about it," I said, without any intention of doing so.

Will cut in, sheepishly. "Honey, we should really see if we can get you a room so you can rest."

I glanced at my watch. It was nearing 9:30 p.m., an hour or so past the time when I was supposed to have escaped the reunion and found myself in Charlie's arms. Instead, I was part of a dead man's investigation, and Charlie had wandered away with another woman.

Albeit his deputy, but still.

"Does it look like the authorities have released anyone else?" Valerie shot back at her husband. "We can't leave yet."

I couldn't handle whatever dynamic was happening here, and I stood to excuse myself, aching to go outside for a breath of fresh air. But as I turned to head toward the door, I felt eyes on me from across the room. Charlie.

He motioned for me, and despite the terrible circumstances,

I felt a little thrill go through me. Charlie wanted me, needed me.

"I could use a second pair of eyes, especially ones with medical knowledge, and I still haven't found a pathologist willing to work for a pittance in Aubergine," he told me as I joined him on the stage, which now consisted of an abandoned microphone and square hay bales that had been part of the décor. He lowered his voice. "We've got the body backstage."

"You know I work mostly with dogs and horses?" I reminded him.

"A mammal is a mammal," he said, his brows dipping inward. "We need to hurry because I want the body autopsied as soon as possible. No one can leave town until we get the results."

I froze. "You're saying that we could be stuck here for days?"

Charlie's expression was hard to read, but it seemed a mix of impatience and, *What part of this don't you understand?* He said simply, "It won't last that long."

My eyes widened at the hard edges of his tone, but I wasn't about to argue here and now.

"Are you going to put everyone on lockdown?" I asked.

Charlie's hands were at his hips as he considered. His tone softened a bit as he explained, "People will need permission to leave the property, and we'll need to know exactly where they are. But for tonight, I've asked Savilla to arrange for everyone to stay on-site while we conduct the questioning."

We. By that I assumed he meant him and the deputy, not him and me. That realization felt like the final emotional jab.

We made our way behind the red velvet stage curtains that hung from the high ceiling. The wings where I'd waited during the pageant were familiar, reminding me of the nerves and comradery all of us contestants had shared. But it was different this time: a man lay dead on a gurney in the wings.

My heart began palpitating as I noticed the white sheet that had been removed from the body. The deputy wasn't around, probably fulfilling other duties, but there was another person with us—Lacy, her hand stuck in one of Brett's pockets.

Suddenly, the memory of the last time I'd seen Lacy and Brett together before tonight came to mind. It was the night before she'd left for college, and he'd shown up at her house with a gun, threatening to use it on himself if she left him. He'd ended up jumping from her second-story window when the police arrived. The gun had turned out to be fake, but Brett's manipulation had been real enough.

I gasped, and Lacy's head shot up, her eyes wide with fright.

"I'm not... it's not what..." Lacy froze in place. "He has something that belongs to me."

Charlie cleared his throat. "Lacy? Can I help you?"

Emotions ran across her face almost faster than I could read them. Fear, hope, anger. My friend was in some kind of trouble.

"You can't tamper with the body," I said, stating the obvious but also trying to prevent this information from coming out of Charlie's mouth. If he spoke the words, they might be followed by, *You'll need to come with me.*

"I wasn't. I swear." Lacy took a moment to collect herself. "He really does have something of mine."

"Something like...?" Charlie waited for her to complete the statement.

Lacy cleared her throat and straightened her shoulders. I knew that look. She didn't want to tell him, so she wouldn't. "Something personal... a piece of paper, a note."

Lacy was lying, I was sure of it, but thankfully Charlie couldn't read her like I could.

He approached her slowly. "I promise we'll let you know if we find anything that could possibly be yours."

Lacy must've realized she had no other option, and with my eyes I begged her to walk away. I did not want to have to pick sides in a fight between the law, aka Charlie, and what I knew to be true of my best friend. If she said she was looking for something that belonged to her, then she was. It might not be a note, but Brett had died with something she needed.

Unfortunately, catching her in the act of rifling through a dead man's pockets wasn't a great look.

Suddenly, a new face appeared between the red curtains. It was Anton. "Lacy? Are you back here?" He seemed distressed, as if he'd thought he'd lost her.

Lacy's face relaxed when she saw him. "Anton!" She started toward him, but she had to pass me on the way. Charlie put out a hand and lightly touched her forearm. "Don't go far, okay? We may need to ask some questions."

I knew that wasn't a maybe, and Lacy did too. She nodded, looked at the ground, and let Anton take her hand and lead her away.

After they were gone, Charlie shook his head as he put on latex gloves and offered the box to me. "Any idea what that was about?"

"None," I said, hoping my tone implied that I wasn't in a mood to speculate.

Charlie seemed to accept my response.

I didn't take the gloves, figuring I could observe best with my eyes. Besides, I had no desire to touch Brett's flesh again. I could still feel his bones cracking under my palms. I'd seen dead bodies before—Momma's in her casket at the funeral home and Mr. Finch's falling out of a stage set during the Rose Palace Pageant—but not one that had expired right in front of me. A chill crept up the back of my neck, leaving prickles, but I pushed aside my own discomfort and summoned my professional training.

I circled the body, first noting the gray pallor of Brett's skin and then the red and purple marks along his neck, a combination of burst blood vessels and scratch marks. I'd cut into my fair share of animals during labs in the first year of vet school, but I'd never stared at a human corpse, trying to discern what the body might be telling me. I tried to do as Charlie had suggested and pretend this was any other mammal, which, in my mind, was a compliment rather than a way to dehumanize the victim. Animals, after all, were often much better creatures than their human counterparts.

"Tell me what you see," Charlie said as he took a step back and waited. I felt very much on the spot, but I made myself focus.

"Burst blood vessels," I noted, pointing to the squiggly red lines. "That almost makes it look like..."

"Like he was strangled," Charlie added.

"But he wasn't," I said. "I heard him, and I saw him. No one touched Brett until..." I listed the people off on my fingers. "Joe tried the Heimlich, and Mina and I attempted CPR. Presley fell to his other side, but I'm not sure she ever touched him." I replayed the moments, grabbing at myself as I'd seen Brett do. "He coughed and held his throat, but he couldn't exactly strangle himself."

Charlie lifted a shoulder. "Right."

I examined Brett's mouth and noticed a slight trickle of blood in the left corner of his lips.

"There's nothing visible in the airway," Charlie said.

"But there's dried blood that indicates some kind of scraping or tearing in the mouth or throat," I added.

"I could see someone choking on ice, but ice wouldn't have torn him up like this," Charlie replied.

"You think it might be poisoning? Like, with some kind of acidic compound? Bleach, maybe?" I paused to consider.

Charlie shook his head. "I don't think it's poison." He tilted his head toward a row of litmus strips on a nearby podium.

"Is that your test kit?" I asked, remembering how he'd talked about buying it for the station even though it was almost a thousand dollars of the county's tiny budget. He'd deliberated for far longer than I would've, but I appreciated how seriously he took his job.

"Yeah, it came in handy after all." Charlie motioned to the tests as he spoke. "I had one of the officers run Brett's glass for different toxins, and everything came back clear."

"How reliable are the tests?"

"Pretty good. Ninety-five percent accuracy for common toxins."

"And uncommon?"

"Hit or miss," he answered. "Just in case, we're also sending the glass to forensics."

"And the coroner will take blood samples," I said, standing back and crossing my arms, trying to figure out what else could've killed Brett so quickly.

My eyes traveled down the body to the dead man's arms, and I crouched low to study his hands, the very ones that appeared to have strangled him as he gasped for air. I peeked beneath the palms and at the fingers, the hairy knuckles and the tiny indentations on the skin. All seemed fine except for... I stopped, noticing the nail beds: a bluish purple. I pointed to them. "This discoloration is likely from cyanosis."

I'd taken one class on animal forensics, and by the end of the semester, I'd known that I couldn't stomach examining cases of animal cruelty even if it was a good and necessary job to prosecute perpetrators. Still, that class had taught me the signs of a lack of oxygen: discoloration of the nail beds, the gums, the tongue. Add that to what I'd seen with my own two eyes as Brett struggled on the dance floor, and I was confident as to how he'd died. Technically, Brett had suffocated from a lack of air to his lungs. That still didn't explain *how* he'd been deprived of oxygen. Whatever the cause, the blood in the mouth and the burst vessels on the neck meant it wasn't a simple case of choking.

"The discoloration could also have something to do with circulation or a heart problem," I added. "You'll need to wait for the coroner's report to know for sure—"

"I know exactly what happened." A voice cut in from the wings.

FOUR

Presley burst in, her carefully crafted appearance now a mess: hair wild, lipstick smeared into a bruise across her mouth. An officer hurried after her.

"Sorry," the deputy said. "She insisted she speak with you."

"That's okay." Charlie angled himself between Brett's body and his girlfriend. "You have information for us?"

Presley came forward, trying to peer around the sheriff before catching a glimpse of Brett's body and bursting into tears, which she dried with the corner of her knuckle. Perhaps unfairly, I was struck by how well grief suited her. Even with the tousled hair and tarnished makeup, she was not an "ugly crier." Her flushed cheeks and gleaming eyes made her almost sparkle.

"Brett and I traveled to Sardinia to meet my extended family a few weeks ago. He was..." Presley sniffled twice. "He was planning to propose, so he was doing a sort of 'meet the family' tour. He thought it would be good for his upcoming show, but while we were there... it didn't go well."

I couldn't help but notice her language: *He was planning,*

he was doing, he thought, his show. Brett seemed to be the only one calling the shots in their supposed relationship.

"How would it affect the show?" I asked.

"We brought the camera crew, thinking that viewers would like to see us traveling. We ate cannoli and granita. We walked along the Cala Brandinchi. The first day was perfect until..." She took a steadying breath. "After the second day we couldn't use much of the footage, mainly because of my *bisnonna*—my great-grandmother." Presley swallowed. "She took us to her spiritual adviser, a fortune teller, who gave us a terrible reading and then took my *bisnonna* aside to say God knows what."

Like Mina had said, if Presley believed in psychics and curses, her great-grandmother's warning could have poisoned their relationship before they could get engaged.

"After that my *bisnonna* despised Brett, said he was a *stronzo*—an asshole—and he would break my heart. She went on and on about seeing him with another woman even though that would've been literally impossible. At first, I assumed she hated him because he isn't Catholic, but then after we spoke for a while, all in Italian and all off-camera, of course, I realized it was because she'd seen *Small Town, Big Romance*. She'd watched him closely all season long and said she knew that he was no good. She was angry that he'd brought cameras to her island home, and she thought that he was corrupting me."

Presley herself had become a household name from the very same show and, from what I could tell, was very Americanized. As Momma would say, this sounded like the pot calling the kettle black if ever there was one.

Presley glanced down now, not meeting our eyes for a moment, but when she spoke again, I realized she was thinking the same thing. "Apparently, she watched the show and knew we were together, but no one had told her about the tape that was released a few months after it ended. My *bisnonna* doesn't go online."

I knew that she was referring to the infamous sex tape, which was not actually a tape but rather a streamed five-minute clip of her – completely nude and in the starring role. I'd always assumed Presley had been the one to release it, since it had apparently secured her ongoing stardom.

"I'm sorry, Ms. Lombardi, for your loss," Charlie said, clearing his throat. "But I do need to understand one thing: What impact would your great-grandmother have had on the events of this evening?"

She glanced between the two of us as if the answer was already sitting right in front of us. "She cursed Brett, of course." Presley pulled a tissue from her cleavage and let out a soft cry.

"She cursed him?" I repeated.

Presley looked from me to the sheriff as she stuffed the tissue back into a pocket, as if she was confused by exactly what part of all of this we didn't understand. A moment later, she covered the distance, took both of my hands in her own, and gazed into my eyes, trying to communicate some deep-seated fear. What she was telling us was not mere superstition to her. No, this was real, applicable in the day-to-day. Like how some Southerners paint porch ceilings "haint blue" to keep the ghosts away or cover mirrors during a wake to keep the spirits from getting trapped. Such cultural practices were silly to me, a person more drawn to science and strategic intervention, but I couldn't deny that they were very real to some people.

As I stared into Presley's unblinking eyes, I could almost feel the fear radiating from her. I tried to calm her with logic. "You said that your family is Catholic, right? I was raised as a part-time Baptist, but from what I understand, they don't exactly believe in magic."

"It's not magic. It's spiritualism," Presley countered, as if I should be able to easily parse out the difference. "And my family in Sardinia certainly believes. They call it the *malocchio*, the evil eye. Perhaps you would call our beliefs a combination of folklore and Catholicism, but to them, to me, it is very real."

Charlie and I glanced at one another. He was certainly doing a better job at keeping his face unreadable.

"My *bisnonna* gave Brett the *malocchio* the few weeks we were in Italy. He'd been suffering from headaches and stomach pains ever since."

"Was he taking any kind of medication for the symptoms?" I asked, knowing the coroner would be able to tell us but that wouldn't be until tomorrow at the earliest.

"No," she hesitated, her eyes flickering. "But he had actually taken up a new diet regimen."

"Supplements?" Maybe that would explain his death. I thought of a sweet cocker spaniel I'd treated whose owner had unsuspectingly overdosed the dog on iron supplements. Thankfully, the pup had recovered, but it had been a long road back. Perhaps I could convince Presley that there was no curse.

I was about to start in about the dangers of unregulated supplements when Presley shook her head. "Twenty-hour fasting. He would eat from ten o'clock in the morning until two in the afternoon, and then nothing again until the next morning."

Hmm... okay. Back to possible murder, then. I thought of the drink he'd held in his hand. That had not been water inside the glass.

"Did he drink while fasting?" I asked. "What about alcohol?"

She titled her head. "He couldn't give up liquor. He would decide to lay off for a day or two, but most evenings he had a drink... or two or three."

"What was he drinking this evening?" I asked.

"And how much?" Charlie followed up.

"He had three beers at the game, and when we arrived, he ordered a cocktail from the bar and then drank most of my glass of wine. I'd just brought him a cup of bourbon before he..." Soft crying began again, and she looked at both of us as if imploring us not to judge Brett—or her—too harshly.

His stomach pains and headaches sounded much more like the effects of alcohol, a lack of food, or even a medical condition, not a supernatural curse, but I didn't think now—with her dead almost-fiancé lying before us—was the time to argue.

Charlie stepped forward. "Ms. Lombardi, we understand, and we appreciate, your input." He ushered Presley away from the body and closer to the stage curtains that would lead her back into the ballroom. "You should sit tight while we make a few notes, and I'll find you soon if I need to ask further questions."

Presley's eyes traveled to the gurney one last time before she bowed her head and stepped through to the other side of the red velvet.

Charlie came back to my side and gestured for the medics to enter and finish loading up the body.

"So," I started. "Should we fly in her great-grandmother for questioning?"

Charlie ignored my quip.

"Sorry," I quickly corrected. When a situation was harrowing, the things jumping around in my head became more erratic, but that was part of how I processed things. "You handled that well."

"Thanks." Charlie gave me a curt nod. "Even that kind of testimony can actually help an investigation. It gives us context, if not of the victim then of the people closest to them."

That was a reasonable explanation, I supposed, but his tone was so frozen that I couldn't help but wonder if, besides my stupid joke, I'd done something really wrong in the past half hour.

Charlie stared at the floor and began to pace. "On first appearances, it looks pretty straightforward, like the victim choked on something. But he was presumably fasting. He was grabbing at his throat, and there was a trickle of blood in his mouth caused by…" His words trailed, uncertain.

"He could've bitten his tongue before I started compressions," I suggested before reconsidering. "But surely I would've noticed. I mean…" I cringed. "At one point my hands were in his mouth."

Charlie nodded as he processed this. "Maybe the blood is evidence of internal bleeding?"

"But what could've caused that?"

"No idea." Charlie sighed. "But it sounds like we need to single out those who were either in contact with his drinks or anywhere in his vicinity when the victim became distressed."

"Makes sense," I said, beginning to feel more like we were on the same wavelength again – even if it was only because we were talking about potential murder.

Charlie began to pace once more. "Run through it with me: Who did you see interact with him right before he died?"

"Joe was on bar, and Presley—as she said—had just gotten him a bourbon and brought it to him. Brett and Lacy were dancing and Anton—"

Charlie took out a notebook and began recording names.

I thought of the appalled—and worse, sad—face Lacy would make if she knew that I'd thrown her or her boyfriend into the spotlight of an investigation. I tried to course correct. "I don't think they had anything to do with—"

"It's just a list of names, Dakota. Doesn't mean anyone is guilty." Charlie huffed out a breath. "Who else did you notice hanging around him this evening?"

I hesitated, feeling like I was somehow betraying these people, but willing myself to trust Charlie's method. "His camera crew was filming most of the night. Brett was dancing with Lacy when he…" I paused, my cheeks heating. "Do not write down Lacy's name."

Charlie looked at me, his eyebrows raised as if trying to

figure out how serious I was. "I told you, this doesn't mean anyone is guilty. Think of it as a list of witnesses, not suspects."

That didn't make me feel better. "Fine. Then add my name to the list since I was at a table only five yards or so from the dance floor."

He huffed out a long breath. "Fine."

I swallowed hard, trying to reframe my thinking and lower my blood pressure. I trusted Charlie. I did. He was a good sheriff, and he'd worked to solve Mr. Finch's murder as well as the case of the missing 2001 pageant queen only a few months earlier.

We could do this. Together. Again.

We just needed to somehow keep from irritating each other to death, which was perhaps a poor choice of phrasing in this moment.

Charlie studied me, and then without another word he turned and walked to the edge of the curtain and poked his head out, likely consulting with his gorgeous deputy.

Fine. I have things to do too, I reminded myself. Things like finding Lacy and asking her exactly what she'd been searching for in Brett's pockets.

FIVE

The medics took Brett's body, and as I watched from the edge of the stage, the room quieted into a kind of solemnity. It was hard to believe that this evening had started with a football game at Aubergine High and ended with a death at The Rose.

When the last medic finally closed the double doors to the ballroom, I released a breath I didn't know I'd been holding and lifted my phone to check in with Aunt DeeDee.

The phone only rang twice before she answered and put it on FaceTime, her preferred method of communication. "Hey, hon. You okay?"

I wasn't sure what to say. I had all my arms and legs and pieces, as Momma would say, but emotionally, I might fall apart any minute.

Aunt DeeDee must've sensed as much. "Joe came down to the kitchen and told me what happened. Brett was always a handful, even as a young'un, God love him." She dabbed at her eyes with the edge of her apron and set the phone on the edge of the counter. She was cutting onions, I realized, and there was a massive pile of greenery stacked next to the sink in a giant rinsing bowl.

"What is that?" I asked, moving the screen closer to my face.

"Rhubarb," Aunt DeeDee answered. She picked up a bowl and started stirring.

Growing up in the South, I knew that rhubarb was used in a variety of desserts, but I hadn't recognized the plant at first, probably because it didn't grow naturally in the hills where Momma and I used to hike. The most important fact I recalled about the plant, though, was that to both animals and humans, the stalks were edible but the leaves were poisonous.

"Joe made a couple of desserts using rhubarb, but he accidentally over-ordered," Aunt DeeDee told me. "He was trying to figure out what to do with the rest. He ended up using it in the signature cocktail."

I thought of the Aubergine Thresher: grape soda, vodka, gin, and rhubarb sticking out of the top. It sounded just as disgusting as when Joe had first offered it to me.

"Why are you still in the kitchen?"

"Folks still gotta eat, especially when tragedy strikes."

Briefly, I considered finding her, if for nothing else than a quick hug, but then I remembered Lacy.

"I'll come see you in a bit, okay?"

"I'll be here." She would. Feeding people was her love language.

I hung up, my thoughts swarming like a hive of bees missing its queen. I needed a moment alone to collect myself before searching for Lacy.

As I skirted the edge of the ballroom, trying my best not to talk to anyone else right then, I spotted Savilla with Presley, both of them crying. Savilla's hunched frame made me wonder if this new death was making her think of her own father's body being taken away during the pageant weekend this summer.

A pang of sympathy rushed through me at the grief she'd endured these last few months, and I could only hope that tomorrow's will reading wouldn't add more fuel to that fire. Maybe I could skip it entirely. Was there a penalty for not attending a will reading? Surely it wasn't an actual legal summons.

I bit my lip, considering this as an option, but immediately my mind went to Savilla finding out the news that we were blood relatives on her own. That wouldn't be fair.

No, I had to be there, and I would steel myself for her reaction, which could go a variety of directions. Maybe Savilla would be thrilled that our friendship was now an actual sisterhood, but maybe she would be confused, frustrated—and perhaps even angry—at having to recalibrate her life again, this time to involve a slightly older sister. I wasn't sure I could deal with those fraught emotions in the midst of a murder investigation.

I slipped out of the ballroom and headed toward the Color Gallery, where the darkened corridor could provide some relief from the sounds and sights, not to mention my own heightened emotions, threatening to overwhelm me.

The hall was empty and unlit. It took nearly a minute for my eyes to adjust to the low light, and as I felt for one of the glass cases to steady myself, I reminded myself to breathe deeply.

Anxiety is strange. It picks and chooses when to rear its ugly head. I'd been fine, steady even, during Brett's entire CPR ordeal. I'd remained composed while the medics intervened and when Charlie's deputy arrived. But now, alone in this hall filled with Finch heirlooms, my figurative seams were coming undone.

Not only was I thinking about Brett's death, but I couldn't help but ruminate over the real reason I'd come home this weekend. Sure, it'd been for the reunion and to see Charlie and Lacy and Aunt DeeDee, but it was also to figure out what came next for me.

This past week, before I'd had any idea that I would be an eyewitness to the death of a former classmate, I'd received two key invitations that could change the course of my future: first, the summons to the will reading and, second, an offer of recommendation to a prestigious fellowship on the other side of the country.

I'd performed well in grad school, really well, even earning an A and then an A- in both of the classes I'd taken with one of the toughest professors in the program. In fact, Dr. Thompson had given me the highest academic praise in the form of a head nod and a mumbled "well done" as she'd passed back my midterm exam.

Then this week, Dr. Thompson had pulled me aside to offer me what could turn out to be the chance of a lifetime.

"I can only select one candidate each year to nominate," she'd said to me. "Even then, there are no guarantees that you'll be accepted, but if you are, it will require a one-year internship and a three-year fellowship in San Diego."

Four years of my life lived across the country. Four years of intensive training far from Aubergine. Four years away from Aunt DeeDee and Lacy and... Charlie. My gut reaction had been to refuse her on the spot, but how could I reject such an opportunity without at least considering it?

"I'll be direct, Ms. Green. Your education trajectory has been nontraditional, but you're the first student I've taught to score a perfect grade on a case study. Your talent shouldn't be wasted in some small-town practice."

The dismissal of my life's goal stung, but her faith in me was undeniable.

"Consider the fellowship carefully," she had said. "I need your answer by Monday."

My mind tried to find a place to land, one that didn't involve the image of my professor's expectant face or Savilla's stricken expression. I tried to remember that these weren't the things I was really anxious about. Or, at least, they weren't the things crippling me with anxiety in this moment. No, it was the image of Brett's gray pallor and purple lips, the death of a man, one who'd been my age, one I'd known for most of my life. Yes, that's what was causing the hum in my head and the thudding behind my breastbone.

Using techniques Momma had taught me years ago, I bent forward at the waist, put my cheek against the cool glass of a display case, closed my eyes, and counted the beats of my breath, trying to lower my pulse. *One. Two. Three. Four.*

After twenty or so seconds, I opened my eyes and released air slowly. My eyes had adjusted to the darkness, so I could finally see inside the case in front of me. It was empty. That was strange. Last time a case had been empty was when the Miss 2001 crown had gone missing this past summer, a signal that all was not well at the Rose Palace Pageant.

I took another slow breath and moved toward the next case, extending a hand to feel the cool glass again. This one was empty too. I moved faster this time from one case to the next to find the towering gems, looking for the jewels and necklaces, the crowns and scepters. All of them were gone.

Did Savilla know? But of course she would know if every single piece was missing. There had to be a reason. Perhaps a cleaning. Was that a thing? Did rich people send out their gems for a polish and shine?

The sound of voices interrupted me. The tones were a mix of resonant and high-pitched, and they somehow sounded like the very definition of technicolor. But then I heard two I recognized, speaking over them. It was Lacy and Anton.

I trailed slowly through the Color Gallery, and as I approached a room with a closed door, I almost jumped out of my skin when I heard Brett speak.

"I'm on this show because there weren't many romantic

options where I grew up. Well, except for one girl, or, uh, woman. She's the one I wrote my song about."

A woman's voice, strangely familiar, came next. "What's she like? This girl who got away?"

I could almost see Brett's dumb grin as he answered. "Super smart, forges her own path, decides she wants something and makes it happen."

My breath caught as I realized that an old episode of *Small Town, Big Romance* was playing. I inched closer and put my eye to the crack in the door to see that the room was a kind of miniature theater, complete with red seats and a screen surrounded by brown curtains that had been swept back and tied. Savilla must've set up this space as another option for guests who preferred a bit of downtime after a night on the dance floor.

The show continued, the camera now focused on Brett, who sat alone in an oversized chair, answering questions from a speaker off-screen. As I listened, I processed each word as if it might contain a clue.

Interviewer: Did you have a girlfriend back home? And did she compete in the pageant?

Brett: I had a high school sweetheart, but we were kids. I never expected that relationship to last a lifetime. And no, she was not the kind of girl who wanted to be in a pageant, even though she was gorgeous. She could run it, but she would never be in it.

I heard Lacy give a short laugh, likely because she knew that in this instance, Brett wasn't wrong.

Interviewer: What are you looking for in your big romance?

Brett: My momma raised me right, so it's not about appearances for me. I want a girl who likes to go to church, who makes me laugh, who wants a couple of kids, who has the all-American values I grew up learning.

Interviewer: Would you ever date a celebrity?

Brett: I mean, yeah, who wouldn't? But that's not what I'm looking to get out of this experience. I want a down-to-earth lady who lets me treat her right.

That did not sound like the Brett Brinkley I knew. I was about to open the door when I heard Lacy and Anton again, though I couldn't see them from my place peeking through the doorway.

"He had it coming to him," Anton said, each word sharp and clear despite the Texas drawl that usually made him sound so charming. "You can't treat people like... that... and expect to get away with it."

"I know," Lacy said, a hiccupping cry escaping along with the words.

Anton and Lacy had met a couple of years ago while Lacy was at a networking conference in Texas. He was working as a waiter, and she was happy when he served her the wrong plate and struck up a conversation. A few months later, he'd moved to Virginia to be near her, which didn't seem like much of a sacrifice since, as far as I could tell, he didn't have a definitive career path. I appreciated that he almost matched me in his love for the outdoors. Tonight, Anton wore jeans and a cowboy hat, and in town, he'd taken over my duties at Straight from the Horse's Mouth Stables. If I had to guess, I would say his pay was going toward buying a ring. I liked the guy from what I'd seen so far, and ever since Brett, I'd been very picky about liking who Lacy dated.

"Brett was clearly a terrible person, and sometimes terrible things happen to those kinds of people." Anton's tone sounded as if he was trying to be reasonable, to lay out an argument, but to what end? To justify his own behavior? That of Lacy? His voice traveled and bounced off the walls as if he was pacing back and forth. "We can't blame ourselves. Brett was the one who was threatening you. You just told him no."

I could picture Lacy nodding along.

"Right, then." The pacing seemed to stop as Anton said the next words: "It will get easier."

Oh, Lord. What was the "it" that would get easier? Seeing a man die? Feelings of guilt? Or—far worse—knowing he had murdered someone?

Anton's words were vague and concerning, reminding me how much I didn't know about Anton or his past. I had no idea if he was the silent type or the jealous type. Did Lacy?

A minute passed, and I couldn't hear what Anton was saying to her, but his tone sounded rushed and urgent.

"Fine. I understand," Lacy finally said, her voice raised briefly before her words were muffled again.

I angled my position at the door, so I could see them. Her head was buried in her hands, her elbows on her knees. I had the urge to throw open the door, to demand that Lacy explain their conversation. But there was something about Anton's mannerisms, about the way he was hovering over her, about the way he struck his hand against his thigh as he spoke that gave me pause.

Anton's movements seemed erratic; even his hair was mussed and standing on end.

"Don't say a word to the sheriff," Anton finally commanded. "Whatever you do, don't tell him a thing, especially not the part about the one that got away."

I hid in the shadows as Anton and Lacy left the Media Room, Brett's interview still playing behind them.

Interviewer: You don't believe in the one?

Brett: There could be a million girls who could make me happy. Good thing too, since the one that got away isn't coming back.

I watched Anton guide Lacy away, his arm tight around her waist like he was afraid she might slip away.

SIX

I reminded myself to take a deep breath and not borrow trouble, as Momma would say. I had enough of my own anyway.

"Lacy." I called to her in the hall. She turned and pulled away from Anton as if tethered between us.

I started toward her, and as I neared, she caught my eye before quickly looking away from me.

"We need to talk," I said, knowing I sounded a bit desperate.

"I can't right now," Lacy said. "Anton needs me to—"

Anton glanced between us. "It's okay." He seemed to sense my need. "You two should talk."

Lacy began tapping her foot as fast as a hummingbird in flight. She didn't seem eager to come with me, so I gently nudged her with my elbow.

"We were heading back to the ballroom because it's Anton's turn. He's being questioned by Charlie's new deputy." Lacy's tone was sharp, which told me she was either angry or afraid—or both.

"I'm fine," Anton reassured her. "Go. You two talk."

This didn't sound like a man with something to hide, which relieved me.

Lacy hesitated only another second before motioning for me to lead the way. I took us past the library and the solarium to a door in the wall. Opening it, we found a narrow stairwell that must've been some kind of servant's back staircase. It seemed a promising place to talk alone.

I started up it, realizing a few steps in that I was already losing my breath. The stairs were steep, and there was no visible landing, the narrow hallway just leading up and up. We must've traveled three stories by the time two doors were visible off the top step.

I opened the door directly in front of us, and there was... nothing. Just thin strips of wooden boards.

"That's weird," I said. "Why would there be a door that goes nowhere?"

Lacy felt along one of the boards and tried to peer through a crack. "Looks like there's stained glass behind here."

"So a window that doesn't face outdoors?"

Lacy shrugged, but fear was pinching her brows. "My parents took me to a house like this in California years ago, remember?"

I recalled a postcard from the place. It had hung on a giant peg board in my room where I kept all of my favorite things in middle school. Obviously, the house hadn't been a fave, but Lacy always was.

"The Winchester House," Lacy continued. "The tour guide said it was filled with spooky secrets. Stairs leading nowhere, rooms that are still being discovered ninety years after it was built. The owner had it constructed after losing her husband and infant daughter."

"A grief house?"

Lacy nodded. "Some people think Mrs. Winchester designed it specifically to commune with her dead loved ones."

I didn't scare easily, but a shiver ran up my spine at those words. I tried to make light of my fear. "You think the original Mrs. Finch built this so that dead pageant queens would have a place to haunt from the other side?"

Lacy didn't laugh and instead looked over her shoulder at the steep stairs behind us. "Maybe we should—"

I knew she was about to suggest we go back down and join the others, so I cut her off. "We need to talk."

I opened the door to the left and was happy to see that it led to an actual room. I let Lacy step inside first and closed the door behind us, realizing only as the latch clicked closed that we'd been sunk into absolute darkness. There were no windows, and I couldn't feel a light switch anywhere along the wall.

I pulled out my phone and flipped on the light beam, so we could get a vague sense of the space.

"I don't like this," Lacy mumbled, turning back to the door and wriggling the handle that didn't give way. "Nope, I don't like this *at all*."

"Don't freak out," I said, trying the handle for myself. It twisted back and forth, but no latch clicked to open it. I released the door handle and held up my phone to check for a signal that didn't exist.

"What?" Lacy asked, her eyes widening.

"I can't call out," I said, lowering my voice and typing out a text to Charlie that I hoped didn't sound too frantic. The phone was sending and sending and sending... before it failed completely.

"Shit," Lacy said, followed by a series of other expletives. Then, she leaned against the wall and sank to the floor, repeating the first word over and over.

I walked around the room, holding up my phone in one corner and the next. Still nothing. "Someone will notice we're missing and come looking for us," I tried with a conviction I did not feel.

In the meantime, I shone my phone around the room until it landed on a large wooden chest, overflowing with what appeared to be lace, tulle, and other fabrics.

Lacy went toward it and tugged at a bunch of material. "Old pageant dresses?" She held up a light purple get-up with seed pearls running across the bodice. "This one looks like it's from the 1940s."

"Looks like it," I said, recalling the times she would dress up in Aunt DeeDee's pageant costumes and twirl around the loft as if she were on the runway. I refused to wear them, but I would occasionally let Lacy braid and twist my hair into all kinds of elaborate up-dos.

Now Lacy flung the dress around her shoulders like a shawl. "It's cold in here." She reached inside the chest again, this time tossing a red velvet dress at me.

"Probably because we are literally in the walls," I said, accepting the garment as a kind of fancy blanket.

She came and sat next to me, and I put the phone on the ground, flashlight up. With the shadows our figures made on the walls, it looked like we were spirits waiting to descend.

"I overheard you and Anton talking in the Media Room."

"You overheard? Do you mean you were eavesdropping?"

"PEE-CAN, peh-cahn," I said, using the phrase we always used to signal that sometimes Lacy and I saw the world differently.

Lacy pulled her knees close to her chest, wrapping her arms around herself in a way that made her look more like her childhood self than the confident woman I knew.

"Anton was telling you not to tell the sheriff something," I prompted. "What is it?"

Lacy looked into my eyes, and I could see that she was warring with herself, but I couldn't figure out why. We'd always treated one another as a kind of confessional, spilling secrets that ranged from crushes to silly white lies we'd told. Lacy tucked her head into her arms and muttered one sentence. "You don't have to know everything."

The words stung me like the bees I'd once so feared. *Wow. Okay.*

Either Lacy was in the kind of trouble that she didn't feel she could trust even me with, or Anton was guilty as hell and she was trying to protect him.

SEVEN

"I didn't mean it like that," Lacy said, a hiccup in her voice as if she might cry.

"How did you mean it?"

Seconds passed as she looked at me, trying to find words that didn't come.

"If you won't tell me…" My voice trailed. I didn't know how to finish the statement, so I decided to go a different route, throwing out something I'd noticed earlier to see if she'd meet me in the middle. "Joe called Brett a 'son of a bitch' when he served me a drink earlier." A tiny flag, not quite red but blush-colored, started to rise in my mind. "Do you know if the two of them are—or were—still friends?"

"Sure, I guess," Lacy answered.

"They were inseparable in high school," I prompted.

Lacy thought for a minute, seeming to soften as we reached steadier conversational ground. "Yeah. If one of them played offense, so did the other. If one of them dated a girl, the other better find a friend."

With a jolt I realized that even though Lacy likely hadn't meant to imply it, this was probably the reason that Joe had asked me on a handful of dates in high school. Out of pity, plain and simple.

"If one of them did a kegger, the other one held their ankles," Lacy continued, sounding more like herself the longer she spoke.

"If one of them stole a goat and left it in the principal's office," I added, "the other took the blame."

"I'd forgotten about that." Lacy's face relaxed only a second before the pinched look returned. "Gross. There were those tiny turds all down the senior hallway, remember?"

"All too well," I answered, before trying one last time to break through whatever shell my friend had been hiding inside. I sighed. "I have to ask again—are you sure that you should listen to Anton?"

Lacy frowned. "About what?"

"About not speaking to Charlie. He's..." I tried to find the words. "He's good at his job, and any little detail could help."

Lacy stared at me, reconsidering before something loosened inside of her. "Tonight at halftime, during the game, Brett spotted me when I was coming back from the restroom and pulled me under the bleachers."

I made a yuck face.

"It wasn't like that," she said, heading off my concerns. "Well, not at first. He said he needed to ask me something. Then, he told me that he wanted a few shots of me flirting with him, said he wanted to create drama for his new reality show."

"What? Why?"

"He said that he wanted to make Presley jealous. I thought it was stupid, but I also wasn't that surprised. I always figured that's how those kinds of shows work. You know, almost every-thing is staged and scripted. I tried to laugh it off and get back to the game, but he wouldn't let me go."

"Exactly what does that mean?" My voice was husky with fatigue, but I was also deeply concerned.

"He blocked my way, told me that he wanted me and Presley to have a big fight over him on camera at the reunion party tonight." Lacy huffed out a breath. "He was so serious, so intense, but when I actually started getting nervous about his request, it was like he flipped a switch and went back to his old self. You know how charming Brett can be."

Um, I must've had a different definition of "charming" because Brett had never been it for me, not even in that god-awful *Small Town, Big Romance.*

"I thought it was over until..."

"Until?"

Lacy shivered, which I suspected had nothing to do with the chill in the room. "Brett kissed me."

"Noooo," I said. "Did you kiss him back?" I tried to sound neither disgusted nor judgmental.

"Of course not." She hesitated. "Or, maybe, for, like, a second, I don't know. It just caught me off guard, and it's... it's Brett, you know? He was my first everything. My first love, the first guy I slept with, my high school sweetheart."

I remembered that fact all too well, mainly because it was the only substantial thing we'd ever disagreed on. Finally I'd had to accept that the heart wants what the heart wants, but I'd been ecstatic when she'd finally moved on and started dating other guys in college.

"Tonight, when Brett grabbed me, I felt a kind of rush. I wasn't afraid of him, but I also wasn't exactly expecting him to... to try something under the bleachers at tonight's game. We're not kids anymore. When I pulled away, Brett was smiling, started talking about how much he'd missed me."

"Basically the exact same thing he wanted you to say to him on camera."

"Right." Lacy rubbed at her forehead as if she was getting a headache.

"Did you tell Anton?"

"Not about the kiss, no, but it took me a while to get back to him, so when Anton asked where I'd been, I did mention what Brett had asked me to do. I mean, who cares about harmless flirting, especially with a high school sweetheart?"

"Um, maybe your boyfriend?"

"I know." Lacy's face fell. "I had no idea how much it would bother him."

I thought of Anton at the reunion party in the ballroom, of how he'd teased her for dancing with Brett but then backed off. He hadn't seemed angry, but something had obviously bothered him.

"I decided I would tell Brett no, and after that I wasn't even planning to talk to him at the party tonight," Lacy continued. "Then, he practically pulled me onto the dance floor as soon as I arrived and whispered in my ear that I had to meet him in the Music Room at midnight. When I told him I didn't feel comfortable leaving Anton alone at the reunion, he held me tighter, said that if I didn't meet him, if I didn't dance with him, if I didn't act like everything was fine, if I didn't..." Lacy was crying now, struggling to let out words that seemed to cause her shame even though none of this was her doing, "Brett said that if I didn't sleep with him tonight, then he had something on me."

Heat rushed up my throat. This was only getting worse. "He wanted you to *sleep* with him?"

Lacy raised her head up and down as if on autopilot, as if she could hardly believe what she was saying. "I don't know if he planned to go through with it, but I..." She swallowed, obviously disturbed by the thought. "I think he wanted the two of us on camera, wanted Presley to catch us in the act."

"So he didn't just want you to flirt?"

Lacy hung her head. "He said he'd scanned the photos, and if I didn't 'play nice,' he would send them to my clients. Those were his exact words: 'Play nice or your career will be over.'"

Lacy had built her event planning business into something impressive, handling everything from school galas to political extravaganzas. The pageant's success—murder and all—had only increased her reputation as a reliable and ethical person who could operate in the most challenging of situations. Her brand was her reputation, and these photos—whatever they were—could destroy all that.

The force of the threat struck me like a slap. Brett Brinkley had been blackmailing my best friend to sleep with him this weekend, threatening her career if she didn't agree. I wanted to yell and scream, and if Brett wasn't dead already, I might've been tempted to take care of him myself.

"How did Brett's 'ask' go from 'Will you flirt with me?' to 'Will you sleep with me?'"

"I have no idea," Lacy answered. "But he seemed almost manic right before he started choking."

"Like he was on drugs?" I asked, thinking this would explain so much.

"I don't think so. More like he was on a power trip."

The two of us were quiet as we considered next steps.

"It's like he doesn't—or didn't—know you at all," I added, thinking out loud. "You would never do something like that."

Lacy didn't speak immediately and I looked at her like I was questioning her sanity.

She quickly clarified. "No, I wouldn't sleep with him, but... I was planning to meet him. I needed to get what he has—or had. That's what I was telling him right before he started coughing."

That would be why she'd been so close to him when he'd started choking and why she'd been rifling through his pockets after he'd died. Relief uncoiled in me even though I'd known she wasn't guilty of anything. She couldn't be.

"So... these photos. What could he possibly have on you?" I asked.

"He has pictures of me, photos I gave him on his eighteenth birthday."

"Like glamour shots?" I guessed but then felt bad because her face told me it was so much worse.

She closed her eyes as if to block out what she had to say. "Like, nudes."

At first words stuck in my throat, and when they emerged, they sounded almost like a groan. "Oh, Lacy, you didn't."

But even as I spoke, I knew she'd done just that. Perhaps even worse, she hadn't told me years ago or tonight, when we'd found her backstage with the body. I've never been one to "slut-shame" – if a woman chooses to use her body as art or a thirst trap or otherwise, that's up to her. But nudes? To Brett?

"I was young and impulsive. I figured it was our last few months together, so I wanted to give him a gift that was... memorable. I set up the old film camera I used the year I took dark-room photography, and I even developed them myself. I gave him three photos, each with a little note from me on the back. Back then I thought I was being smart by not texting the pictures." Lacy's eyes swelled with tears. "When we broke up, I figured he threw them away or burned them or something, but he didn't."

Lacy was growing more and more flustered. "He told me..." She sniffed, blinking several times, as if she couldn't believe the next few words were true, "he told me that he would send them to all of my clients on Saturday at midnight, that he would anonymously send them to TMZ and tell them that I was a former girlfriend of Brett Brinkley. He said I had until midnight tonight to decide if I would be a part of his... charade."

"What an asshat," I muttered, imagining him whispering threats to my friend. "What a dickhead, creep-o, dysfunctional... asshat!"

Lacy's anxiety and anger were becoming my own, and the urge to protect her pulsed through me.

"How was he planning to send the photos?" I asked. "Email?"

Lacy nodded. "He said it is already scheduled to send. The last thing he whispered to me was, and I quote, 'If you don't do as you're told, then the only person who can stop me is the one who got away.'"

"What does that even mean?"

"At first, I thought he was talking about me. Like..." Lacy pointed a finger and imitated Brett. "'Only you can stop this.' But now, I'm not so sure."

"So when you were going through his pockets, you weren't just looking for the photos?"

"I was looking for anything that might give me a clue to this elusive person who broke his heart, or damaged him so much that he would consider such a thing. A long shot, maybe, to think that there might be evidence on his person, but I couldn't think of where else to start." Lacy's face crumpled as she began to cry again.

I hated Brett, even if he was dead, for making her feel ashamed and anything less than an amazing human being. My heart pounded in my chest, but I tried to steady my own breathing so I could approach things reasonably. For her.

I wrapped my arms around Lacy, pulling her close. "This isn't your fault," I whispered, wishing I could shield her from whatever was coming next.

"But I'm the one who took the photos and gave them to—" Lacy cried harder, choking out the words.

"—to someone you trusted," I reminded her. "He's the one who was using them in the wrong way."

Lacy settled a bit at that realization and wiped her nose, still sniffling as she said, "This weekend was not supposed to go like this."

"Definitely not," I agreed, checking my phone again for a

signal. Nothing. As I reminded myself not to panic, we heard steps outside the door.

I didn't even take a second to think about who would know about these stairs and why anyone would attempt them when there was another hundred thousand feet or so of the mansion to explore. "Hello?" I yelled. "Is someone there? We're stuck in here."

"Help!" Lacy said, jumping to her feet and overlaying my words with her shouts. "We can't open the door."

More steps. We heard someone try one door and then, blessedly, our own.

The door was flung open and there stood Savilla. I'd never been so glad to see her face, which was almost as surprised as our own.

"Thank God," Lacy breathed.

"How did you know we were here?" I asked.

"I was looking for you," Savilla said, before realizing that didn't really answer the question. "And I use these back stairs as a shortcut around the house. I thought I heard voices. How did you two get up here?"

"We needed a quiet place to talk," I said, deciding not to give away any of the confidences that Lacy had entrusted to me.

"I guess you found one," Savilla said, flipping on a light switch that was three-quarters of the way up the wall. The room was suddenly bathed in yellow light from a lamp that hung from the ceiling in the corner near the chest. "I used to play dress-up in here, so Daddy had a light fixture installed." Savilla gestured at the dresses flung over our shoulders for warmth. "I guess you found the pageant extras. My grandmother had a stash of accetrements."

I narrowed my eyes, trying to decipher her actual meaning. Accessories? Accoutrements?

Savilla didn't miss a beat. "She kept that trunk full in case anyone got a last-minute stain or tear, and when I eventually inherited the vintage pieces, Nanny Kate suggested I keep them in here. It was our hideout for a couple of years."

Savilla's face softened with the memory as she looked around the room. My guilt at keeping our sisterly connection a secret twisted inside me. That, combined with worry about Lacy and frustration over Charlie's distance, wasn't a good mix. But my emotional state didn't matter right then.

Someone in this house could be a murderer, and that had to come first.

EIGHT

Before making my appearance at the homecoming and reunion celebrations this weekend, I'd picked a bundle of wildflowers from the hiking trail and settled it in front of Momma's headstone at the graveyard.

"I haven't told Savilla," I'd said, continuing our ongoing conversation. "And, honestly, I blame you for having to deal with any of this."

Even dead for almost a year and a half, Momma was still the person I told my inmost thoughts to, especially the angry ones.

"If you'd told Mr. Finch that I was his kid before you died, then we could've dealt with this together, but instead, I have these weird pieces of my childhood—and Savilla's—to work out."

I'd imagined Momma nodding along and asking me what I planned to do now.

"You kept me away from the Finches for my entire life, and I get it. You didn't want me caught up in their wealth and all the drama that came with it. But... I just think it would've been nice to know that I had a sister, especially after watching you and Aunt DeeDee have such an amazing relationship."

I'd run a finger along Momma's name engraved into the stone, thinking about all the times I'd almost picked up the phone to call Savilla with the news. I'd been too chicken, though, which was probably the same excuse Momma would've given for leaving me news about my paternity in a letter a year after her death.

The graveside conversation came to mind now as Savilla led Lacy and me back down the stairs to the first floor. When we were in the main hallway once again, Lacy excused herself to find Anton.

"Charlie might be wondering where I am too," Lacy added, giving me a look.

She wasn't wrong. As soon as he had a free minute, I was pretty sure he'd want to ask her why she'd been going through a dead man's pockets. I hoped she would find the courage to tell him the truth, because I didn't want to have to keep a secret from him.

Either way, Lacy's absence meant that I was now stuck with my secret sister.

"Speaking of Charlie," Savilla said, looking in the direction of the ballroom to make sure no one else was nearby. "He asked me to show you around."

"Me?" A prickle of nerves went up my arms. I hadn't told Charlie about the will reading or that Savilla was my half-sister. I needed to process the information fully on my own first.

"I don't have time to give you a tour of the entire house right now," Savilla said, glancing at her watch as if she were a real businesswoman. "I asked one of the staff to start demartricu-lating people into rooms."

I ignored the strange word combo, but I couldn't keep from giving her a quizzical look.

"I need to make sure everyone gets settled so I sorted the guests based on how well they know Aubergine. It's a good practice run in hospitiality since I'm thinking about converting

The Rose into a grand hotel in the new year." Savilla smiled as she said the words, but it was forced. She seemed tired. "Depends on what I find out at the will reading tomorrow. I think I know everything, but there can always be surprises."

My stomach flipped. This was my chance, my "in," but I just couldn't do it. I wasn't ready.

"I know." Savilla's eyes lit up and she raised a finger. "It's not at all the same, but I can show you the general layout of the house in about ten minutes." She motioned for me to follow her as she took out a small ring of keys and we headed toward the vestibule and out the front door.

The darkness and cool air would've been perfect for an autumnal stroll, but in the middle of the chaos of this weekend, it felt more inconvenient than anything else. Savilla took me to the door of what appeared to be a two-story garage around the side of the home.

"There's a replica of the estate in the old carriage house," she said by way of explanation, as she inserted a key into the lock on the front door. "The main house has four floors—or, six, depending on how you're counting."

I squinted one eye. "How can you not know how many floors are in your own house?"

"Easy. There's the first floor, which is where we came in and has the ballroom, the solarium, the library, the kitchen, the Color Gallery." Savilla ticked the rooms off on her fingers. "And the second floor, where we have the Music Room, sitting rooms and parlors, several guest rooms."

My ears perked up at the mention of the Music Room, the place where Brett had asked Lacy to meet him at midnight.

"The third floor is mostly for family and guest rooms, and the fourth floor was for servants but now houses rooms for close friends and family, and Daddy's old office."

I knew this to be true from my time at the pageant this summer. "And the other two floors?"

Savilla flipped on a panel of lights that illuminated a high garage housing a fleet of transportation vehicles ranging from a motorcycle that looked like it was straight out of a 1970s episode of *Happy Days* to an actual carriage.

"The basement has a couple of storage rooms, the bowling alley, a pool."

My eyes widened. "You have an indoor pool?"

"You're so funny," Savilla said, with a grin.

Am I though?

"There's a pool in the basement, but it's empty right now." Savilla shot me the same look her parents must've given her as a child. "It's very dangerous without water, so do not go down there alone."

"Deal," I agreed. "And the sixth floor?"

"The sub-basement. That's where they put storage, the wine cellar, the boilers, and for reasons I'll never understand, a small hall for hosting get-togethers." Savilla's eyebrows turned down. "A man died down there once. A butler, when Daddy was a little boy. We're pretty sure it's haunted."

She said the words so matter-of-factly, as if it was an unavoidable reality for one's home to feature a ghost or two, but in a place with the history and scale of the Rose Palace, maybe it was inevitable. I'd also caught how her voice had changed on the word "butler." It wasn't disrespectful exactly, but it was removed, as if the servants were *them* as opposed to *us*. I didn't like that, particularly since my family roots—or at least the ones I'd grown up knowing about—would've placed me here as a scullery maid rather than mistress of the home.

"Come on, this is what I wanted to show you." Savilla directed me toward the far corner and pulled off a tarp to reveal a six-foot-high dollhouse. "It's the exact rooms and proportions of The Rose. Daddy made it for me when I was a baby, so I grew up with it in the nursery. At some point in my teen years, it got moved out here to be out of the way, but I thought it might be the fastest way for you to get a feel for the full scale of the place."

I began studying the structure, which was definitely impressive—and detailed. There were pots and pans in the kitchen, a plant with plastic leaves in the entryway, and miniature furniture in every single room.

I fingered the labels on each room, running my hand over the ones reading *Vestibule*, *Color Gallery*, and *Primrose Ballroom* before bending down to the bottom floor, which must have been the sub-basement Savilla had mentioned.

"That's the hall. It's officially called the Vampire Room," Savilla said, coming to stand over my shoulder.

I studied the label and, sure enough, she was right.

"That's just what we call it, not because there are actual vampires. No one has actually ever, like, sucked anyone's blood down there."

"Then why call it *that*?" Despite myself, I felt a shiver run down my spine as I remembered the local lore surrounding a tunnel collapse at one of the mines in the early 1900s. A lone, bloodied figure with pointed teeth had run out of the coal mine, and when the rescuers had chased him down to the graveyard, he'd disappeared into a mausoleum. Of course, it wasn't true, but the childlike part of my mind still wondered, *What if it is?*

"My great-grandmother traveled to the Balkans on her honeymoon and was obsessed with the legends about vampires, so she came back here and decided to host a themed event for Day of the Dead that year—1925, I think. She had an artist come in and paint all of these dark murals."

"How have I never heard about this?"

Savilla shrugged. "I guess the tours we did in school didn't think it was kid-friendly."

"Kids would love that," I said, my voice rising in pitch even as fear crept up. Part of me wanted to descend to the Vampire

Room that very moment to see it for myself, and the other part of me wanted to run back home right that minute.

Savilla's phone rang and she took it from her pocket, answering monosyllabically and hanging up after less than a minute before turning back to me.

"I've gotta get back, but take your time. Just turn out the lights when you're done, and I'm sure I'll see you back in the ballroom later. Seems like that's the headquarters for the investigation." Concern flitted across her face and she stared at me, frozen for a brief moment in the reality of the weekend. "I can't believe Brett's dead."

"Me neither," I said in a quiet voice.

Savilla took my hand and squeezed it tight, signaling with her resolute expression that it wasn't my fault and we would carry on. A moment later, I watched her walk away.

I hadn't been able to save Brett, but I couldn't fail Lacy too. With a little more than twenty-four hours until his email was set to expose her, I needed answers fast.

NINE

As soon as I walked back into the ballroom, it was clear Charlie had been looking for me. His eyes were heavy from working a full shift, and I considered that he'd likely been looking forward to a late night with me as much as I'd been looking forward to it with him. He could be warm and caring, I reminded myself, thinking of the last time he'd come to visit me in New York and we'd driven out to Buttermilk Falls State Park in Ithaca before walking to a local cemetery for a picnic.

"This is your idea of romantic, huh?" Charlie had asked, as I'd spread a blanket in the walkway between two rows of graves.

"Momma wrote me one letter a month for the first year after she died, all of them asking me to go out and do something. One of them said that Lacy and I should picnic in a graveyard, and we had a great time."

He'd lifted his soda can and bumped it against mine. "Cheers to living, I guess."

We'd eaten cheese and crackers and an assortment of fruit, stopping every now and then to steal a kiss. Afterward, we'd packed up everything and wandered through the headstones, pointing out our favorite epitaphs that the dead had left behind.

At the end of the weekend, when Charlie had stood at the door to my apartment waiting for an Uber back to the airport, he'd studied my face as if trying to memorize the turn of my lips, the bridge of my nose.

"What are you looking at?" I'd teased, tucking my head into his neck.

He'd nudged me away so he could properly look into my eyes, and my stomach had somersaulted.

"You," Charlie had said simply. "I'm looking at you."

Now, I was so confused by Charlie's aloofness. I supposed I should chalk it up to him simply doing his job. But did he have to do it without any compassion? Without so much as a hand on my shoulder? A steadying look into my eyes?

Charlie spoke now, his flat voice bringing me back. "Because you and Mina Davis attempted CPR, I'll need an official statement from both of you."

I inhaled and exhaled, trying to stay calm rather than exploding at him. "So, we're now suspects because we tried to help?"

He didn't answer my question, saying instead, "I've spoken with Lacy, Anton, Presley, and Joe. It's your turn now."

I glared at him.

Charlie closed his eyes for half a second too long. "Look, it will just take ten minutes, and one of my officers has to be with us because of our... relationship. If you don't want me there at all while you give your statement, then I'll understand."

"Fine."

I lagged several yards behind as he led me through the ballroom doors, past the Color Gallery where the overhead lights blared against the empty cases, through the carved wooden library doors, past the rows of shelves, and into an alcove that turned into a short hallway that led to a small gallery filled with portraits and art, as well as a couple of sitting areas.

The windows were stained glass, featuring tulips running in

a horizontal line at eye level. The glass petals were a deep red, and the rest of the room was charcoal from floor to ceiling. With the satin curtains drawn, no moonlight streamed in. Directly across from the couch hung the focal point of the room: a giant Finch family portrait with an expressionless Savilla and staid Glenda Finch, Savilla's stepmother, both seated. Mr. Finch towered behind them, both of his hands on his daughter's shoulders.

As I sat, I thought about saying something that I hoped would be charming, to get me and the sheriff back on more solid footing despite the circumstances: *Come here often?* Or perhaps one of the cheesy pickup lines I'd seen someone post recently: *Is it autumn? Cause I think I'm falling for you.* Before I could showcase my witticisms though, Charlie gestured for me to take a seat, and like magic, the deputy appeared with Mina right behind her.

Charlie smiled at his second-in-command in a way I didn't like, and my heart felt like it might flutter out of my chest, either from nerves or longing for him to smile at me that way again.

"Thanks for joining us, Deputy Wright," Charlie started.

Lovely. Her name was literally Ms. Wright.

As soon as the thought entered my mind, I hated that I'd gone there. I was not someone who viewed other women as competition. Momma and Aunt DeeDee had taught me by example that it's much better to live in a kind of sisterhood with other women than to fight against them. And even if Deputy Wright was competition, what would we be vying for? Charlie was not a prize to be won. He was flesh and bone, a man who was looking at me strangely as my eyes finally moved away from the woman in uniform.

The deputy gave a nod of acknowledgement and extended a hand to me. "Are you *the* Dakota Green? I've seen you a couple of times, but I don't think we've officially met."

I nodded, words caught in the back of my throat.

"Sheriff Strong has asked me to take the lead in our conversation tonight," the deputy said, her eyes flitting from him to us. "Now that you're both here, I'd like to thank you for trying to resuscitate Mr. Brinkley." Deputy Wright's expression was full of understanding and compassion. "It can be harrowing to attempt medical aid, especially when it's unsuccessful. The end result does not diminish the fact that you were the only two people who actively tried to save him before the medics arrived. You should be proud of your efforts."

My eyes began to fill at the words, and I felt silly as I quickly wiped them. It would take some time to be able to process the fact that I hadn't been able to save someone when it really counted, and the acknowledgement that I'd tried meant more than I could say.

"Can I get the spelling of both of your names?"

I gave her mine and Mina followed. "M-I-N-A, D-A-V-I-S."

Mina's voice had deepened with the late night, and I thought I recognized something in the timbre. Or maybe it was the way she tilted her head an inch to the right that was so familiar.

Putting the pieces together, I asked, "Are you any relation to Doris Davis? As in Miss 1962?"

Mina's features relaxed at the mention of the older woman, who'd been a sassy balm for my soul during the pageant investigation during the summer. "She's my grandmother."

Of course. She looked just like the younger photos I'd seen of the 1962 Rose Palace Queen, Doris Davis. My mouth turned up at the recognition of her features in this younger version.

"When I saw the job posting for this gig, I thought I might get the chance to come back to where she'd won. I never expected..." Mina's voice trailed off.

"Have you been here, to The Rose, before tonight?" the deputy asked.

"I grew up in California but every summer I would stay

with Gram during the month of July, so I could come to the pageants with her. It's how I recognized Mr. Brinkley's hometown when he was on *Small Town, Big Romance*."

"I understand that you both performed CPR on Mr. Brinkley?" Charlie said, bringing us back to the real issue. He was sitting on one of the wingback chairs, his pad and pen ready to record anything of note that we said.

"I began CPR," I answered. "And Mina jumped in to help." As I spoke, I noticed that Mina's chin quivered as she inhaled, like a kid trying to contain her emotions.

"I'm sorry." Mina wiped at her eyes and tried to catch her breath. "I feel bad because I'm sad for Brett, I am, but my grandmother..." Mina began to cry softly.

"It's okay, take your time," Deputy Wright broke in, extending a reassuring hand to Mina's shoulder.

It took several moments for Mina to collect herself. Finally, she took a tissue that the deputy had pulled from a pack in her pocket and blotted her eyes and nose with it before continuing. "I think I'm even more emotional because my grandmother decided this week not to continue chemo." Mina took a couple of deep breaths and put both hands in her lap. She sat up straighter, trying to regain her composure.

"I'm sorry. Illness can be... devastating," the deputy offered, her voice steady and calm.

"Miss 1962 is quite a personality," I added to break the silence, suddenly recalling how it felt to get the news of my mother's diagnosis. Doris had seemed immune to such things as cancer, but of course, none of us were. My heart ached for her and Mina. "Your grandmother gave me all kinds of advice during the pageant."

"That sounds like her." Mina gave a small chuckle. "I wouldn't be such a mess except that I'm really the only one that Grammy has left. And now I'm stuck here this weekend instead of being with her."

I caught myself warming faintly at hearing the pragmatic judge called something as endearing as *Grammy*.

"Where is your grandmother now?" Charlie asked.

"At a hospital in Richmond, but they're supposed to be discharging her soon. I'm going there as soon as I leave. I want to speak with the hospice nurse to see if we can get her home in time to..." Mina began crying again, and I felt her pain like a tear in my own chest. I knew this feeling too well—I'd wanted Momma to die at home, but an emergency had landed her in the hospital and then in the hospice facility instead. She never saw our house again.

"Are you living with her right now?" the deputy asked.

"Kind of. I have an apartment in L.A. since that's where I get most of my gigs. After Grammy was diagnosed, I flew back once every couple of months for her appointments, but recently, I've been staying with her. That's why I was glad that Brett wanted to film nearby for a few weeks." Mina seemed to suddenly realize to whom she was speaking and covered her mouth with one hand before letting the words rush out of her. "This is not what you need to know for the investigation. I'm so sorry to bother you with my family stuff."

"Is this your first time at The Rose? I mean, in recent years?" Charlie asked patiently.

"No," she answered, concern furrowing her brow. "Grammy invited me here when she was judging the pageant two or three years ago. I actually helped pass out programs." She smiled at the memory. "It was quite a circus."

That was an appropriate way to describe the hustle and bustle of pageant weekend.

Charlie sat up and glanced at the deputy before recording something in his notebook.

"I've also filmed a couple of things on-site, one of them being Brett's home episode for *Small Town, Big Romance* two years ago." Mina looked from him to me to the deputy, her nerves obvious. "Why? Is it bad that I've been here before?"

"He writes down anything and everything," the deputy said as she smiled at him in a way that felt too familiar. "It's how he works."

It was like she knew him better than I did.

"It's true. I'm a stickler for details. It drives some people crazy," Charlie said, his eyes fluttering to me before going back to Mina. "I've already spoken to Dakota, but Miss Davis, can you tell us in your own words what happened this evening?"

Charlie had his pen ready, and in that moment I thought I understood something. Maybe he had brought me here not to question me but to be privy to one of his interviews. Not that he thought Mina was guilty, necessarily, but maybe he wanted me to see the kinds of things that he and the deputy asked, the kinds of things he needed to know. When we'd been thrown together in our first case at the pageant this summer, he had learned that as a layperson I could get information he couldn't, and enhancing my skills now could only increase the kind of intel I could provide.

Mina began detailing things just as I remembered them, everything from the coughing to the passing out to me beginning CPR and her joining me on the ground to take over every other round of compressions. But then she added something that I hadn't noticed at the time.

"I actually didn't give him breaths during the last round because I thought I saw blood in his mouth."

"Blood?" Charlie asked, as if he hadn't been aware of the thin trail we'd noticed at the edge of Brett's mouth. "Why do you think he might've been bleeding?"

Mina bit her lip, taking the question as seriously as if she were a medical expert weighing in. "I would guess that he bit his tongue when he fell to the ground. Or maybe he hadn't been choking—or at least, not just choking. Maybe something else was wrong with him?"

Charlie nodded and recorded what she'd said, which matched what we'd observed of the body. "Are you certified in CPR?"

"Yes—or, no, not officially, but I learned by watching videos when Grammy was diagnosed."

"You thought you might need it for her... cancer?" Charlie asked. I hated that he sounded skeptical, and I hoped Mina wasn't picking up on it.

"No. I mean, she has ovarian cancer, and as soon as she was diagnosed, I read every article I could on it. The list of complications from the treatment is almost as scary as the diagnosis. I can't control much in this whole process, but I can know how to do a few helpful things. Or, at least, I thought I could while she was still undergoing treatment."

I'd done something similar when Momma was diagnosed, and I was picking up everything Mina was putting down, being reminded again of the same sense of powerlessness that I was certain she now felt. The knowledge that the end was coming for my momma had carved a hole in my chest that would never quite mend. Mina was on her own journey of loss, and I couldn't even help her, except perhaps in one way.

"I think that's enough for now," I said. I stood and shot Charlie a look.

His gaze met mine. "One more thing. When you were here with your grandmother and later for the filming, did you ever see Brett interacting with any of the people here tonight?"

Mina considered the question. "When we were here for the home episode, he spoke to Presley, of course. She was on the show," she clarified, which was probably a good thing since Charlie wasn't the reality TV type. "And Joe. He was here that weekend as well." She bit her lip and looked to the ceiling.

"Other than that, I don't think so. You could look back at the credits to know for sure."

Charlie recorded the info in his notebook. Joe's name stuck in my mind, specifically because of how he'd called Brett a son of a bitch at the bar earlier that evening. His tone hadn't been admiring, as in "that lucky son of a bitch." No, it had definitely been frustrated, perhaps envious, but not light-hearted. It couldn't go unnoticed either that Joe had been the one making drinks, which Brett had potentially choked on.

Mina's phone rang, and I saw that the caller was *Richmond Methodist Medical.*

"You should take it," I said.

Charlie and the deputy both nodded in agreement.

"Am I dismissed?" I asked, as Mina moved to the corner for a moment of privacy.

Charlie gave me a curt nod. "I need to address the crowd. I'll see you back in the ballroom."

I wanted to do the exact opposite of whatever he wanted. I suddenly had the urge to grab my keys, get in my car, and drive off into the night. Yes, this was an immature and ridiculous impulse, but I was over this night and this weekend and this season of life when decisions needed to be made about what came next. All I wanted was to run away.

Charlie's eyes caught mine, asking a silent question. He wanted me there, despite everything.

"See you in there," I said.

TEN

"Was that the doctor calling?" I asked Mina, as I found her in the hallway outside of the den, heading back toward the ballroom. I tried to keep my tone low enough that no one else could hear if they passed us.

With one hand, Mina worried at the bottom of her striped shirt, now untucked from her wide-legged jeans. She'd wiped under her eyes, and her makeup had rubbed off. Her face was slightly puffy, and her eyes red. "No, it was Grammy calling from her hospital room. She told me not to worry and that she's feeling fine and turning in for the night." She sniffled but tried for a slight smile. "Not that I believe her, but it was good to hear her voice."

"Did you tell her what's happening here?"

"Briefly." Mina's head swiveled to Charlie and the deputy several yards in our wake. "I told her that Brett Brinkley died and that the police are questioning witnesses, but I didn't tell her that I might be a suspect."

"I don't think that's what Char—or the sheriff—intended," I said, hoping I was right. "If that was the case, he might think I'm a suspect too."

Her eyes met mine as we neared the ballroom, and I could tell that she'd caught on to me almost calling the sheriff by his first name. "You two seem... close?"

I didn't confirm or deny the statement.

Mina didn't seem to want to pry. "Well, you were the first one who tried to help, which has to count for something."

I thought that fact should matter too, but I wasn't sure that it would when it came to Charlie's investigating rules of conduct. He had put my aunt behind bars, after all.

"Did Miss 1962—your grandmother—did she know Brett?" I asked, as we stepped through the ballroom doors, back to the scene of the crime.

"I'm sure she ran into him—Gram said everyone in town came to the pageant." Mina's eyes were piercing as she looked at me. "Regardless, do you think anyone actually *knew* him? Or Presley?"

The way Mina asked the question made me wonder how she felt about Brett. She was a woman about my age with long black hair and a willowy frame. Her profession kept her behind the lens of a camera, and for however long, her subject had been Brett Brinkley.

Had she felt some sort of connection to him?

"Lee and I..." Mina glanced in the direction of the person who'd pulled her away earlier to look at some footage. Her shoulders relaxed as she made some sort of decision. "We were on the show. Well, not *on it* on it. Lee was the jib operator, and I was basically a glorified gopher – did some off-screen, behind-the-scenes work, acted as an assistant, that kind of thing."

The fifty-something-year-old man was crouched in the corner. His expression was difficult to read from this far away, but he seemed concerned. Mina went silent for a few seconds as she processed our situation. Then, she turned back to me, more pensive as she spoke.

"Years ago, I worked as an extra on this police procedural

that never actually made it past the pilot, but in the episode, the detective had a piece of dialogue that stuck with me. He said something like, 'In the court of law, you're innocent until proven guilty, but in the interrogation room, it's just the opposite.'" Mina squinted, considering her line of reasoning. "I think you're right. I think the sheriff sees us as suspects, along with everyone else."

I wanted to argue with her, but my defenses sounded so ridiculous:

But I'm his girlfriend—or at least someone he's been dating.

I attempted CPR—even though it didn't work.

I helped him solve his last big case—and then left town.

Nope, none of those would hold water.

With the overhead lights on and the reunion attendees quickly tiring, we appeared a rather motley crew. Charlie stepped onto the third step of the stage, projecting loudly enough to be heard, while the deputy remained on the floor, her frame facing the crowd as if acting as a kind of bodyguard for him.

My former classmates and their plus-ones stared back at him with crossed arms and narrowed eyes, and I realized that to at least two-thirds of them, Charlie was an unknown quantity.

"Folks, I realize that tonight has been tough," Charlie began. "Brett was not only a member of the class of 2015 but also a good friend to many of you over the years."

I noticed Joe, still behind the bar, frowning, which made me wonder even more about what kind of friend he'd been to Brett. Yes, Brett had been buddies with Joe throughout high school, and yes, dating Lacy had gotten Brett admittance into a lot of social circles, but were these people Brett's friends?

"His death was sudden," Charlie continued. "Over the next few hours—and into tomorrow—we'll be conducting a full investigation of the events."

"You think someone in this room murdered him?" Will Hurt, Valerie's husband, called from the back. I was surprised she'd let him speak.

"Not necessarily," Charlie answered, putting out a steadying hand. "But the body does show clear signs of something beyond a mere choking incident."

"Like what?" Joe asked.

Once again I saw that Presley was standing only a few feet away from Joe. My eyes trailed to her, and from my angle I spotted a red light from a camera just over the woman's shoulder. Mina's partner, Lee, was filming the sheriff's speech.

"I can't get into those details right now," Charlie answered.

I wondered if he'd noticed the camera, but since he hadn't shut it down, probably not. Despite the uncertainty I was feeling about our relationship, I didn't want something caught on tape that shouldn't be public information. I started along the back wall toward Lee as Charlie continued to address the crowd.

"As I was saying, I know that some of you have lost someone very important to you."

"Tell them about Brett's body," Presley interrupted. Joe stood behind her now, his hand extended to her shoulder as if he were gently pulling her back. "Tell them about the signs of foul play."

"As I said, I can't go into specifics right now but"—Charlie's attention flickered to me as I scooted along the periphery of the crowd, but it didn't linger—"as soon as we have any more information from the official—"

"He was killed," Presley cut in, her tone certain. Joe did pull her back this time, but not before she ground out three final words: "By someone here."

Silence descended and the entire room seemed to hold a collective breath. I was the only one moving an inch, but even I paused, realizing that Presley had apparently either changed her mind about her *bisnonna*'s supposed curse, or now believed that there'd been some kind of human help involved in carrying it out.

"We don't know for sure that Brett was killed," Charlie corrected, breaking the silence. His tone had taken on a slight edge that others not attuned to his voice might not even hear.

"We all saw what happened," Valerie called to Presley. "No one touched him."

"There are other ways to kill someone," Presley shot back.

As I inched past Presley toward the camera, I noticed that her eyes were dilated, indicating that she'd had more than one drink from the bar.

Charlie didn't respond directly to Presley, saying instead, "We'll need an accounting of everyone before we let you head back home or to your hotels, so most of you will likely be staying here overnight. Savilla Finch has been kind enough to allow all of you free accommodations. If we haven't already spoken to you, we'll call your name soon, and if we have, please sit tight. We may have further questions."

A murmur spread across the room and a couple of people asked follow-up questions, but I was no longer paying attention to the details because I'd reached Lee and the steady red light of his camera. I tapped the cameraman on the shoulder, startling him.

"Hey," I said. "It's Lee, right?"

The man took his eye away from the viewfinder but didn't answer or turn off the camera.

"Why are you still filming?" I asked, moving in front of the lens so Charlie would be blocked.

"Presley told us to keep filming, said she could use it. Just following orders."

I tried to think whether or not Presley Lombardi currently had her own reality show, but came up with nothing. I wasn't exactly a TV aficionado. Presley could be airing herself nude every night on cable, and I, stuck in the lab with a dissected cat's heart, would have no idea. Regardless, it didn't really matter because the point was that Presley Lombardi was asking Lee to film something that certainly required consent from law enforcement.

She was also using the moments after her boyfriend's death as a kind of entertainment.

Brett was dead and she was the single star. Camera gold.

I stuck out a hand and lowered the camera. "You can turn it off for now, okay?"

"I don't think you have the authority to make that kind of decision," Lee said, standing to his full height, which was a few inches taller than me.

I started to tell him exactly what he could do with his camera when Mina intervened. "You're primarily the lighting guy anyway, Lee," Mina said, her voice easy as she took the camera from his shoulder. "And it's probably a good idea if you tell Dakota what you told me."

Lee's eyes shot from Mina to me, and he stuck out his bottom lip.

"She's good people, just trying to help," Mina said about me. "Go ahead."

Lee cleared his throat, suddenly seeming nervous. "We... Mina and I... we..." His voice was so low it was almost a whisper. "We filmed Brett's death. Accidentally."

I froze. The crime—or at least the end result—had been caught on film. That was the real camera gold, at least for investigators.

"We didn't mean to film it," Lee said. "We were just doing our job."

"Lee was getting a pan of the room," Mina added.

"I was checking the lighting so we could get different angles after the party was in full swing. Then Brett started..." Lee's words were coming rapidly. Maybe he was anxious about reliving the memory or perhaps he was more concerned about being seen as withholding evidence. "I dropped the camera when Mina ran over to help with CPR, but it was still filming."

That was odd. Why would he drop the camera if he wasn't the one hurrying to help with CPR?

"Where did you go during all of this?" I asked Lee, trying not to sound judgmental.

"I was..." He blinked several times as if trying to recall. "I was here, in the ballroom. I just... I was so flustered, I don't really remember..." He couldn't finish his sentence, couldn't come up with a reasonable answer, which made him seem guiltier than he might be.

"We need to give the footage to the sheriff," Mina said, her words firm as if she were finishing a conversation she'd already been having with Lee. "Maybe it has something that can help the investigation."

"I don't know." Lee frowned, looking at her with concern. "Although... it could clear things up." He rubbed at his jaw. "Especially because it makes one person in particular seem pretty guilty."

The hair on the back of my neck rose. "Presley?" I asked.

Lee shook his head. "Some Black girl dancing with Brett."

My eyebrows rose to my hairline and my mouth went dry at the way he'd thrown out the generic description with derision. *Some Black girl.* Not for the first time that night, I had the urge to slap a person.

I knew that Lee was talking about Lacy, one of three Black students in our graduating class. Aubergine High wasn't exactly a melting pot, and she was also the only person of color at the reunion who'd been dancing with Brett.

"Still..." Lee moved as if to take back the camera from Mina. "We can't just hand over footage that belongs to the production company."

"It's the Finches' production company, and yes, we can." Mina's tone was sharp as she stuffed the camera inside a bag and held it out to me.

I took it as four words stuck in my mind: *The Finches' production company*.

ELEVEN

Lacy was innocent. I knew this because she was my best friend, and I'd known her almost my entire life.

In second grade, I'd told her my biggest secret at the time: I had a crush on Joe—yes, *the* Joe Larson—primarily because one day on the playground he'd found a baby bird that had fallen from a tree and gently wrapped it up in a napkin, climbed the tree, and put it back. I'd had no idea that I wouldn't think about Joe in that way again until our junior year of high school when he asked me to prom. Our "relationship" had lasted until three weeks later when he burped the national anthem at a softball game, and I just couldn't see him like that anymore.

Back in second grade, though, I would draw very bad pictures of horses and give them to my friends. After the baby bird incident, Trudy Livingston had found one I'd made of me and Joe as horses with hearts around our heads and, during math center time, she'd passed it around for the entire class to see. When seven-year-old Lacy had realized what was circulating, she'd snatched it out of a kid's hand, stood on a desk in the middle of class, and begun to passionately belt out "Part of Your World" from *The Little Mermaid*.

It was Katniss volunteering as tribute, it was Abraham sacrificing his son, it was beautiful.

The rest of the day had been spent talking about Lacy's song, discussing whether it was brave or the s-word (stupid), and forgetting about the lovey-dovey horse versions of me and Joe.

I would always remember how Lacy had helped people turn their attention to her instead of pointing fingers at me, and now I needed to ensure that she wasn't unduly accused. So as not to withhold evidence, I would show Charlie the footage, but I would watch it with him, arguing her case as needed.

I made my way to the stage and got Charlie's attention, lifting the camera bag up for him to see.

"Mina said they were getting shots of the room when Brett started coughing. There's footage of the death."

Charlie took it from me and glanced around. "This way."

He led me to the sound booth and closed the door behind us. It was the first time we'd been alone all evening without a dead body in between us.

Methodically, Charlie removed the camera from the bag, and familiarized himself with the controls.

I tried to keep my hands still and my heart from exploding as he found the video and pressed play. I wanted to see the footage, but I didn't want Charlie to view it the way Lee obviously had—as if Lacy might be to blame for Brett's death.

The small screen came to life with familiar figures. There was Lacy, her and Brett dancing as the camera panned past them to take in the full length and breadth of the Primrose Ballroom.

For several slow seconds, the lens lighted on Jemma singing her heart out, on the paper-mache flowers hanging from the ceiling, on the disco ball hanging above the center of the dance floor, on Presley heading toward the back of the ballroom as if she had other business to attend to.

Then, it was back to Brett and Lacy, her arm draped over

his shoulder, her hand dangling over his cup. Brett turned toward her, a big grin on his face, and spoke into her ear for several seconds. As he talked, Lacy's body language shifted, and though I couldn't see her face clearly, I was fairly certain that she elbowed him in the stomach before responding.

A figure's hand entered the screen. Then, half a head made an appearance. It was Anton. It seemed as if he was about to step onto the dance floor, but Lacy looked straight at him and shook her head. Anton stayed where he was.

Oh, Lord.

I made myself keep watching, hoping that Charlie was somehow seeing all of this differently than it first appeared.

There were other people milling about on-screen, confusing the eye. Valerie stood on the outskirts of the dance floor next to Will Hurt, her arms crossed. Mina held a light meter a few feet from their subject. Joe spoke to a passing server. Jemma kept on singing.

Brett bounced to the beat of the music and tried to put both of his hands on Lacy's hips. She pushed him off and took one step back. He laughed and then he was downing his glass in one gulp.

Seconds later he began to clutch at his throat.

Presley came back on-screen at Brett's first wheezing cough but didn't immediately rush over.

Lacy, her eyes wide, scanned the room and backed away from Brett as his hand went to his neck and he began clawing at his throat.

Less than thirty seconds later, the camera fell, the world tilting sideways as the crowd made a circle around Brett. It was hard to see much of anything clearly anymore, but I could vaguely hear myself telling Lacy to call 911 as I started CPR.

The camera caught the sounds of me compressing, counting, and breathing into Brett's mouth before Lee picked up the device, looked straight into the lens and cursed.

Then, the screen went dark. That was the end.

I didn't want to be the first to speak, so instead I took the camera from Charlie's hands and restarted the video. My heart hammered a steady rhythm.

"What are you doing?" Charlie asked, his brows furrowed as if he thought I might delete the footage.

"Playing it again," I said, sure that the late hour and my pounding headache had clouded my thinking, certain that I had to have missed something.

"You saw it too?"

"What do you mean?" I feigned ignorance. "What did you see?"

"Lacy," Charlie answered, his tone heavy and resigned. "Her hand, and the way she backed away when Brett started making noises."

I didn't answer as I peered down at the camera, watching the terrible tableau unfold again, pausing it every two or three seconds.

"I have to question Lacy again, maybe even detain her," Charlie said, sounding more and more official with each word.

I clenched my jaw. Did Charlie always have to act immediately? Couldn't his conscience take a half-hour break? Couldn't his reactivity wait until morning?

"She obviously had opportunity," Charlie mused. "Motive too, with their past relationship."

I looked up from the video and into his eyes. "What do you know about their past?"

"When I interviewed her earlier, she mentioned that they'd dated," he said, staring back at me. "Things ended badly."

That was an understatement.

"They were eighteen, and lots of relationships end badly," I said in her defense. "Anyway, Brett was the one who would have a motive against her, not the reverse."

"Why is that?"

"She was the one who left," I answered, my tone implying it was obvious. *The one who got away*, I thought, but didn't say.

"He ended up going away to school that fall too," Charlie argued back.

He was right, of course. I remembered Lacy telling me back then that Brett had gotten off the waitlist at Virginia Tech at the last minute. With the amount of partying he'd posted on Snapchat, admission to college had seemed to heal whatever wound their breakup had inflicted.

"Maybe Lacy regrets letting a reality TV star escape?"

"If you think Lacy cares about fame, you don't know her," I scoffed.

"That's the thing: I don't really know her," Charlie said, and for perhaps the first time in our relationship, I realized that was true.

Charlie, as they say, wasn't from around here. He didn't know my friends, and I didn't know his. I'd never heard of his former partner, the gorgeous new deputy, until I happened to run into them at the diner months ago, and I hadn't met her properly until tonight. In the brief span of our relationship, with half a dozen trips to visit one another and snatches of time on the phone, we'd only ever had time to get to know each other, and now I was beginning to wonder how well we'd done at that.

"Look, Dakota. I have to do what's in the best interest of the law." Charlie's voice was both preparing me and pleading with me to understand.

I hushed him with a wave of my hand. "Give me two minutes, that's all I ask." I let out a long breath and continued watching the video, and that's when I saw Brett's cup tilt, something long falling from the glass.

"Did you bag this up?" I asked, pointing at the screen.

Charlie studied the image. "The garnish? Yeah. I had one of my officers test it before sending it to the lab."

I thought back to the drinks Joe had been serving. My chat

with Joe at the bar. My FaceTime with Aunt DeeDee. Two images came to mind: the thin stalks sticking out of Joe's drink concoction and the pile of leaves near the sink while Aunt DeeDee stirred the contents of her mixing bowl. "It must be rhubarb. I saw mounds of it in the kitchen, and Aunt DeeDee said the caterer over-ordered."

"And Joe was the caterer?"

I nodded. Charlie already had his phone out and was looking up the plant even though I knew what he would find.

"The leaves are poisonous," I told him. "But it only causes stomach upset if ingested in bulk."

"There's no way it could've poisoned him so fast," Charlie muttered almost to himself.

"Regardless," I said firmly, "with this footage and with the rhubarb garnish you found in Brett's drink, you should probably focus on questioning Joe, don't you think? He was the one making the drinks, after all."

"I have questioned Joe," he said. "And I see what you're doing."

"I'm not doing anything," I said, with faux innocence.

I longed to escape to any room with a bed and sleep for the next twelve hours.

Charlie shot me a curious look. "I'll talk to Joe again, but afterward I need to confront..." His words trailed away.

Neither of us wanted him to finish that statement.

"I'm sure we'll have more sufficient evidence soon enough." I said the words with more confidence than I felt.

Instead of bustling out the door, Charlie leaned back against the wall and rubbed a hand across his brow in a childlike gesture. His usually bright eyes were tired and his shoulders were weighted with the burden of a man's death, but he still needed my help.

Maybe that was enough for now.

TWELVE

After Charlie and I parted with curt nods to one another, I started toward the kitchen, where Joe had spent the afternoon with Aunt DeeDee before guests had arrived. Maybe that space held some kind of clue. I just had to find it first.

I wandered through the house, passing various rooms and halls—the solarium, the library, the Color Gallery—that were becoming more and more familiar, before stumbling into the kitchen.

It was as large as any I'd imagine in a restaurant, and it was covered in state-of-the-art, stainless-steel appliances. At the back appeared to be a walk-in fridge, and everything was industrial-sized.

I spotted Aunt DeeDee standing at a long island wearing an apron with red strawberries scattered across it, hand-beating what looked to be whipping cream. A dishwasher was working a few yards away, the countertops were laden with half-empty trays of canapés and finger foods, and a server was leaving as I walked in.

"Oh, Lord, Dakota," Aunt DeeDee breathed as she set

down the bowl. "I'm half afraid to come out and be carted off to jail like last time."

I attempted a faint smile. "I think you're in the clear, though Charlie and the deputy will probably have questions for you at some point."

Aunt DeeDee raised her eyebrows at the mention of the deputy. "I met her. Seems like a nice enough gal, but very..."

"Pretty?" I finished.

My aunt lifted a shoulder. "You have to trust your man."

"Right, well, Joe's in the ballroom now with the other witnesses, detailing what they saw, so I thought I'd take the chance to look around in here."

Aunt DeeDee nodded easily. "I can tell you this: Brett didn't have a single thing to eat from this kitchen." That matched with what Presley had said about his strange eating habits, but Aunt DeeDee was speaking so quickly that I couldn't get a word in. "I already had one of the servers confirm it, which was a relief, and, apparently, that man never ate anything except for a few hours a day. I don't know how a body can live like that."

I knew Aunt DeeDee, who loved to serve any person within a mile a large helping of down-home cooking, would be appalled at such a notion, but in this instance, I was glad she could provide confirmation—albeit second-hand—of his fasting, because that meant that whatever had killed Brett had to have been either in his glass or from some other direction we hadn't yet considered.

It was still hard to wrap my mind around the reality of Brett's death. Not that I was inexperienced with the concept of death—in fact, my entire course of study was how to treat creatures whose bodies were betraying them. I'd also watched my own mother struggle for breath at the end of her life, and I'd been the one to find Mr. Finch's body. Brett's death felt different though. Someone my age, whom I'd known for most of my life, was gone.

"You okay, doll?" Aunt DeeDee asked, putting aside her mixing bowl and coming to stand next to me. "You need to talk about something?" She put a reassuring hand on my shoulder, and with the other, she stroked my hair out of my eyes, the same thing she'd done to help me fall asleep as a child.

I leaned into her. "It's just... I don't know what to do."

"About?"

Where to start? My future career? Charlie's odd ambivalence toward me? The fact that I'm Savilla's illegitimate half-sister?

The last one actually made the most sense. I hadn't yet told Aunt DeeDee about it, for two reasons: first, I didn't want to burden her with news I couldn't quite process myself, and second, I didn't want anyone in my life, especially my aunt, to look at me differently after learning I was a member of the richest family in the state.

But how could I say all of that in between watching a man die, suffering a panic attack, and investigating a potential murder? I supposed, as Momma would say, I just had to spit it out.

"I got a letter from Momma soon after the pageant, and in it... she told me some news."

Aunt DeeDee tilted her head, waiting for me to continue.

"My father was..." I swallowed hard.

Aunt DeeDee's hand froze in mid-air.

I decided to go for it, spewing everything at once. "Momma told me that my father was Frederick Finch, which means Savilla Finch is my sister. Also, tomorrow is Mr. Finch's will reading, and I've been asked to attend."

Aunt DeeDee's cheeks puckered as if she'd bitten down on a lemon. She reached out a hand to steady herself on the steel counter, and nearly a full minute passed before she spoke.

"Mr. Finch was your father," she said slowly, trying out the information. "And Savilla is your sister."

I couldn't tell if Aunt DeeDee was appalled or pleased.

"What are you thinking?" I asked.

She handed me a bottle of water and placed a pecan bar on a napkin in front of me, almost by rote movement. "Eat something. You look peaked."

I took a small bite and the nuttiness hit my tongue, reminding me of when she'd made the same treats for me after school when I was a kid.

Aunt DeeDee took a tiny bite as well before pushing the dessert out of her line of sight and straightening her shoulders. "Well, darlin', that's big news for a night like this, but I suppose that's how life comes at you. All at once." She breathed in deeply. "I can't say I'm too surprised, though I have no idea why your momma waited till she was in the ground more than a year to inform you of your parentage."

"You're not shocked?"

"Not entirely." Aunt DeeDee considered. "Mr. Finch would ask me about you. Check in, I suppose. I thought it was small talk, but I can see now that perhaps he had a distant sort of fatherly interest. As for your momma, she avoided him like the plague—her standard approach to exes— and she never would talk about her one-night stand." Aunt DeeDee clicked her tongue and gave a slight chuckle. "The timing makes perfect sense. I don't know how I didn't see it all these years."

"I know how," I told her. "It's because it's crazy. Momma was everything Mr. Finch was not."

"Maybe, though people are complicated. And layered." She motioned toward a tall confetti cake, and I understood the metaphor without her having to spell it out. "Your momma and Mr. Finch had a brief connection and it made you. That's a pretty good outcome, I'd say."

Aunt DeeDee touched her forehead to mine and placed a dollop of whipped cream on my nose.

I laughed, relieved that she was carrying the weight of this secret that I'd kept for the past few months so easily. It made me kick myself for not telling her earlier.

"As for the will reading, I wouldn't expect too much," Aunt DeeDee said, pulling back. "Mr. Finch was sometimes stingy with family, although... maybe that was just with greedy women who wanted to murder him."

"I have no expectations," I said, wiping off the whipped cream and touching her hand. "And thank you."

"For what?"

"For not freaking out."

"At my age, I've seen too much to even consider freaking out over something as small as an illicit father and a secret sister."

I smiled before my eye caught the kitchen clock and I suddenly remembered that I'd come down here to find out more about Joe.

"I'd love to talk to you about some other topics," I said. "Plans for my job, mainly, but that can wait. First, can you show me where Joe put his things when he arrived this evening?"

Aunt DeeDee studied me. "Dakota, hon. You should let the sheriff do the investigating."

I gave her a mock shocked expression and pointed a finger at her. "That's not what you said last time."

"Last time I had no choice," Aunt DeeDee countered. "I don't want you getting wrapped up in something dangerous. Men like Brett..."

"What about men like Brett?"

Aunt DeeDee shook her head. "I'm not exactly sure. It's more of a feeling I got after watching him on that silly TV show."

"You watched *Small Town, Big Romance?*" I said, incredulous.

"That's the one." Her nose crinkled. "Brett was always just so smarmy."

That was a word I hadn't heard her use to describe anyone until now. Still, I wasn't backing off of the investigation.

"Listen, I think I'm safe, and I'm pretty sure that anyone trying to kill Brett wouldn't be after me."

"Unless you get too close."

"I'll keep the appropriate distance," I told her, knowing that this vague promise was a very subjective line. I couldn't help being involved, though. Brett deserved justice. He might not have been a good person, but hours before he'd had a whole life ahead of him.

And solving the mystery of his death might be the only way to keep suspicion off Lacy.

Aunt DeeDee sighed. Squaring her shoulders, she continued: "When Joe came down here to tell me what happened, I told him that people would be hungry, especially for comfort food, if they have to stay here tonight, so we should keep sending out platters of goodies periodically."

"Did Joe seem upset?"

Aunt DeeDee tapped her nails on the counter and squinted. "Joe was sad, but I could tell he was trying to keep it together."

"For you?"

"For himself, and maybe for the gal who was with him."

"Who was with him?"

"Cute girl. Dark hair and eyes. About your height. Name was... Priscilla?"

"Presley?" I asked.

"That's it. Like Elvis, not his wife." Aunt DeeDee turned and dropped a cup of blueberries into a batter of some kind that was in a bowl on the counter. "You know, sweetheart, Joe's been through some things."

I had no idea what my aunt meant, unless she was talking

about the time Joe got suspended for squeezing super glue in all the locks on the doors to the academic classes—as if he actually thought the administrators would let us only attend our electives the rest of the school year.

"Joe's always been a sensitive boy, probably wanted to study theater because of that, but look where he is now. Trying to start a business and make ends meet. Life doesn't always go as planned."

I knew this to be true.

"Anyway, I guess kids don't often know other kids' struggles," Aunt DeeDee said almost to herself as she added a pinch of salt. "Youth can be very near-sighted."

Growing up in Aubergine hadn't been perfect, but I supposed that for me, with Momma and Aunt DeeDee seeing to my every need, it had been kind of idyllic. It made sense that this wouldn't have been true for everyone.

I waited and when she seemed reluctant to continue, I prompted her. "What happened to Joe?"

"Not one single thing. Just..." Aunt DeeDee looked to the high ceiling before staring back at me. "You had a good childhood, right?"

The question was even heavier now with the recent news about my father.

"Sure," I answered. "I knew you and Momma loved me, had my back. I didn't feel like I was missing anything, not really."

"Right. So... Joe's was good too until he was about nine and his dad injured his back. A pain doctor in the city started his father on opioids, and after that, he went the way of a lot of citizens in small-town America twenty years ago. I heard about it as an ongoing prayer request on the roster of First Baptist. From what I can tell, Joe's dad still struggles."

I winced. That would've been when we were in third or fourth grade, my era of *The Suite Life of Zack & Cody* and hatching baby chicks for a science fair project, not watching a parent struggle with addiction.

"I'm just saying," Aunt DeeDee continued, "each person has been through something, regardless of whether or not it's visible."

"I hear you," I said. "But the more info I have about Joe, then the faster I can help Charlie eliminate suspects."

Aunt DeeDee folded her arms and considered my logic. "Joe's a good kid. I'm sure he's innocent, but if you want to be certain that you can cross him off your list, then fine, take a look at his things."

Honestly, I didn't want to cross him off. I wanted to find out he was guilty. Then I could stop doubting my best friend. For Aunt DeeDee's sake though, I would give Joe a chance.

Aunt DeeDee lifted a thumb and pointed over her shoulder. "He put his stuff in a locker in the back of the kitchen."

"Thank you," I told her, before planting a quick peck on her cheek.

THIRTEEN

Aunt DeeDee went to grab some extra plates and napkins from storage, and I headed toward the kitchen staff's lockers, planning to quickly look through Joe's possessions to see if he had anything that might make it seem like he'd wanted his oldest friend dead. Maybe he had a bottle of undetectable arsenic rolling around in the bottom of his bag?

The lockers were in an alcove in a narrow hallway off the kitchen, and as soon as I reached them, I began trying the metal handles. The first four were completely empty. The fifth contained car keys; the sixth, a wallet with a couple of dollars and a debit card inside.

I knew the seventh must've been where Joe had dropped his things earlier in the day because the first thing I saw was a stack of photos of Joe. As I flipped through them, I quickly realized they were professional, black-and-white 8x10 headshots. At the bottom of each photo, in which he appeared far more handsome and far less goofy than how I pictured him when he came to mind, was printed his full name, Joseph Andrew Larson, and on the back was his resumé with castings and dates ranging over the last two years.

The very first one listed was *Small Town, Big Romance* in the part of "Brett Brinkley's friend," which made me think again that the show must've been heavily scripted. The rest of the list consisted of appearing as an extra in five movies I'd never heard of, and one Netflix show.

Under "Representation," his agent was listed as Presley Lombardi, which was strange, particularly since, as far as I knew, Presley wasn't an agent. Maybe she was unofficially representing him? Could that be the reason that she and Joe had seemed so close earlier this evening, their heads practically touching as he'd leaned across the table and whispered to her?

I held the photos and tried to wrap my mind around what Joe was playing at. As far as I knew, he'd mostly performed odd jobs around Aubergine to make ends meet, and apparently, he'd tricked my aunt into thinking he was a good enough guy to deserve help starting, of all things, a catering business. But his first major gig had ended in the death of his best friend.

Joe was looking guiltier and guiltier to me, but for Aunt DeeDee's sake I needed to give him the benefit of the doubt. Besides, I wasn't sure how seriously Charlie would take my hunches. I needed proof of something, anything.

I put the photos on the bench and turned to the remaining contents of the locker, all the while keeping an eye on the door to ensure I wasn't caught unawares. There was a backpack, and inside I found a yearbook from 2015, which would've been strange if the reunion wasn't this weekend. Maybe Joe had planned to pull it out and reminisce. I opened the cover and spotted several signatures, including mine.

There was also a note from Lacy, dating back ten years:

To the biggest weirdo. Take care of Brett at V Tech next year.

—Lacy, 5/24/15

Brett and Joe had been admitted to the same school—or, to be more accurate, Joe had been recruited to play football for them. Although I'd never cared about team sports, I did remember that he'd led our fearless Aubergine Fighting Farmers to victory at the state championships our junior and senior years.

Joe had come home from college after only one semester, though. From town gossip at the Christmas tree lighting that year, I knew it had something to do with him being caught with an illicit substance. There were even whispers of Brett's name too, but he'd stayed and graduated right on time.

Something had happened, possibly something involving Brett Brinkley, that had derailed Joe Larson's college career.

I smelled motive, and the scent was revenge.

Next to Lacy's entry, in different handwriting, was written *valedictorian*, which seemed strange enough on its own. But while some people might've gone back and labeled people that they didn't want to forget as they aged, Joe certainly didn't seem the type.

I went back through the pages and spotted Savilla's 2015 message to Joe:

Get rich and marry me. Or not. JK.

XOXO—Savilla

I scanned the rest, which seemed like inside jokes and ridiculous allusions to our twelve—thirteen, if you counted kindergarten—years together. It made me glad I'd grown up in Aubergine, a close-knit community.

Maybe too close-knit sometimes.

I came across a comment that, based on the initials and the creep factor, must have been from Brett Brinkley.

Your mom was fun last night. I'm coming for your sister (the hot one) next.

—BB

Ew.

Brett had been dating Lacy when he'd written that—they hadn't broken up until right before both of them left for college. Even if he hadn't been, though, it was still not okay. I shuddered at the kinds of things that were normal for boys to say only a decade or so ago.

I flipped through the pages of the yearbook and landed on one that had been dog-eared. It was a photo of Brett and Joe in football uniforms, sweaty and exhausted after a game, their arms thrown over one another's shoulders—except that Brett's figure had been Xed out with a thick, black marker.

I set aside the yearbook and quickly pulled out the rest of the contents from the backpack: a Swiss Army knife, a receipt for an oil change, a pack of gum that was mostly empty, and a case with one silver CD inside. *How very early 2000s of him.*

I flipped the case over to see handwriting that matched the loopy scrawl from the yearbook: *Our Big Romance.*

It was part of the name of Brett and Presley's reality TV show from two years earlier but with the possessive plural pronoun added. I considered the implications, which depended on the answers to a few key questions. Whose romance, exactly? And was the tone intended to be nostalgic? Sarcastic? Derisive? The show playing in the Media Room earlier that night came to mind. Did this CD also contain footage of *Small Town, Big Romance?* I needed to find out, and since I didn't have anywhere to put it, I lifted the back of my shirt and tucked it in the waistband of my jeans.

As I began to stuff the other items back inside the bag, someone stepped forward.

It was Presley, a puzzled expression on her face. "Dakota?"

I stared blankly at her.

Jutting her head like a schoolmarm who'd caught a kid cheating, Presley said stiffly, "Can I help you?"

I didn't immediately answer because I was confused as to why she was asking if she could help me with Joe's things. What business was it of hers if someone rifled through Joe's personal belongings?

I grabbed the closest thing within reach, which happened to be Joe's headshots, inventing a feasible lie, something I'd never been good at. As Momma always said, I was a born truth-teller. My face, if not my words, gave me away.

"I opened the wrong locker," I said.

She glanced down at the open backpack. I wasn't fooling anyone, and we both knew it.

"What are you doing all the way in the kitchen?" I asked, realizing that perhaps I could turn the questions around and stump her.

Presley straightened and then crossed her arms. "I was looking for Joe."

I raised my eyebrows to study her, and now she was the one to squirm.

"All of this has been so..." Presley's eyes began to fill quickly, and her shoulders crumpled forward as she sank onto the bench next to the backpack, which still had the yearbook sticking out of the top.

Her tears bought me time to think. I wasn't sure if I should try to comfort her or demand answers about why her name was on Joe's headshots. I sat down next to her, at a loss for how to proceed and feeling defeated by this whole terrible night. I placed the headshots in her hands and decided to let her tell me what she wanted, when she wanted. I was almost too tired to do otherwise.

"Joe wants to be famous," she said, taking them from my

hands and hiccupping. Presley put a hand over her lips and smiled down at the image of him. "He's so much like Brett."

I knew that look: the same one Lacy had when she turned to Anton; the same one I likely had whenever Charlie came into view. So it was true. Brett's girlfriend had eyes for his former bestie. I could only wonder how far these feelings had gone.

"Is Joe actually like Brett?" I asked, struggling to see the similarities. Of course, they'd always been buddies, and they'd always gotten into trouble together. But Brett had struck me as a self-obsessed jerk while Joe seemed to have a couple of redeeming qualities. He could carry on a conversation without making it all about himself, for example. And Joe was a hard worker, even if he couldn't ever seem to find his calling in one particular career.

"He and Brett were always competing, even for me. That's why I told him I'd help him get a foot in the door in Hollywood. What he doesn't understand is that a foot is never enough. You have to give over your whole self, every ounce, every inch." She shivered and drew her arms around herself. "It's like being eaten alive, bite by bite."

The words Lacy had said to Anton came back to me: *I know how to handle a man who bites.* My heart beat faster, and I inhaled deeply. Those words didn't mean anything. They didn't.

I watched Presley wipe at her eyes with a clenched fist and decided to slightly redirect our conversation.

"I bet Joe was pretty jealous when Brett's song became a hit," I suggested. "Do you know if he wrote 'The One That Got Away' about Lacy?"

"I thought so, but when I asked..." Presley shook her head. "He wouldn't tell me."

That was odd, to say the least.

Presley's eyes were bloodshot, and there were rings under her eyes, which were also smudged with mascara. Her obvious signs of fatigue reminded me that time was running short, so I decided to go straight to the key information.

"Do you have any idea what Brett's email password might be?"

Her eyes squinted, as if she were trying to get her bearings in the middle of a conversation she didn't know we were having.

"His password? How would I know that?"

"You are his girlfriend," I reminded her, hoping, even though I knew it was a long shot, that they were the kind of couple who shared passwords.

She laughed in my face, a kind of half-cackle, half-amused sound. "Yeah, no. We weren't that *close*." The words were mocking, as if she were communicating a message far beyond the words, as if they hadn't even been friends, much less a couple.

More and more, Presley and Brett's relationship seemed to be built on secrets and hidden things, two features no real relationship could bear long term. I observed her, noticing the way her tears caught the light.

"It's eleven fifty-eight," Presley said, as she glanced at her watch. Then, her eyebrows shot up as she thought of something else and stared straight at me almost as if in a trance. "Almost midnight," she mumbled to no one in particular. "The witching hour."

With that, she stood and hurried away, leaving me there to wonder what else Brett hadn't told her—and what she hadn't told him.

PART II

Saturday
After Midnight

FOURTEEN

I made my way out of the kitchen, passing the vestibule and spotting Savilla, who stood behind a marble desk handing out keys to reluctant guests. She caught my eye and waved me over as Will Hurt took a key and went back in the direction of the ballroom, presumably to find his wife.

"Hey," I said, "do you have an old computer? Something that would play this?" I pulled the CD case from the back of my jeans.

Savilla took a beat and then lifted a finger, calling over a staff member and giving them quick instructions to take over for her.

"Come with me."

We headed to Aunt DeeDee's old office in the library. With the pageant officially only on hiatus, her ancient computer would still be there—perfect for reading decades-old technology.

Savilla opened the office with one of the keys on her ring. "I think this will work," she said with a wink.

I sat behind my aunt's desk and Savilla hovered over my shoulder, her voice eager. "What are we looking for?"

I gave her a two-minute rundown of the past hour or so, realizing all the while that I was talking to her as easily and openly as I would've with Momma, Aunt DeeDee, or Lacy. With each word, her face grew brighter. Even if she didn't know about our connection, she was enjoying being part of my life. That, at least, boded well for the will reading.

"Oooo... snooping," Savilla said when I finished. "Love it!"

I turned on the computer, which didn't require a login or password, and pressed a button to open the disc drive before sliding the CD out of its case and reading the cryptic hand-written message again: *Our Big Romance.*

Savilla spotted it over my shoulder. "Is that footage of the show?"

"We're about to find out."

After a couple of minutes of infuriatingly slow loading, the icon for the drive popped up and I clicked on it to find a list of video files that seemed to be in no particular order. I pressed play on the top one, named "STBR_Episode 8," and a clip from *Small Town, Big Romance* came alive on the computer screen.

Mr. Finch and Brett were wandering around the lawn at the back of the house, interview-style with a camera in front of them, though it wasn't clear who was interviewing whom. Mr. Finch wore khaki pants and a short-sleeved polo, and I watched him with renewed interest now that I could identify him as my biological father. I studied his nose and eyes and chin, trying to see something of myself in him—or of him in me—but I came up short. Momma's genetics had thankfully been the overbearing kind.

Brett wore faded jeans and a T-shirt that sported the image, perhaps ironically, of the farmer mascot that was splashed across all Aubergine High paraphernalia.

What was your favorite thing about growing up in Aubergine? Mr. Finch asked, his voice calm and clear and interested.

Probably the family values, Brett replied.

Um, yeah, those had sure served Frederick Finch and the Rose Palace well—if you didn't count philandering judges or missing pageant queens. I refrained from saying as much because Savilla's face was a mixture of loss and longing.

"Is this the first time you've seen your dad on camera since...?" I didn't finish the question, but Savilla nodded once, wiping away a tear. Compassion welled in me, and I reached to pause the footage.

"It's okay." Savilla touched my arm. "Let it play."

We picked back up as Brett was asking Frederick Finch a question.

Why did your family, after making so much money, decide to build a permanent residence in Aubergine? Brett was playing the inquisitive type as soft music sounded beneath what I guessed was supposed to be an intimate get-to-know-you.

My family earned their wealth in the diamond business in the late 1800s, Mr. Finch answered. *My grandfather came from Scotland in steerage, just him and a few coins to his name. After he saw the crowded New York tenements, he decided to go west. He wanted to find a place that looked more like the Highlands he loved, so he went out to the Dakotas to see if he could make his way in the world. Through a shrewd game of poker, he ended up with the deed to a mine near Spearfish, and it just happened to be filled with diamonds.*

I could imagine the commercials that must've run when this episode aired: *Finch diamonds for that special someone who may someday murder you.* Okay, maybe that wasn't their slogan, but it did seem to be the theme of this family.

I pushed aside those musings as I suddenly realized that I was not only listening to Mr. Finch talk about his ancestor – I was also hearing part of my family history, the half I'd never known.

Mr. Finch was detailing the life story of Savilla's—and my—

great-grandfather in Spearfish, South Dakota. Was that why I was named Dakota? A feeling of faintness washed over me, and the room tilted ever so slightly.

The disparity between the two branches of my family tree couldn't be more different: one had owned a diamond mine and founded a well-known jewelry company that provided the crowns for the oldest pageant in the U.S., and the other had worked in a Virginia coal mine for a pittance.

"Are you okay?" Savilla asked this time, catching my eye as she reached across me and pressed pause.

She had no idea that I was learning about a branch of my family tree for the first time, and I wasn't ready to tell her.

"They're just talking about Grandfather Gordon," Savilla said easily, misreading my fraught emotions as mere curiosity. "He died in 1953 at ninety-two years old, and was apparently quite a character. Wore only navy blue and red to show his American allegiance, and he proposed to his wife after he spent some time with her in a house of ill-repute in the Dakotas. A bit eccentric."

A great-grandmother prostitute? Wow. My origins were becoming more and more interesting.

"Gotcha," I said, trying to sound uninterested as I pressed play again.

On-screen, Mr. Finch and Brett walked past the hedge maze that I now knew housed an underground tunnel that might still be marked with Mr. Finch's blood. It was the place that had led me and a couple other pageant contestants toward unraveling the mystery of his death this past summer. The camera panned out to show the two men walking up the white stone portico to the back of the house.

A second later, the camera cut to a space that I didn't recognize, but with the grand piano, I could guess.

"Is that the Music Room?" I asked.

"Yep, second floor. Did you see it in the dollhouse?"

I nodded distractedly, realizing that this was where Brett had asked—or demanded—that Lacy meet him at midnight.

Savilla's phone lit up with multiple texts and she frowned as she read them. "Shoot. Looks like they can't find the keys to the residential wing of the house." She glanced at the computer and at me, explaining, "The original rooms use the old-fashioned brass keys rather than the scannable key cards. Will you be okay if I run back to the front and show them where to find them?"

"I'm good," I reassured her, even though I wasn't thrilled about being in this darkened area of the house by myself after midnight. Still, I wasn't one to believe in things that go bump in the night.

Savilla scurried away, and I turned back to the computer to finish watching whatever was on this CD, speculating about whether Joe or someone else had burned it.

I dragged the mouse across the screen to the CD menu, and I spent the next thirty minutes clicking through highlight reels from *Small Town, Big Romance*.

I stopped on the final episode in which Presley was being interviewed by an off-screen woman.

Interviewer: How are you feeling about tonight?

Presley: Good. Nervous. Excited.

Interviewer: Can you unpack that a bit for us?

Presley: Sure. I mean, Brett *could* propose, right? But he probably won't. Imagine, a proposal on live TV. I'm not sure I'm ready for that.

Interviewer: Are you feeling conflicted about how you might respond?

Presley: I know I want to be with him. We would be a fabulous power couple. Can you imagine?

Interviewer: I can. So, is that why you're still in it? To be a power couple?

Presley: No, that's not what I meant. It's just… I think we're good together, you know? We have the same aspirations, ambitions. But there's also… love.

Interviewer: Is there?

Presley: Is there what?

Interviewer: Love?

Presley: Of course.

Interviewer: What about the song he wrote? About the one that got away.

Presley: We all have that person, but obviously it didn't work out. Maybe they weren't compatible long term. Maybe they wanted to go different directions. Maybe they just couldn't make it work, you know?

Interviewer: I do know. I really do.

Next, I started watching a deleted scene, this one back in the Music Room at the Rose Palace. On-screen again, Mr. Finch pressed a button on the mantel and out of it slid a record collection ranging from Bach to the Beatles to Britney Spears. He held one record after another out to Brett, who looked on admiringly, glancing up every now and then to point out a classic to the camera. I had to give it to Brett, he was a natural.

Finally, after two full minutes of admiring records—I could see why this scene hadn't made it into the show—Mr. Finch held one up to the camera and grinned broadly.

Do you recognize this one? Mr. Finch asked Brett.

He smiled sheepishly. *That's not what I think it is, is it?* But by his smile and the gleam in his eye, he obviously knew it was his single, "The One That Got Away." He'd recorded it only months before, in early 2023, and the song's popularity had likely been the thing to cement Brett's place on the show later that fall.

And we just happen to have the writer and performer here. Mr. Finch winked at the camera. *What a great coincidence.*

I leaned closer to the screen, looking for something, anything, that might offer a clue about this song's origins or inspiration. All I saw was the two men's cheesy grins as they preened for the camera, Brett grabbing a guitar that just happened to be behind him. He sat on a stool and began to play, the words and chord progression as basic as always.

Mr. Finch stood behind Brett for the entire fifty-second verse and chorus of the song, an unabashed plug for whatever Brett was selling: charm, goodwill, or actual merchandise. The entire scene was clearly staged for Brett to perform his runaway single because in the corner, a QR code had popped up.

I paused the clip, taking out my phone and holding it up to the code. A website appeared for a company I'd never heard of, but in large letters visitors were encouraged to *WATCH THE MUSIC VIDEO for "The One That Got Away."* I scanned the page for the fine print, reading aloud the name of the production company: Petal Productions.

The logo was a wreath of green leaves with a rosebud in the center. Petals, like on a rose. The Finches certainly remained on brand.

If Petal Productions had helped Brett, that meant that Mr. Finch had had a hand in pushing Brett into the limelight. It would make sense for Mr. Finch to want to pull an up-and-comer under his wing. He'd done it with Dr. Bellingham, the disgraced plastic surgeon and pageant judge who had then taken part in a plot to murder him. Mr. Finch obviously hadn't been a great judge of character, but it would stand to reason that he would see potential in a young Aubergine resident in his daughter's class and try to bolster him, give him a head start in life. It would also make sense in terms of Mr. Finch's expansion into various streams of income from diamonds to pageants to plastic surgery. A production company for pop-culture trash would fit right in.

I wondered if there might be clues to the identity of the one that got away, so I opened the chord chart for the music, which contained the lyrics to the now-infamous song. I read all the way to the bridge when he referred to "the pretty face with all the frills and lace, my young rose, full of love and grace." No wonder Lacy first thought the song was about her. As I read, I pressed the link for the music video to follow along.

There was Brett standing with a guitar and full band in front of the rose hedge maze at night, the mountains barely visible in the distance. I studied each of the band members, but I didn't recognize a single person. Maybe that wasn't surprising since the group had disbanded as quickly as it had come together.

Brett had been the truest definition of a one-hit wonder.

I thought how strange it was that he—and apparently Mr. Finch—had put so much time and effort and money into this one song and then never recorded another note: according to the Internet and a quick search on Spotify. But then, I supposed the timing didn't make sense to pursue a music career when soon after he landed a spot on a show that became such a sensation. Brett had obviously been far less passionate about music than he was about fame in any form.

The music video was straightforward—Brett wandering the

estate, singing to camera. But when he hit the bridge, a woman in white appeared in the peach orchard. Ethereal in a gauzy dress, she kept her back to the camera. Just as she turned, about to reveal her face, she vanished. In her place, Brett's hand opened to reveal a rose-pink stone before the camera pulled back to show him alone by the hedge maze.

Right before the camera screen went to black, though, there was a woman's voice, low and sonorous, whispering the last line of the song: "The one that got away."

Goosebumps rose on my arms. I recognized that voice. I rewound it and played it back. Then, I did it again.

I could swear that was the same voice in the interview clips, the same voice I'd heard echoing through the speakers in the Media Room earlier that evening when I'd stumbled on Anton and Lacy. I played it again, even more certain this time that the voice of the woman in the music video was the same as the interviewer off-screen in *Small Town, Big Romance*.

But that timing didn't make sense. This song had been produced before he'd been on the show.

I considered what this might mean. The date of the files confirmed the fact that the music video had been finished a few months before *Small Town, Big Romance* even started filming. But the voice unmistakably belonged to the same woman.

Did that mean that Brett had known the interviewer before he arrived at the show? Or had this person been a convenient actress for the recording of the video? Had she somehow also gotten the gig as the interviewer on *Small Town, Big Romance*?

FIFTEEN

I took the CD out of the drive and made my way back out into the hall.

Almost immediately I found Anton, leaning against the wall, his head drooping. He was drunk and held a full drink in his hand as if he'd decided to get one to go. I approached him with caution as I would a wild horse who might buck if startled.

"Anton," I said as I stepped closer. "Hey, Anton!"

He turned then and almost stumbled, using the textured wall to prop himself up.

"You okay?" I asked, genuinely concerned.

He squinted one eye as if trying to focus on me.

"Looking for Lacy," he slurred. "She went to the Music Room."

"Lacy? But why—" I didn't finish my question out loud. *What is she doing in the Music Room?* I checked my watch. 1:32 a.m. "She should be in bed. You too."

"She said she needs to look for something." Anton's voice was low and his words thick. He pointed a finger at himself and mimicked Lacy rather badly. "I need to deal with some things from my past. Alone." Despite the subpar impersonation, the words sounded like something she would say.

"I'm supposed to meet her in our room in a half hour." Anton fumbled in his pocket and lifted his key card. He looked at me, eyes heavy. Anton was handsome, with a cleft in his chin and curly dark red hair. Lacy had joked about dating a ginger for the first time, and then when she'd actually fallen hard for him, she'd started to imagine how adorable their babies might look someday.

"Tonight was sad," Anton continued, before taking a few beats to rethink his statement. "Lacy's boyfriend came to steal her." He sneered the last few words, but with his Texas drawl and drunken state, they didn't sound totally threatening.

"You're her boyfriend," I reminded him as he began to slide down the wall. I yanked on his arm until he was in a standing position again. He might not be able to get back up if he got all the way to the floor. "Why don't I help you to your room? Then I can find Lacy and send her to you."

"One more sip," he slurred, before finishing off the glass in one gulp.

Stairs were not in Anton's foreseeable future, so we started down the hall and through the Color Gallery toward the elevator. We passed a couple of uniformed men and one old classmate, and I hoped it didn't look like I was taking Anton upstairs to get in bed with him.

"This way," I said, steering Anton toward the elevator that led to the newer guest rooms.

He had to lean on me to steady himself, and when we got inside the elevator, I breathed a sigh of relief that he couldn't escape. Anton pressed his face against the cool metal of the elevator, and I was fairly sure he snored at least once between me pressing the button and the doors opening again.

I grabbed his arm and tugged him out of the elevator.

"Lacy?" he asked, startling at my touch.

"It's Dakota," I reminded him, hoping that Lacy might already be in their room and I could deliver him safely before checking in to see what she'd found in the Music Room.

"Dakota." Anton sniffed the air like a hound dog as if he might know me better by scent.

"Come on, Tex. Hand over your key." I checked his hands. "You still have it, don't you?"

He'd tucked it in the cuff of his long-sleeved button down, and when he popped it out, he grinned. "Magic."

Fantastic. Anton was not only pitiful, he was also a bit of an obnoxious drunk.

I checked the hall placards against the key card. We passed the *Sun-Sprinkled Suite* and the *Carefree Beauty Suite*. My goodness, why couldn't they just number the rooms like a normal hotel?

"Your boyfriend asked us *all* the questions," Anton said, peering at me through one eye as he slumped against me.

"Not my boyfriend," I said firmly.

"Charlie and Dakota sitting in a tree. K-I-S-S-I-N-G."

Oh, Lord. This has to stop.

"Okay, he can be my boyfriend," I relented. "What did Charlie ask you?"

Anton screwed up his face so it looked ridiculously severe and tried to stand up straight. It was impersonation time again. "When did you last see Brett? What was the na... na"—he grasped at the air as if trying to catch the word—"na-ture of your relationship?"

"What did Lacy tell him?" I asked him.

Instead of answering, Anton started singing, belting out the titular line of Brett's song: "The one that got away!" Then his face turned serious again and he was back to Charlie's questions. "Did you put anything in his drink?"

"Did you?" I asked.

"I plead the fifth," Anton said, starting to... giggle?

I rolled my eyes. That response and that laugh looked great for ruling him out as a suspect.

After we passed the eighth room, I spotted their room name, *The Blue for You*. How fitting. I knocked several times, practically begging my friend to come to the door. When Lacy didn't answer, I swiped the key card and turned the handle.

I held the door open with my foot while gesturing for him to walk inside. "In you go."

He didn't budge and instead leaned against the doorframe, looking at me owlishly. He spoke softly. "She loves me."

"I know she does." I was telling the truth. Though their entire relationship had happened in the window of my mother's diagnosis, death, and a year of grieving, I could see how Lacy beamed when he entered a room and how she considered his needs when making decisions. Not in a *my life is all about Anton* kind of way, more in a *he's a person I love so I'd like to hear his opinion* way. That alone told me that she respected his thinking, which meant a lot for a person as intelligent, competent, and capable as my friend.

"Brett is her small romance," he said, his one open eye drooping. "Anton is her big romance."

Perfect. We'd moved into the third-person narration stage of drunkenness, and it proved that whether or not Anton showed it, there was jealousy lurking beneath the surface. Regardless, I wasn't about to hop on the "everyone is a suspect" train that Charlie rode during an investigation. I had my list of suspects: Joe, the caterer; Presley, the girlfriend who seemed to be a bit too cozy with Brett's former best friend; and maybe even Lee Frank, the quiet camera man watching life through a lens. I refused to add Lacy or Anton.

I took a breath, digging deep for my patience as I used my body weight to shove him toward the bed. He made it a few steps forward before his legs gave out beneath him and the bed caught his fall.

I positioned his head so that he wouldn't choke if he threw up, and I made my way out of the room and back toward the elevator. As I waited for it to arrive, I rested my head against the wall and closed my eyes, taking a beat to steel myself for what I might find in the Music Room.

SIXTEEN

I stepped off the elevator and onto the second floor. In front of me was a huge, windowed terrace overlooking the gardens. Even in the dark of night, the view of the mountains was striking, the moon and stars illuminating the ridges like a backdrop on a film set.

The second floor was surprisingly difficult to navigate, rooms practically running into one another and too many doors to choose from. I was glad that Savilla had shared her to-scale dollhouse with me or I would've been completely lost.

I ended up wandering through an art gallery, complete with what appeared to be authentic Monets and Renoirs. Next, I stumbled across a sitting room with pockets of wingback chairs and massive fireplaces at either end before I hit a dead-end storage room filled with cutlery and china. I passed signs for a handful of rooms: The Bachelor's Hall, which ran into both the Billiards Room and the Smoking Lounge, and ended in the simply and aptly named Music Room.

The space was more like a grand hall to host small concerts of fifty or so, and I recognized it from the footage of Brett's home visit, where he'd played his hit song.

Rows of chairs were arranged in a circular formation around a grand piano, and as I walked into the room, I spotted Lacy in the corner on her knees in front of a tall storage cabinet containing twelve narrow drawers. Pages of sheet music were spread around her; she was so focused that she didn't even realize I'd entered.

"What are you doing up here?" I said, quietly enough to try not to startle her.

I failed. Lacy jumped and grabbed her chest. "Oh my God. I'm glad it's just you." She puffed her cheeks and bent forward at the waist, shuffling pages again.

"Have you taken up an instrument that I don't know about?" I knelt beside her and thumbed through one of Bach's concertos. "Started rehearsing for a debut performance at Carnegie?"

Lacy looked at me with an expression that said she didn't have time for jokes. "You were right. Brett was such an asshat."

"Yep," I confirmed, thinking of our junior year when he'd temporarily broken up with her on her birthday, dated a cheerleader for six weeks, got dumped, and then asked her out again on Valentine's Day, probably just so he wouldn't be alone. Years ago I'd asked Lacy what she saw in Brett, and she'd given the most astounding answer: *He's broken and he doesn't mind who knows. He just is who he is.* Perhaps that kind of transparency and self-awareness is attractive to some people, but personally, I don't mind a few repressed feelings, especially if they reek of animosity.

Still, that had been more than a decade ago. We were adults now—and, more importantly, Brett was dead—so why was my friend in an obscure room of the Rose Palace, rifling through a music cabinet?

"Okay, so you were supposed to meet him here at midnight."

"I'm looking for..." Lacy stopped, dropping one of the

pieces of music she'd been holding, and stared into my eyes, trying to tell me something beyond the words she was saying. "I thought he might've... I don't know... left behind something, anything, to help me hack into his damn email account." She was desperate enough that her line of reasoning made sense. "He said if I met him here and did what he wanted, then he would hand over the login information to the email account that he planned to send the pictures from. It was, like, a twisted game to him—not only did I have to agree to his conditions, I also had to login into his account and delete the email myself. Since I didn't find anything in his pockets, I thought he might've put the password somewhere in here before the reunion party started. I had to at least look." Lacy's face fell and her shoulders rolled forward as she dropped her head into her hands, her voice growing shaky. "Anton was angry, so I left him downstairs with a drink."

I'd been so focused on figuring out who might've murdered Brett that I'd left my friend to figure out how to save her reputation on her own. "What's the account name?" I asked, redirecting my full attention to her now.

She hesitated as if she didn't want to say it out loud.

"Lace, it's me," I reminded her.

She took a deep breath. "The account name is allmyladies@mail.com."

My stomach turned.

"I already tried to hack in. It didn't work, but I did get this." Lacy held up her phone to show the password hint to the account: *diamond numbers, hashtag, lowercase, name of the one that got away.*

"That is nonsensical," I said, before taking a beat to reconsider. "Except, Brett did tell you that the only one who could stop him was the one that got away. Maybe this is what he meant?"

"That's what I was thinking." Lacy nodded. "Earlier tonight

I asked Presley if she had any idea what it meant. She looked at me with these big eyes and asked if Brett had threatened me."

I thought of how I'd spoken to Presley in the kitchen earlier that evening. She'd also claimed to have no idea about the identity of the person who'd inspired Brett's hit single or his email password.

"I didn't feel comfortable explaining everything to her, but I think she, like, somehow knew about Brett's threat, but then we got interrupted by the police needing to question her again." Lacy's expression was pained. "I know he stayed at the estate occasionally, even recorded some music here, so I was looking for something by him or about him. This is all I found." She held up a piece of paper with typed lyrics.

"Ugh. 'The One That Got Away' again?"

"Yep." Lacy handed it over to me. At the bottom was scribbled Brett's signature, a date, and a message.

"What's that say? *To my...*" I was struggling to read his handwriting.

"I'm pretty sure it says, *To my dark lady: a rose for the rose that got away.*"

"My dark lady?" I asked, recoiling. "He doesn't mean..."

"It's not me," Lacy insisted. "I'm sure of that. I think he meant it as a reference to Shakespeare's Dark Lady."

"Which is?" I tried to recall a detail I was pretty sure I'd never paid attention to in the first place.

Lacy had always been the more literary of the two of us. "It's the mistress who inspired a bunch of his sonnets. We don't know who she was."

I studied the words and date right after the dedication: *To us & June 2021.* "That would've been during one of the pageants, right?"

"Probably. Number ninety-six?"

"Do you remember if Brett came back to Aubergine for that one?"

"God, who knows? Maybe. He and Mr. Finch seemed weirdly close, so I guess he could've been at any of them."

I gave it some thought. "And he released his song almost two years later, in early 2023."

Lacy tapped at her phone to look it up. "It hit the charts and stayed there for a few weeks."

"Did you see him in between that time at all?"

Lacy shrugged. "I don't think so."

I stood and walked to the piano, quietly beginning to play the melody line on the sheet music. Aunt DeeDee had forced me to take piano from fifth to eighth grade, and while I remembered only the most basic musical terms, I could still pluck out the notes from a score. I played through the chorus before speaking again.

"So, he came to the 2021 pageant, he recorded the song in early 2023. Then, he made his TV debut on *Small Town, Big Romance* in fall 2023."

Lacy narrowed her eyes at me. "What are you thinking?"

"I'm thinking that if we can find the person he called *his rose*, the person he would've known in June 2021, then maybe we can figure out his password—and perhaps better understand who might've had something to do with his death."

"Who else would've been here at the pageant *and* here this evening?" Lacy asked.

And as soon as she said the words, we both knew the answer.

SEVENTEEN

I remember Savilla clearly on that first day of school. She was the smallest one in the class and terribly shy, with no indication of the boisterous, outgoing person she would become.

"Why don't you say hello?" Momma had said as she nudged me forward to meet Savilla.

The girl had been with her nanny, Nanny Kate, whom I would get to know well in coming years. I'd stepped forward and held out a miniature plastic penguin that Aunt DeeDee had given me the night before—*to help you break the ice.*

Savilla had studied the object in my palm and hurried to her backpack, taking out a stuffed lion with a soft mane, which she'd held next to my penguin. She'd given Momma and me a wide grin, one tooth already missing. "Look. They're the same."

I'd looked up at Momma, who had shrugged as if to say, *Just go with it.* At five, though, with my literal way of seeing the world, *going with it* hadn't been a possibility for me.

"They're not the same," I'd insisted, taking her animal and holding them both up to the light in case she needed glasses. "My penguin is smooth and your lion is furry."

"Do you love your penguin? What's her name?" Savilla had asked, completely ignoring my explanation.

"Yes," I'd answered, with the childhood affinity for any object smaller than me. "Her name is Poppy the Penguin."

"This is Harriet the Lion," Savilla had said, grabbing her stuffy and combing back the fur with two fingers. "And I love her too, just the same as you."

That's when I'd realized that Savilla hadn't been referring to the objects as being exact replicas of one another; it was the feelings we'd assigned to those objects... and, okay, I hadn't realized this at five, but I did now, and it gave me a bit of insight into the way that my half-sister's brain worked. She was very big picture, very much not detail oriented, which was where I came in.

Maybe channeling some of my half-sister's way of thinking could help me solve Lacy's blackmail problem as well as Brett's murder. I thought about all of this as I followed Lacy to her room with a promise that we would figure out everything in the morning when we were in a more rested and less distraught state of mind.

"It's gonna be okay," I tried to assure her.

"I just keep seeing The Worst," Lacy whispered, as we reached her door. I knew she was referring to a thought experiment we had made up in high school in which we would imagine the absolute worst-case scenario to its final end. Like, if I failed my biology final, I would get a C on my report card, which meant that I wouldn't be salutatorian and I might struggle to get into vet school and then decide just not to attend college at all, which would mean I'd be working at a chicken coop for the rest of my life and I'd probably be so desperate that I would marry Joe Larson and have twelve babies and hate my life.

We would usually end up in a fit of giggles, stress

temporarily relieved, but today The Worst was having naked pictures sent to her clients, potentially losing a lot of her hard-won business and causing contention with Anton, though I hoped the last part wasn't true. I hoped he would be the kind of guy who would see the past as the past and support Lacy come what may, but the reality was that I didn't know him that well.

I hugged Lacy goodbye, my heart aching at her brave attempt at a smile as she disappeared into the room where Anton's snores already filled the air.

I wanted to sleep too, but first I needed to find Savilla.

Thankfully, it wasn't hard since she was back in the vestibule, handing out keys to the few remaining guests who must've just been released by Charlie and his crew.

"Find anything useful on that CD drive?"

My mind was swirling with so much information that I actually wasn't sure. "Maybe." I paused, uncertain how to broach the question I really wanted to ask. I decided to be direct. "Were you here for the 2021 pageant?"

"I don't think so." Savilla bit her lip, thinking back. "Wait. At least not for the last exhibitionist."

I was certain Savilla wasn't using the right word, but I let it slide as she continued.

"One of my friends had a gallery opening in New York that same night, so I left before the final pageant show." Savilla tilted her head, questioning me. "Why?"

"I was just wondering if you happened to see Brett that year."

"Not that I remember, though he would show up on occasion, especially when we were kids. Everyone used to volunteer back then. *All hands on deck*, Daddy would say."

"Any idea who he might've written his song about? The one that got away?"

"Sorry, no idea." Savilla shrugged.

I couldn't tell if the way she'd answered was dismissive or avoidant, but I was so tired that I probably couldn't read anyone right at this point.

Savilla turned to the brass keys. "I put you in The Original. It's down the hall from mine, so if you need anything, I'm only a few steps away."

Hooray. It could almost be like a sister-sleepover, except I was starting to suspect she knew more than she was saying—and she still didn't know we were sisters.

"Do you want him in your room?" Savilla asked sweetly, a hint of teasing in her eyes.

"Who?"

"Charlie."

"Um..." I had no idea how to answer, much less how Charlie would want me to answer that question. "Whatever he wants."

"I already asked him before he started questioning every-one. He said it's totally up to you." Savilla smiled. "He's a true gentleman."

I swallowed hard, aware of the fact that she'd been talking to him about me. Like we were in middle school. "Sure, yes, then. We likely won't get much sleep anyway."

Savilla raised her eyebrows as if I hadn't meant that we'd be awake to discuss a murder investigation, not to engage in other delights. "I'll put two toothbrushes along with other toiletries in the bathroom. I'm doing the same for the guest rooms and the cottages out on the green." She leaned forward and whispered, "Charlie told me which people I should keep in the main house, and I'm pretty sure it's because they're the most suspicious. Except for you and me, of course."

I didn't have the heart to tell Savilla that to Charlie, everyone was a suspect.

I took the key and turned to leave, then pivoted back to face Savilla. "Actually, I was hoping to ask you one more thing," I said. "About Joe and Brett. You've kept in touch with both of them over the years, right?"

"Mostly." Savilla traced the edge of one of the room keys with a finger. "I don't think it's any secret that Joe was super hurt when Brett got him kicked out of college."

I leaned closer. I'd suspected this but had never actually heard this part of the story.

Another guest, Miss Most Likely to Drop Out (she didn't), approached and took a key from Savilla, and I waited until she was out of earshot before continuing our conversation.

"What did Brett do to Joe?"

Savilla took a step closer to me and spoke in low tones. "At Virginia Tech, Joe made the football team but Brett was red-shirted. Halfway into the season, one of the coaches found something in Joe's locker—something that wasn't his—and they kicked him out."

"What did they find?"

"Steroids." Savilla tisked. "A big no-no."

I could believe Joe would be dumb enough to use an illicit substance—but maybe weed, not steroids. He had been a natural athlete from the time we were in fifth grade, already tall and broad for his age. He'd always been fast too, a typical dumb jock, a stereotype that he seemed to embrace.

Something about the expression on Savilla's face told me that she didn't believe he'd been doping either.

"You think Brett planted the steroids in his locker?" I asked, though it was less a question and more a realization.

I thought of Brett's short stature, the way he'd bulked up almost immediately after graduating high school, the way he'd been trying extreme health regimens. Could he have been using steroids and planted them in Joe's locker? If so, what was the purpose? To get Joe kicked off the team? Out of school? Such a tragedy would've changed the entire trajectory of Joe's life. It would've kept him stuck in a town where he'd watched his parents—especially his dad, I now knew—struggle.

Wrecking his life would've been reason enough for Joe to crave revenge.

I'd found possible motive.

"Why don't you ask him yourself?" Savilla said, nodding toward a man entering the vestibule from the direction of the ballroom, his sneakered feet not making a sound as he strode into the entryway. It was Joe, and right behind him was Presley Lombardi.

"I came to get my key," Joe said, putting his hand on the small of Presley's back before catching my eye and yanking it away.

Savilla first handed Presley a plastic card with a room number written on the paper holder. The plastic card meant she was not in the residential wing, which likely meant Savilla didn't trust her and Joe to be that close by. Made sense.

Presley, her eyes wide as if she were forcing herself to prop them open, nodded her thanks then turned and loped toward the elevator.

Next was Joe, and Savilla was placing him far from the residential wing as well.

"Can I have a key to Presley's room too?" Joe asked, his eyes flitting to me as he tapped a hand restlessly against the marble desktop where Savilla's computer faced her. "I want to check on her."

Savilla shook her head and kept an even tone. "That's not our policy."

I could feel my eyebrows rising even though I told my face not to give anything away.

"Fine, I'll take a second key to my room. Just in case I lose it."

Savilla didn't bat an eye as she handed him another key, and I admired her seeming neutrality. She would make a discreet hotelier if she decided to turn the Rose Palace into such a thing. "And Joe, Dakota had some questions for you."

Savilla blinked innocently between the two of us, and I realized that she thought she was being helpful: I had suspicions, and I could ask him directly about my concerns. In her mind, this must be the most direct route to get answers, but from my perspective, I'd rather watch from the sidelines and make my own conclusions. Murderers weren't usually forthcoming, after all.

Joe crossed his arms and tilted his head as he examined me. I noticed for the first time that he had purple circles under his eyes, either from extreme fatigue or crying. Maybe both.

"I really want to get to my room," he said, looking in the direction that Presley had just wandered.

"Maybe you two could take a walk and chat first?" Savilla suggested, as if we were two old friends going for a stroll instead of suspect and interrogator going off alone. "Or we could see if the sheriff is available to arrange a better time to chat?"

The words were perfect, the right level of threat and encouragement.

Joe hesitated one more second before realizing that I was the better option than actual law enforcement. "Sure." He put on a fake gentlemanly tone. "A moonlight stroll in the garden, perhaps?"

"What about the solarium?" I suggested, swallowing back the lump of fear rising in my throat. Did I really want to be alone with a potential murderer? I found my voice. "It's still moonlit, but out of the chilly night air."

I didn't add that it was also close enough to the ballroom for an officer to hear if I screamed. *A ridiculous thought*, I chided myself. Even if Joe had something to do with Brett's death, he wouldn't dare threaten me. I was the girlfriend—or whatever—of the lead investigator, after all.

Then I thought of Dr. Bellingham and Katie Gilman alone

together at the back of the property four months ago, and about bursting out of a hidden tunnel to find him hovering over her, threatening her despite the fact that they were both pageant judges and Katie was related to a Finch. Some men had no qualms about hurting women, regardless of their position or rank.

But no, this was different. It had to be. I knew Joe. I did.

EIGHTEEN

Stiffening my back and my resolve, I tromped quickly through the Color Gallery toward the back of the house and took a left, Joe silently following behind me. After a few minutes, we were walking down stone steps and into the glass-paned solarium, which didn't seem to have been properly cared for in the months since Mr. Finch's death. Only the innermost rows of plants, the succulents, remained alive, while every potted plant by the windows was either completely gone with brown stalks proceeding from dry dirt, or struggling between life and death.

The familiar spider design of the archways rose above us, the structure like eight legs meeting in the center of a giant arachnid. The moon was bright and streamed through the high windows between the arches, and several old-fashioned lamps hung from the ceiling.

I stepped into the center of the room, where two chairs faced one another. As I nudged one chair, Joe passed behind me and I bumped into him. Because he was several inches taller than me, my shoulder wedged him in his rib cage.

"Watch it." Joe scowled at me.

As he took a seat, I could see all the different versions of Joe

I'd known over the years: the six-year-old who'd rescued a bird, the class clown in middle school who couldn't keep out of trouble, the boy I'd really liked for about three ridiculous weeks in high school, and the wanderer who couldn't seem to get his life together.

"*You* watch it," I told him, falling back into our childish dynamics. Perhaps it was a defensive instinct, a response to the fear of being alone with him, or perhaps I was just finding my courage. Regardless, I was determined to get answers in the next few minutes. This guy was guilty of something, and I wasn't about to let Lacy—or anyone else—take the fall for a crime she didn't commit.

"What's your problem with me?" Joe asked, leaning forward to place his elbows on his knees.

"Besides the fact that Brett Brinkley died after drinking a cocktail you made him?"

Joe shook his head and settled back into the wicker chair. "I didn't kill Brett."

That's what a murderer would say.

"Whatever," he breathed, as if he could read my mind. "I'm exhausted and need to check our inventory in the kitchen before getting a few hours' sleep."

"I was in there earlier, talking to my aunt," I said, not mentioning the fact that I'd gone through his things and taken a CD. "I noticed that you had a pretty big order of rhubarb."

He squinted at me, likely trying to figure out what I was playing at. "Yeah, so I over-ordered. I'll use it for a couple of pies tomorrow and throw out the rest."

"The roots and the leaves are poisonous. I saw a bunch of stalks with leaves still attached."

"Everything is poisonous in large enough quantities. Apple seeds, peach pits, tomato leaves." Joe listed them off on his fingers as he kept his eyes on mine. "That doesn't mean that I somehow used a giant pile of rhubarb to... what? Kill Brett?" He almost laughed as he realized what I'd been thinking. He inched closer to me. "Is that what you suspect me of? You think maybe I dried out the leaves, ground them up, slipped a fine powder into his drink when he came to the bar? He ordered two or three drinks, so maybe I'd been slipping it in all night until it finally took effect."

I squirmed uneasily. I didn't like this Joe. I much preferred the one who would down an entire bottle of ketchup on a dare.

Joe was just getting started though, his eyes widening as he mocked me. "Maybe I even made sure that my bartender would call in sick, so I would have to fill in for him. That way I could act surprised that I needed to be on bar while I did my deadly deeds."

Joe looked like he was about to issue a maniacal laugh just to make fun of my line of reasoning, but when he saw how uncomfortable his words were making me, he pulled back. "Look, I don't know if you're jealous that DeeDee's been helping me with the business or—"

"You think I'm jealous?" I couldn't believe his nerve. So what that my aunt had been helping a young entrepreneur get a start? So what that I was flailing about what to do when I graduated and hadn't even broached the topic with her?

A rush of heat crept up my throat. Shoot. Was Joe right? Did I want my aunt to be helping *me*? Did I want her to work by *my* side to get a practice up and running? I hated that Joe might be more aware of my motives than I was.

"When's the last time you spoke with Brett?" I asked, shifting the focus back to him.

"Is this an interrogation?" Joe huffed out air and reclined in his seat, already tired of talking to me—and probably realizing that he was under no actual obligation to do so. "Because I've already answered the sheriff's questions."

I crossed my arms. "I'm sure Charlie will have more."

"Okay." Joe laughed darkly. "In addition to sleeping with

him, you speak for him now, too? I wonder how his pretty new deputy feels about that?"

That was a punch to my gut, and he seemed to know it.

Joe's lip curled. "Your life and everyone else's in Aubergine has been practically perfect."

I started to interrupt him, to correct him, but he stopped me. "Comparatively perfect," he clarified. "Do you know where my dad was on the night of our graduation?"

I swallowed hard. This wasn't the direction I'd wanted this conversation to take.

"He was at the hospital because he'd OD-ed the night before. Someone found him passed out behind the wheel on Drake's Road. At first they thought he was drunk, but when the ambulance arrived, they realized he'd given himself so much oxy that his pulse was practically nonexistent."

The words hit me hard, mainly because I hadn't realized that I was the kind of person who could be that oblivious to the pain of someone so close to me. I guess with the pranks and the crude humor, I hadn't registered what Joe had been dealing with, but this was exactly what Aunt DeeDee had been talking about.

His eyes were glassy now, but I could tell it wasn't from drinking. He was on the verge of tears. "Before we went to the after-grad party, Brett stopped by the hospital with me, said that he wanted to see with his own two eyes that my dad was okay since he used to coach us both in peewee football. Brett was a good friend – at least, I thought he was until..." Joe's voice trailed off and he sniffed.

"Until what?"

Joe shook his head as if trying to rid himself of painful memories and said simply, "We had a falling out in our first semester at college."

I braced myself for his reaction to my next question, but I

had to ask it. "Did he get you kicked off the football team? Out of college?"

Joe blinked at me several times, his jaw clenched. "I think we're done here." He made as if to stand, but I put out a hand.

"Please."

Joe forced out a big huff of air but he sat back down, though this time on the edge of his seat as if he might leave any second. "Brett put steroids in my locker, which was the one and only thing that could actually get you kicked off the team and out of school. It sent my entire life in a different direction. No more football. No more scholarship. I never forgave him. Is that what you want to hear?"

It was. Kind of. I stayed quiet, hoping he would keep talking.

"Brett apologized, tried to throw me a few bones here and there. Job opportunities, girls he didn't want to sleep with anymore." Joe's face contorted into a grimace. "When we were kids, I had no idea how selfish he was, how he used people, how he was using me." He lifted a hand and pointed at his own chest. "Did you know that I trained him? I spent hours on the field, throwing the ball with him, trying to get his arm in shape for college try-outs. It didn't come naturally to him, and he barely even made it on the team. After he got me kicked out of school, he quit the team, said he wanted to focus on his studies. But it was because I wasn't there to compete with anymore. He just wanted to make sure I didn't succeed, and once I was back home, ashamed of something I hadn't even done and my college prospects ruined, he felt free to go his own way."

"When's the last time you spoke to Brett?" I asked, gentler than I'd been moments ago, in part to encourage him to keep talking but also because hearing his story brought out compassion that I didn't know I had for this guy. "I mean, before tonight?"

Joe hung his head and sighed, a sort of resignation settling across his face. "He called me last week to tell me that he was bringing Presley. He asked if I had a date, and I told him I'd be working."

"He didn't know you were catering tonight?"

"Not as far as I know." Joe shifted in his seat. "He probably called just to remind me that he was dating this amazing woman, and I have..." Joe didn't finish the sentence, so I waited. "No one. Not really."

"Except you're staying next door to Presley and got an extra room key for her."

Joe sighed but didn't deny the fact. "It's complicated."

NINETEEN

After Joe left me alone in the solarium, I was catching my breath for a few seconds when I heard the faint sound of raised voices coming from outside. I turned to the door that led to the back gardens and listened again.

I grabbed the doorknob that led to the portico and opened it slowly so as to not be overheard by whomever was out there.

"We'll have nothing to show for months of work," the man's voice said loudly enough for anyone within fifty yards to hear. I was pretty sure it was the cameraman, Lee Frank. Even though I couldn't get a visual on them, I caught the scent of tobacco coming from the direction of the rose hedge maze. I wondered if Charlie or any of his officers were keeping an eye on them.

"I was an idiot, letting him string me along like that." The man's voice sounded desperate, frantic even. "I even used my own credit cards on travel because he promised to reimburse us."

A second person cleared her throat and spoke in an even tone. "I think we should go to our rooms and talk about this in the morning." It was Mina.

"No one is depending on you for a roof over their head or

their next meal," Lee argued. "I've got three kids in school, and this was supposed to be my way to break into the industry. You know how hard it is to join the union. You have to wait for someone to die to get your name on the list."

"I'm sure Presley will make sure you get paid," Mina reasoned.

"That's easy for you to say. You don't need money like I do." Lee raised his voice. "Anyway, I know what she'll say: *Ask the production company.*" He said the last line in a singsong voice as if mimicking someone.

"Look, if they don't pay you, I'll loan you the money myself. I've been living with my grandmother and have some savings." Mina's tone was calm and gentle as she walked from one end of the hedge to the other.

"That's not good enough." He sounded desperate as he followed her. "The production company is bust, and I can't wait for Presley to get her shit together. I need that money now." He paused as if realizing something. "Did Brett pay you?" There was a tinge of bitterness in his tone. "What are you not telling me?"

"What? No, I—" And that's when Mina began to scream.

I ran past the portico and onto the green lawn, stalking quickly toward the rose hedge maze. Suddenly, I spotted Mina's shadowy figure, struggling away from Lee's grasp. A cloud moved past the moon, and I could see him grabbing her arm, yanking her back with such force that her torso flung back sideways.

I turned to call for help and spotted an officer on the high stone steps at the back of the house. "Help! Over here," I called, waving my arms to catch his attention.

The officer rushed over at the same time that I neared Lee, who now had Mina on the ground, his hands clenching her arms as he shook her, demanding answers she didn't seem to have. My presence wasn't stopping him.

Mina's eyes were wide with fear, and she choked back a sob as the officer grabbed Lee and pulled him off her. She scrambled away from him.

"I'm okay," Mina said with a tight mouth, as if she was trying to keep from crying. "Lee just lost his mind for a second."

Mina said the words as if this had happened before, as if there might be a long history of threats.

"Sir," the officer said, addressing Lee with a sharp edge to his tone. "I'll be happy to escort you to your room. You'll be staying there indefinitely, and I'm sure the sheriff will want to have a few words with you."

"You've got to be kidding." Lee looked from the officer to Mina and began to laugh. "I'm not the criminal here."

"You assaulted this woman," the officer said in an even voice as he motioned to Mina. "But, regardless, it's time—"

Lee cut him off, his arms flailing only a second before the officer pinned them behind his back. "Brett Brinkley is the criminal! He's a thief, owes me nearly twenty grand in back pay and reimbursements."

"Sir, I'm going to ask you only once to come quietly," the officer said, clicking handcuffs on the man. "Otherwise, I'll use force."

Lee was fuming. "This is ridiculous."

The officer pressed a button on the walkie-talkie attached to his shoulder and called for backup that he probably didn't really need. Lee seemed angry, yes, but also incapable of inflicting much harm at this point. As soon as he was restrained, his fighting stance gave way.

"I'm going to lose everything," he moaned, as he was hauled into the grand house. "And it's all Brett's fault."

Mina and I were left in the dark garden, watching as the officer escorted Lee to his room. For the first time, I realized that the estate must be crawling with a police presence, and I wasn't sure if it comforted or unnerved me.

I shook my head in disbelief. "What was that?"

In the moonlight I could see red finger marks appearing on Mina's upper arm and she absentmindedly rubbed at them. "He's under a lot of stress, but he usually doesn't take it out on me. He has three kids, and his wife has been sick for a couple of years."

I'd been right. They did have some kind of history, or at least enough of a relationship to share about their families. "Has he ever grabbed you like that before?"

Mina huffed out a long breath. "He's upset. We both are."

I tilted my head and studied her. "You seem to express your emotions very differently."

"We haven't been paid for this gig, and now that Brett's... gone, we may never be. I'll be fine, but he... who knows?" Mina lifted her head and looked directly at me for the first time. "I know you probably couldn't tell, but Lee was—is—my mentor. Took me under his wing when he was a cameraman on an episode of *SVU* and saw me cut from the scene. I'd been trying to make it in Hollywood, and I'd gotten parts here and there, but that day I was playing an actual named role. Until I wasn't. They decided to rewrite my part and give it to a guy. I was standing off-stage crying, and Lee spotted me, distracted me by asking if I'd ever tried operating a Blackmagic URSA."

At that, I must've made a face because Mina clarified, "It's a camera. Lee let me hang out and watch him, got me clearance to shadow him. Over the next few months, he taught me the tools of the trade. I figured it was the next best thing to being on camera, and it was kind of nice, learning from someone who'd been in the business for a couple decades. We became friends."

The interaction I'd just witnessed didn't seem too friendly, and she must've read as much on my face.

"I know," she sighed. "When COVID happened, it shut down almost everything for a year, and he's been struggling to make ends meet ever since. He's worked in the industry since he graduated high school, so I think seeing me get paid more on *Small Town, Big Romance* and then me being the one to get this gig for us to—"

"Wait." One line in particular stood out to me, and I interrupted her. "Why did you get paid more on the reality show?"

"I got a few lines – nothing that actually helped my acting career, but it bumped me up to a different tier." Mina looked toward the house where the officer had taken Lee. "I think he feels like he's losing his edge, that I'm just a kid getting him opportunities instead of the other way around. To him, it's all... I guess, a load of crap."

What I was hearing was that Lee was not only desperate for money, but he was also frustrated by the lack of control he had over his life, his finances. I understood the strain and the toll such a thing could take on one's mental state. Even now when my phone lit with a voice message, I had flashbacks of demanding debt collectors.

"When the sheriff was speaking to everyone this evening, Lee said that Presley wanted us to keep recording, but it was really his idea," Mina continued. "He was hoping we could make some kind of documentary out of all of this, but the sheriff shut that down real fast."

Mina bit her lip as if contemplating her next steps. She started to speak again but then looked at me and hesitated, before finally saying, "Look, I don't know if I should be saying this to you, but you seem to have some kind of rapport with the sheriff, am I right?"

I nodded once. "I helped him with the investigation at the summer pageant, and we're... kind of... together."

"Kind of?" Mina asked, studying me before she gave up. "Never mind, none of my business." We started back through the garden and toward the house, pausing for a beat as we reached the stone steps. "Just... if you get a chance, tell the sheriff that Lee was freaking out, but really, he's a decent guy."

I couldn't help but shoot her a questioning look. The way he'd shaken her hadn't seemed *decent*.

Mina put up both hands. "I know, I know, but I've never seen him violent before. I didn't know he had that kind of fight in him."

"Now that you do, do you think Lee could've been angry enough to hurt Brett?"

Mina squinted as if trying to see exactly what I was after. Finally, she shook her head. "What would be the point? He was hoping that Brett would pay us any day now. It wouldn't make sense to kill the income source."

Mina's logic was sound, but as I told her to get some sleep and watched her walk away, other reasons Lee might've wanted to kill Brett leapt to mind.

Maybe Lee had planned to make some kind of documentary, like Mina had suggested. Or maybe he planned to wrest the back pay from Presley's hands. Maybe he was just fed up and wanted to off his boss.

There were many reasons a desperate man might murder someone like Brett Brinkley.

TWENTY

It was well after 3 a.m. and I was moving like a zombie. I made it upstairs to the residential quarters, which were bathed in a soft yellow light that came from the sconces shaped like old gas lanterns along the wall.

As I neared my room, I took out the large key Savilla had given me. I fingered the cold brass, imagining that I looked like the Rose Palace warden as I stumbled down the hall with it in hand.

I struggled to slip the enormous key into the lock, jostling and wriggling it at various angles as I turned the handle on the door with a plaque reading "The Original". I didn't know exactly what an original room in this estate might mean. Feather mattresses? Wash basins? Chamber pots? Whatever. As long as there was somewhere semi-soft for me to lay my head, I'd happily take it.

I was still angling the key when I felt a movement behind me. In one move, I jumped, pulled out the key, swung around, and held it in front of me, my arm outstretched as if wielding the tiniest weapon known to man.

Charlie's eyes were wide but his lips turned up as he threw

both hands in the air. "I'm unarmed." My eyes dropped to the gun holster at his side, so he clarified, "I won't use any weapons on you."

My head was starting to ache just behind my eyes, an effect of the combination of travel plus murder investigation. It was too much for one day. I put a hand to my head to ward off the lights that seemed to be coming at me rather than glowing warmly.

"I was planning to bunk with you," Charlie said, before adding, "if that's all right?"

I peered at him with one eye closed. "I thought you were all business this weekend." I needed to find my footing here. Was Charlie planning to stay in this room with me as a... boyfriend? A partner? A bodyguard? Did he simply want to rehash the specifics of the case? Maybe these weren't the questions I should be asking at the end of this interminable night, but I wanted to know where I stood with him right then. "What exactly are you doing here?"

"Sleeping. Very soon, I hope." Charlie's voice was husky with fatigue. For the first time I noticed that he too looked as if he might collapse if he didn't find a bed soon, and I had sympathy.

He motioned to the key. "May I?"

I held out the so-far useless object to him but I hated needing rescue, even for something as simple as an old lock.

Charlie slid in the key and smoothly turned the handle before holding out an arm to invite me to go first. Of course it had worked for him.

The room was dark, and I felt along the wall to find... nothing. No switches or flips or chains to yank. I stepped further inside, pressing the light on my phone just as I ran into a piece of furniture – I grabbed at my shin.

"You okay?" Charlie asked, hearing me curse under my breath. He took out a flashlight and shone it waist high, and I spotted a lamp a few inches from me. I found a switch under the shade, and as I turned it on, I could see the bronze base and green and blue stained-glass design reminiscent of peacock feathers. According to *Antiques Roadshow* episodes I'd watched on repeat after Momma's death, this was a Tiffany Studios lamp, and the light from it revealed an entire room that looked exactly how a room from the early twentieth century would appear.

The bedspread had a gold and ivory print with a matching canopy and curtains. The ornate mahogany bed frame appeared to have been carved into the wall, ceiling, and floorboards. A curtain could be drawn around the person tucked inside.

"It's like a room fit for the king and queen of Versailles," Charlie mused.

"Hopefully without the beheading," I added.

He turned off his flashlight and scratched at his jaw. "That would be preferable."

The rest of the furniture was simple—a writing desk, a wardrobe, two wooden chairs that were so large as to appear throne-like. Every item kept with the royal antiquity theme.

"Do you think the Finches understood that there was actually no such thing as American royalty?"

"Definitely not," he answered, standing only inches inside the doorway, his face asking if he could step inside. He was a gentleman, if nothing else.

I took in the worry lines etched into his forehead and the wrinkled uniform. "It's fine. You can bunk with me."

Relief settled across Charlie's brow as he closed the door behind him and plopped down on the edge of the bed to pull off his boots.

I took a couple of deep breaths and forced myself to release any expectations, conversationally or otherwise. We were both done with this day. Still, I thought I saw his eyes flash with emotion when he glanced back at me, though I couldn't tell if it was suspicion or desire.

"Dakota," he said, his gruff voice making the three syllables resonate.

Despite how conflicted I felt about our earlier interactions, a rush of warmth crept into my chest when he said my name, but I refused to feel lovey-dovey after this terrible night.

"Did you and your deputy finish interviewing everyone?" I asked, trying to sound professional and removed as I sat down on the bed too.

He nodded but didn't answer, staring at a fixed point on the rug that stretched wall to wall. I had the sudden urge to shake him out of his intense focus. Surely he could do his job while also sounding human?

"And?" I asked, prompting him to continue.

"We made pretty fast work of narrowing down who we'll be questioning more extensively tomorrow."

I hated his use of the "we" pronoun to reference himself and his deputy, but even as the thought struck me, I knew it was ridiculous. This man couldn't change the entire English language to navigate my ridiculous jealousy. God, I needed to sleep.

"Do you feel like you have a good lead on who might've been involved?" I tried again.

"I've got a few names." He wasn't giving anything away. "What about you? Who's on your list?"

He knew I had one, even if I didn't like to talk about it. I wanted to tell him that he had to go first, but he was the sheriff —and by default, the lead investigator—so he didn't actually have to give me anything.

"Joe's still at the top of my list," I admitted. "And I'm keeping a close eye on Presley and Lee Frank."

"That's it?" he asked. "Three suspects?"

He could read me, and he knew that there were others that I didn't want to name.

"I think I have an idea of which guests had opportunity, and I have a few theories on possible motives."

"Right." He sucked his teeth and let out a heavy breath. "Regardless, until we know the actual cause of death, the method can't exactly be proven. And until we have the method confirmed, we can't get much further in terms of identifying the perpetrator."

We weren't getting anywhere fast, personally or professionally, with this line of conversation. I moved my hands behind my back, placing my palms against the soft comforter. "I found something downstairs in the kitchen."

"Really? My guys didn't see anything there."

"It was actually in one of the lockers for the staff," I told him. "In a backpack belonging to Joe Larson."

"I can't exactly condone searching property without a warrant." Charlie lifted an eyebrow. I'd seen that look a lot four months ago during the last investigation here.

"That's fine, *I* will condone it," I told him, rubbing my fingers on my left temple. It was wonderful to be dating a man so honest and aboveboard, except when it came to following stupid rules that actually prevented progress. "Inside, I found an old yearbook with some notes from when we graduated, a stack of Joe's headshots, and a CD." I reached into the waist of my jeans and took out the CD, still wrapped in the case with the handwritten message.

"I haven't seen one of these in years," Charlie said, taking it from me. "Probably not since I downloaded songs from Napster and burned them in 2009."

"Illegally?" I teased him.

"I was in college," he said, reminding me that he was a few years older than me.

"Right." I smirked at him. "Even though this CD is illegal

contraband, I watched it in my aunt's old office, but don't worry: I won't show any information to you unless it's absolutely necessary."

"Anything helpful?" Charlie asked, ignoring my holier-than-thou tone.

"Honestly, I have no idea." I put both elbows on my knees and dropped my head in my hands. "It's like I drank from a fire-hose of information tonight, and I can't quite organize the details into a clear through-line."

"That's a good way to put it." Charlie leaned back onto the bed. "This isn't the weekend I expected," he finally said, in a near whisper.

I looked into those eyes that I loved... er, um, liked. Heat rose to my cheeks, and I hoped that in the low lighting, he wouldn't be able to tell.

"What did you expect?" I asked, genuinely curious, as I dared to lie back on the bed next to him. From my lower angle, I turned my head toward him, noticing the stubble lining his jaw.

We didn't have luggage or a change of clothes, and despite the fact that Charlie and I had spent as many nights together as we could, this strange place and our lack of normalcy made us awkward. Still, there was something between us, some fine thread that tugged at the core of me, nudging me toward him. If he would only let down his guard.

Charlie sat up for a moment, took off his shirt and his belt, and placed his holster on top of the end table. When he lay back down, he was on his side and turned toward me. He put out a hand and as he tucked a strand of hair behind my ear, my body shivered at his touch.

"I was hoping for something more like you and me, and a pint of Phish Food," he said, his voice low. "A show at my place."

"What show?" I asked, drawn to his alternative universe. I wanted to hear what could've been.

"Maybe the BBC *Pride and Prejudice*? It would have to be one of those British romances where I can only understand every other word."

"That's what subtitles are for," I reminded him.

"Right." His hand trailed across my cheek and down my neck to the bare skin on my arm. "But it wouldn't really matter since we wouldn't make it past the opening scene."

"The inciting incident," I said softly.

"As one of them insults the other very politely, we'd be... otherwise engaged." Charlie said the last two words with an accent that came out more Cockney than posh.

I laughed despite this weekend and the bizarre way it was unfolding. Charlie's warmth, that's what I'd been missing. This closeness, this way of understanding one another, this laughter. All of the missteps and my encroaching jealousy fell away as soon as we were alone together.

Charlie studied my lips as he continued his aristocratic charade. "Since your lady's maid hasn't made an appearance this evening, I'd be delighted to help you off with your outer garments."

I chuckled despite it all and moved closer to him, almost collapsing into him as I inhaled his cedar scent.

If only it could be like this, if only he could avoid becoming so absorbed in his work that he almost switched personalities; if only I could squash my instinct to always question his motives, then this could work. But that was a big ask on both of our parts.

Regardless, I had him—what I'd come to think of as "the real Charlie"—until dawn. I didn't want to waste the few hours, so I kissed him long and hard, waiting for his hands to slip the fabric from my skin.

PART III

Saturday
Morning

TWENTY-ONE

Charlie was asleep almost as soon as he lay his head on the pillow next to mine, and I followed him into that sweet abyss in what seemed like seconds. My conscious and subconscious were churning over so many things as my eyes closed: that I needed to be alert and awake enough for Mr. Finch's will reading downtown where Savilla was about to find out I was her half-sister, that Lacy and I needed to find Brett's email password before midnight tonight, that Monday's decision about the fellowship recommendation was less than forty-eight hours away. And that didn't even include solving a murder.

Death becomes familiar when you're a vet. Between both my medical training and the personal experience of watching Momma fade away, I'd learned to accept its inevitability. Still, the harrowing events of the day came out in my dreams, manifesting the fear and uncertainty I hadn't yet been able to vocalize. I competed on a reality show in which I had to eat a bowl full of bugs while treading water. It was almost a relief to awaken to semi-normal anxieties seven hours later, around 11 a.m.

I woke to the sound of the door closing and sat up straight, gripping the sheets to my bare skin and calling out the first thing that came to mind. "Who goes there?" Apparently I was a maiden living in a medieval castle.

There was no response, so I leaned over and poked at the other side of the king-sized bed, hoping Charlie would come to the rescue, but his place was empty and the bed cold. His clothes and his holster were gone too.

I dropped my head into my hands, rubbing away sleep from my eyes as I realized that I'd likely heard the sound of the door hitting Charlie on his way out. Great.

Any doubts about our relationship that I'd managed to quell last night came roaring back with a vengeance. I took my own advice and let myself play out The Worst. He was probably on his way to find Deputy Wright and tell her that he'd been wrong to sleep with me in the early morning hours. He was probably going to confess his love to her and propose before the end of the day. They'd have a baby within a year. Life would still go on.

I reminded myself to breathe as I felt for the Tiffany lamp on my side of the bed and pressed to switch on the now-electric light bulb. When it brightened, I spotted a note.

Meeting with Wright this morning to discuss case. —Charlie

Oh God. That did nothing to dispel my ridiculous fears. A man of few words sounded romantic and brooding until you received a note like this.

After the sleep of the dead, he'd walked out the door without a kiss or a goodbye, and he was heading straight for a woman with beautiful eyes and dark hair, and more importantly, with an address that wasn't hundreds—much less thousands—of miles away from him. I crumpled Charlie's note into a ball and threw it across the room.

I pulled the down comforter over my head and was contemplating hiding out in my room all day when a knock sounded at the door.

"Who is it?" I scrambled out of bed, grabbed the jeans I'd worn yesterday, and pulled them on as I went to look through a peephole that didn't exist.

"It's Savilla," the voiced called. "I have clean clothes if you want them."

I opened the door to find her standing in a brown leather skirt with a matching fitted top and boots. She looked amazing, nothing like the host of a party where a man had died last night.

"I thought you might want a few things." She held up an outfit and let it dangle from her hands. It was a pair of soft worn jeans and a flannel shirt, and I caught the scent of linen detergent. She knew me.

"That would be great actually. Thanks."

I took the clothes and started to close the door, but she put out a hand.

"Don't be silly. You get dressed, and I'll drive us into town. I cleared it with Charlie."

"Into town? Why?"

She raised an eyebrow. "Um, for our meeting."

"Our meeting?"

Savilla crossed her arms and looked at me as if she wasn't sure why I kept repeating her words. "With Mr. Froble."

I was startled. I didn't think Savilla knew I would be present at the reading of her father's will.

"You're the unbiased witness," Savilla said matter-of-factly. "That's what Mr. Froble told me when I checked to make sure that he'd heard from the prison about Mommy and StepMommy's visit."

The words were coming at me so fast that I struggled to keep up with the meaning behind them. Not only was I disoriented from just a few hours' sleep, but waking up to an empty bed had put a nail in whatever coffin I'd wanted to crawl inside.

My mouth tasted sour, my headache had only dimmed with sleep, and all I craved was the biggest cup of coffee known to man.

"I can wait in your room or out in the hall," Savilla said with an expression that told me she wasn't planning to leave.

I let her wait inside while I brushed my teeth, showered, and changed into the clothes, which fit perfectly. When I emerged from the bathroom, Savilla added mascara and lip gloss to my face like I was a helpless pageant contestant, and as soon as I'd slipped into my boots, Savilla shoved me out the door.

"So, Mr. Froble told you that I'm..." I let the words trail off, hoping she'd finish them. I noticed then that Savilla's cheeks were flushed, her hair had a couple of flyaway strands sticking out in different directions, and her hands were constantly moving. She'd either had a lot of coffee or she was nervous. Maybe both.

"An unbiased witness," she repeated, forcing a smile.

"And that's common at a will reading?" I asked, hoping I didn't make her suspicious, but also wondering if she still hadn't figured out that there might be another reason I'd been invited – namely that I was related to her.

"I'm glad you'll be there. It's the first time I've seen Mommy and StepMommy after their sentencing."

So that was the reason for the nerves. "You haven't visited them in prison?"

Guilt washed over her face. "I was too... I don't know. It was all too much."

Knowing her mother and stepmother had plotted to kill her father—and succeeded—would be too much for anyone.

I stopped and took her hand, giving it a quick squeeze and meeting her eye. "I'll be there the whole time."

Savilla squeezed my hand too and lifted her chin. "Thank you." As we reached the stairs, she changed the subject. "I didn't sleep a wink last night. I kept replaying everything with Daddy, how he died. I think that seeing Brett brought it all back."

Her sleepless night had been worse than my reality show dreams.

Tears welled in Savilla's eyes as we started down the stairs side by side, and she sniffled several times as she ran a hand along the wall. "It's just... today I'll find out if Daddy left all of this to me, and I have no idea what to do with it."

"Do with it?" I repeated weakly. "I mean, you live here, right? At least part of the year."

Savilla frowned at me as if I could never understand the plight of the enormously wealthy, which was fair. Momma had always said that the richer someone becomes, the less secure they feel, a sentiment I'd tried to debate several times. But maybe she was right. Maybe having and maintaining all of this opulence created burdens I didn't comprehend.

I'd never expected to know that kind of dilemma, though I did wonder if Mr. Finch might've left me some little piece of his wealth. I wasn't desperate for money like I'd been during the pageant, but I couldn't deny that cash offered options that a lack of it did not. The pageant winnings had helped so much, but after paying off Momma's house, paying back Aunt DeeDee for the debts she'd incurred from Momma's experimental treatments, settling with the credit card collectors, and covering all of my expenses for a final year of school, I only had about ten grand in the bank.

According to my professor, the fellowship in San Diego came with a low but livable salary, or when I graduated, I could get a job with an established practice, but unless I wanted to go into debt again, I couldn't open my own practice without another influx of cash. I kind of hated that this was where my mind went as I entered the main vestibule next to my secret half-sister, but practicalities mattered.

The two of us paused as we took in the view from the wide windows at the front of the house. There were my blue mountains, the haze already burning off as the sun rose higher in the sky.

"A man died here." Savilla breathed out as she turned away from the windows and her eyes scanned her home. Her tears were still coming, and I wondered suddenly if she was emotionally stable enough for the day ahead.

"Have you eaten anything this morning?" I asked, channeling Aunt DeeDee.

Savilla shook her head, but I wasn't sure if she was answering me or still stuck in her train of thought. "Brett died only four months after my own father died. Here, at my home." She reached out a hand and grabbed my forearm. "What if Presley is right? What if there's some kind of curse? On The Rose?"

The statement caught me off guard, but I supposed October was the season to think of scary things going bump in the night. I tried to reassure her with logic.

"Your father died because three people"—three people very close to him, I wanted to add but didn't—"were determined to get revenge on him, and Brett died because... well, we don't know, but I'm one hundred percent sure it's not because of a curse." I stole a glance at her. "You don't actually believe in those kinds of things, do you?"

Savilla wiped away tears and studied the ground for a moment as if weighing her answer. "Presley told me last night that she'd been thinking about breaking up with Brett for a while, that she'd even contacted a shaman who told her that she needed to get out of the relationship while she could."

The idea of a relationship shaman sounded on-brand for Presley. "Were those her exact words?" I asked.

Savilla looked straight at me and then nodded. "She told me

that I should meet with this lady, talk to her about my... troubles."

The last word rankled me even though I knew the response wasn't fair. Savilla might not have many visible troubles as far as I understood, but she did have numerous family issues. A frustrated mother and a vacuous stepmother who'd actually been sisters working together to kill Savilla's father. That was enough to keep any therapist employed for years to come.

This wasn't the thing that bothered me the most about our conversation, though. It was Presley and her desire to get out of her relationship with Brett. I'd learned that people's murderous intentions could spring from all sorts of reasons, but if the pageant investigation had taught me anything, it was that the impulse often came down to love or money.

Presley, presumably, had once loved Brett—maybe even still did—but she'd also seemed very cozy with Joe last night, whether it was because she was acting as his agent, which I found doubtful, or something more. But if Presley had simply left Brett, a rising star, for Joe, a no-name, part-time, aspirational actor/caterer... how would that decision look to the public? Wouldn't Presley get more sympathy and publicity by tragically losing the man she loved and, after an appropriate amount of grief and time, falling into the arms of an Ordinary Joe?

Maybe that was reason enough for both Joe and Presley to want Brett dead sooner rather than later.

TWENTY-TWO

By the time we reached Mr. Froble's office, it was noon, which meant we were right on time for the reading of the will. My heart thudded, and I tried to keep my anxiety at bay, especially as the police escort arrived with two killers who still stood to inherit something from the man they'd murdered.

Gathered in the small assembly were the lawyer, me, Savilla Finch, the police escort, StepMommy Glenda Finch, and Savilla's biological mother Katie Gilman, aka Nanny Kate. The distinguishing features of the latter two attendees were the orange jumpsuits and the guard between them. The two women had been brought in from the prison they now called home.

The lawyer, Mr. Froble, was an ancient man, nearing a hundred any day now, but he still sported a tidy white mustache and a full head of hair that stuck up in all directions. He'd survived two bouts with cancer, one of them pronounced terminal according to Momma, but he'd recovered from both.

We sat down across from the lawyer, the four of us ladies in a row. Until the will was read, I couldn't bring myself to meet anyone's eyes, especially Savilla's. She was the one whose reaction I cared about, the one who stood to lose the most by having a sibling.

Thankfully, within a minute of arriving, Mr. Froble dove right in, reading from the page in front of him. "I, Frederick Finch, being of sound mind do declare this to be my last will and testament."

Silence blanketed the room as we listened to the instructions concerning the bulk of the estate. My jaw dropped with each word. All property and financial holdings would be split evenly between Savilla Finch and Dakota Green.

As Mr. Froble finished reading the first section, I dared a glance at Savilla. I'd expected a piece of jewelry at most. Certainly not half of an entire estate. I wasn't sure whether to laugh or cry.

My eyes fell on Glenda Finch's face, which turned from peach to pink to red. As I watched the progression of color, I noticed that the woman's eyebrows hadn't been plucked in quite some time. How traumatizing for her.

Savilla looked at her two matriarchs, and though at first I assumed she was waiting to mirror their reactions, I soon realized that she was simply trying to gauge their level of distress so she could jump in and calm them. For perhaps the first time, I saw that Savilla was bearing a heavy load carrying the emotions of these two.

"That's wrong. It must be wrong. Check again," Glenda said, her mouth a grimace as she gave me a hard stare. "Dakota doesn't deserve a dime."

"I assure you," Mr. Froble said in his thick Virginia drawl, "years ago your late husband confided in me that he had suspected he might be Miss Green's father. When her pageant application came across his desk, he hired a private investigator who all but confirmed that suspicion."

"How? How would he confirm such a thing?"

"Apparently Dakota did an ancestry kit not too long ago,"

Mr. Froble said. "The investigator found that information among other indications that Dakota might be Mr. Finch's child."

The shock of the news froze me. I'd done that DNA test with Lacy as a lark. When we'd gotten the results, we'd laughed about my supposedly "elite athletic genes" and her alleged "tendency to procrastinate," neither of which were remotely true. My report had said nothing about a secret father.

I swallowed hard and stared at Mr. Froble's wrinkled jowls as I tried to process this new information. Mr. Finch had been a fixed figure in Aubergine for most of my childhood. I always knew he was there in the back of my mind, but could he have also been keeping a close eye on me as I grew up? And what about the fact that he'd hired a P.I. to look into my paternity? What did that even mean? I wasn't sure whether to feel frustrated over the invasion of my privacy or grateful that Mr. Finch cared.

Confused, concerned, overwhelmed. Whatever else I was, I was now rich. Like, very, very rich. All I wanted to do was talk to Momma, but instead I had a brand-new sister – whose enthusiasm outweighed my uncertainty.

"A sister? I have a sister!" Savilla shouted, springing from her chair. Gleefully, she threw her arms around me and rocked both of us from side to side. My body went from rigid to relaxed as her warmth spread. Savilla was happy, thrilled even, to have me as part of her family. Relief flooded me. "I knew you weren't just an unbiased witness."

Savilla hadn't known that, but regardless, she knew it now and seemed completely fine with her new reality. More than fine, even. Unfortunately, the rest of the party didn't seem to share Savilla's enthusiasm for my inclusion in the ragtag Finch family.

Mr. Finch tapped his hand against the desk to draw our attention back to the matter at hand. "There are two other items here," Mr. Finch said, pushing glasses up his nose. "The Miss 2001 Crown shall be shared by Glenda Gilman Finch and her sister Katie Gilman."

"A crown?" Glenda interrupted. "That's all my husband left me?" She spewed her words directly at me, ignoring Savilla's display of affection.

"If you ever get to claim that item," Mr. Finch reminded her. "You are both guilty of his murder, after all." He turned back to the page. "And the Rose Diamond shall be passed on to Brett Brinkley upon the occasion of his engagement."

I perked up at the unexpected detail. Why would Mr. Finch have left anything to Brett? Much less an item that seemed to shock Katie and Glenda as much as my inclusion in the will?

"Brett Brinkley gets the Rose Diamond?" Katie asked, her voice trailing off as if she was struggling to understand, albeit with much less anger, how she and her sister could've been kept from everything of real value.

Glenda pointed a finger at Mr. Froble as if he were to blame for the will, and her voice was icy as she leaned forward. "We will fight this."

The officer touched Glenda's shoulder to remind her of her fragile place in it all. He could escort her out any time.

"What's the Rose Diamond?" I asked, leaving out the other half of the question: *Why would Mr. Finch leave it to Brett Brinkley?* I know it's wrong to think ill of the dead, but the more I heard about Brett, the more convinced I was that he'd remained a jerkish butthole if there ever was one.

Still, I wasn't exactly in a position to argue over who should and should not inherit.

Savilla put a possessive hand over mine, and with the other, she held up her phone to show the screensaver: a photo of a light pink gem slightly smaller than a child's palm, about the size of a rose bud.

"It is—or, it was—Daddy's most precious stone."

"More importantly, it's the fifth largest diamond in the world," Glenda clarified through clenched teeth. "Easily worth fifty million. Maybe seventy-five."

"All the best jewelers have one signature piece, and this is ours," Savilla continued. "My great-grandfather mined and cut it."

A Finch man who'd been a rich but amateur stone cutter. That must be the reason for the misshapen petals and nicked ridges. Nonetheless, the sharp angles caught the light in a way that made it beautiful.

"The Rose Diamond isn't quite as valuable as the Hope Diamond," Savilla added. "But it's ours."

The use of the word *ours* made me wonder if she was including me. I wasn't courageous enough to ask, so I looked to Mr. Froble, who sat with his hands folded over his stomach, watching our exchange.

"The will says that Brett is supposed to use the stone for a very specific purpose, right?" Katie asked anxiously.

Mr. Froble pushed his glasses back up to the bridge of his nose and consulted the document again. "Yes, for his engagement. Directly after Mr. Finch updated his will, Mr. Brinkley was notified by a lawyer of the terms of the will, but now that Mr. Brinkley is dead, the stone will revert to being included in the estate's holdings."

Katie and then her sister gasped.

"Dead? What do you mean?" Glenda demanded, looking from Mr. Froble to Savilla. "That boy was the picture of health. Just the other day I saw a photo of him on page six in the *New York Post*."

I narrowed my gaze. Why had Glenda Finch been keeping tabs on Brett Brinkley from prison?

Savilla glanced at the officer for permission before placing a hand on both women's arms. "Brett passed away last night. At the reunion. He..." Her eyes flickered to me as if to communicate that I should back her up. I felt the first tug of a sisterly connection between us. "He choked. It was so sudden, but I know he would want you to know how much he appreciated everything our family did for him."

This was a misrepresentation of the events, which I was convinced involved murder, and I had no idea if Brett was grateful to anyone besides himself. I couldn't back up Savilla, but I wouldn't interfere at least. I stayed quiet while the women took in the news.

"He was like a son to my husband," Glenda said, putting a hand over her mouth as though to keep back a cry stuck in throat.

A sick feeling crept into my stomach. Had Mr. Finch spread his seed even farther? Was Brett his son? My half-brother?

"Exactly how close were Brett and your father?" I asked Savilla, trying to steady my voice. "Was he your... or our..." I had no idea how to ask the question in a subtle way.

Savilla tried to understand my meaning. "Was he my... ? Oh, Lord, no." She pointed at me. "Your face." She laughed lightly. "Don't be ludiotic."

Hmmm... Ludicrous? Idiotic? Either worked.

"Brett was *like* a son," Katie clarified, taking pity on me. "But, I swear, he was not."

Okay, that was comforting, I guess. Although, no one had known about me until now.

"That's correct," Mr. Froble confirmed. "Brett Brinkley had no biological claims to anything as far as Mr. Finch knew."

"My husband saw himself in Brett," Glenda said, as she wiped at an eye. "He was such a lovely boy."

The words were strangely comforting, largely because I trusted Mr. and Mrs. Finch's judgment of people zero percent. I could see the two of them thinking Brett hung the moon; I could see them pouring time and energy into him, especially if they thought they would get publicity or fame in return.

Glenda turned her focus back to her primary concern—that of her own well-being. "What about the stocks I purchased? Or the paintings I collected?"

"Those purchases were made with Mr. Finch's family money, and everything goes to Savilla—" Here, Mr. Froble shook his head once as if he didn't quite believe the piece of paper in front of him either. "And Dakota Green." He blinked at Glenda as if he wasn't shattering her world, finishing feebly, "But the crown technically belongs to you and your sister."

"And we get to share it," Glenda said with a smirk. "Just like we shared everything else."

"But he wrote his will in 2001, the year I won..." Katie protested.

"The year *we* won," Glenda corrected, shooting her sister a look that said too much time in the same penitentiary might not have been good for their relationship.

The reminder was said casually even though it was actually a piece of the mystery I'd solved last summer. Katie Gilman had originally won the Miss 2001 crown, but then fled at Mr. Finch's threats, passing on the title and perks to the runner-up, which happened to be her sister, Glenda Gilman. Within the year, she was Glenda Finch, the first phase of her revenge plot against her husband.

"I saw him sign the will more than twenty years ago," Glenda added. "I was here, in this room with him. Why would he cut me out after all our years together?"

The unanswered question lingered in the stale air of the law office, and I didn't feel like it was the right time to suggest that perhaps Mr. Finch had sensed his wife's murderous plans.

"He told me I would be provided for," Glenda said in a low voice that was almost pitiful enough to elicit sympathy, if I didn't remember his empty eye socket or the trickle of his blood running in a tunnel under the estate.

"You know I'll take care of both of you when you're..." Savilla's hands fluttered as if she were trying to bring the temperature of the room down several degrees.

I knew that Savilla had planned to finish the statement with *when you're out of prison*, but after conspiring to murder Mr. Frederick Finch for his money—and a smidge of revenge—it was unlikely that the two women would be awarded early parole for good behavior, which meant both had years behind bars in store for them.

"I don't want you to take care of me," Glenda replied brusquely. "I want what is owed to me for putting up with that man for more than two decades. I gave him his medicine, I listened to him snore, I had sex with him—"

Katie cut in, "I bore his child."

"He's a monster," Glenda finished, which I thought pretty ironic, considering who'd killed whom. "And the crown, it can't be worth any more than... what? A hundred grand?"

Mr. Froble consulted his notes. "A hundred and twenty."

That's a lot of ramen and socks from the prison commissary.

Even though I kept from saying these words out loud, Glenda scowled at me. "You and your mother were nothing to Fred."

I couldn't help myself. I laughed out loud. She thought this was an insult?

"Ladies," Mr. Froble said, putting out one shaking hand. "Let us remain dignified. The proper documentation can be submitted to the court if it comes to that, though it is clear that the man himself had no such qualms when he updated his will. Rest assured that Mr. Finch was in his right mind when he made these changes."

Glenda was not assured by this fact, but I wouldn't let myself be pulled into her narcissistic tantrum. Katie kept her eyes averted from me, so I had no idea how she was taking the news.

"I just don't understand..." Glenda pouted. "What kind of man changes his entire will because of... a bastard child?"

Savilla inhaled sharply. "That's enough." She stood and stepped forward as the guard watched her closely. "Perhaps it is a surprise, but, as I said, I swear I'll take care of both of you. I've already hired the best lawyers who are working night and day to get your sentence punctuated."

"*Mitigated*, dear," Katie corrected.

Savilla didn't miss a beat as she took a knee in front of her mother and aunt. "I swear to do my best to keep us afloat."

"Your best isn't going to be good enough," Glenda scoffed, throwing off Savilla's hand and standing, her arms flailing.

As soon as she was on her feet, the guard was on them, gripping Glenda in a kind of manual straight-jacket as he called for the officer standing watch outside the door. In seconds, the other guard had Katie's arms behind her back, and the men were leading the women, one sister screaming and belligerent and the other resigned and sorrowful, out the door and into the waiting police car.

Mr. Froble, Savilla, and I watched it all unfold in stunned silence, my mind circling Brett's inclusion in the will as the room emptied. It didn't make sense why Mr. Finch would've left him a dime, much less a diamond worth many millions.

The mystery of this man and his death was getting muddier than a pigpen, as Momma would say.

TWENTY-THREE

Mr. Froble raised both palms in the air as if to say he couldn't even begin to fathom what he'd just witnessed: two distraught sisters who'd once been upstanding members, even leaders, of the Aubergine community, carted away once again in handcuffs.

"I'll have the official paperwork sent out on Monday, and we'll be able to move everything from the trust into both of your names in coming days." Mr. Froble tapped mindlessly at the sheet of paper that had caused such uproar before addressing Savilla. "I'll arrange for the Miss 2001 crown to be kept in a secure lock box at the bank until Glenda and Katie's potential... or eventual... release."

The man stood to his full height, which couldn't have been more than five feet and some change, put on the hat that had been resting at his elbow, and walked out of the room. He probably needed a nap after the excitement, and even though it was only 1 p.m., I thought I might need a stiff drink.

Once we were alone in the office, Savilla threw her arms around me again, and the nerves I'd been feeling about her finding out we were sisters finally disappeared completely.

"I always wanted a sister," she squealed, squeezing me tight. "And we're almost, like, twins, which is twice as good."

Except we didn't share the same mother or the same birthdate. I supposed we could be Irish twins—of a sort. Regardless, the thing that mattered was that Savilla seemed ecstatic rather than resentful about sharing her role as an heiress, even though I had no idea what exactly that might mean in coming days. If only there was some kind of book for dummies, a kind of *Heiress's Guide to Death & Diamonds*.

"We have so much catching up to do. Oh. My. God. I have chills." She held out her arm to prove the fact. "It's like I knew without knowing. I'm, what's it called, precious?"

"*Prescient*," I corrected.

"See! You can even finish my sentences." Savilla studied me with slack-jawed amazement, even though I was pretty sure that any kid studying for the SAT could've figured out that one. "You can move into the west wing of the house and you can run the stables, because that's totally your thing. I could also use some help with the accounts because I do not do math."

Savilla giggled as if bleeding money from an estate like The Rose was the best joke ever.

"Every night we can eat dinner together and watch movies —the classics are my favorite. *Clueless, Mean Girls, Ten Things I Hate About You*." She inhaled and thought of another benefit to our new relationship status, waving her hands in excitement as she spoke. "Aunt DeeDee can come too. Can I call her Aunt DeeDee now, since we're, like, totally family?" Not waiting for an answer, Savilla spun around in a full circle. "This is the best thing since that time I met the Jonas Brothers in Cancún and one of them asked me to marry him. I had to turn him down because our auras didn't align, but it was a thrilling week."

When her words ran out, she looked at me expectantly. I wasn't quite sure which thing I should address first: moving into the Rose Palace, the fact that none of those movies were classics, the Jonas proposal, or the auras?

"I think I might be a little overwhelmed," I said, lifting my thumb and pointer finger to show her that I was freaking out inside. "How about we take some time to digest the news and then we can figure out details?"

"Of course, yes, you're right. I'm being too much. So, so, so sorry." Savilla stopped beaming and her perfectly tailored eyebrows dipped into a concerned V. "I get like that when I'm excited, and my words get all jumbled too. Why don't you take a minute and then we'll go grab coffee and work out the details?"

It wasn't what I had meant by a request for time to process, but *que sera*.

"Sounds good," I said, wondering how, after the news of my inheritance, I was ever going to focus on figuring out Brett's email password or who might've actually killed him. Savilla was right. It was *all* too much.

Savilla threw her arms around me one more time and yanked me close. "I'm going to be the best sister ever. Just you wait."

"Half-sister," I corrected without thinking.

"Silly girl. I don't care about demantics."

Oof. That was a tough one.

"*Semantics?*" I dared to correct.

"Details or semantics, neither matter in family affairs," Savilla said. "Family is what you make it, and I make you my full-hearted sister."

I knew how Punnett squares tracked genotypes, and none of what she was saying made scientific sense. Savilla's kindness was endearing though.

"Look, I appreciate your generous... welcome, but this weekend has been a lot. I have no idea what comes next for me, much less how to figure out who..."

Savilla's ears perked up as she finished my sentence. "... who killed Brett?"

"Well, yeah," I said. "I wasn't sure if you actually believed there was a murderer with what you told your mom and stepmom."

Savilla waved a hand. "I didn't want to upset them until we know something for sure. They can be... fragile."

That description did not add up with what I'd seen of Glenda and Katie. Erratic, perhaps. Unstable, even. But not fragile. Perhaps this was the *demantics* of which Savilla spoke.

"Glenda said that Brett was like a son to your father. Did he help him get his start? Produce the music video? Get him on the reality show?"

"Yep, they were close. Daddy started Petal Productions, his last madcap attempt to make us rich and thrust Brett into the spotlight." Savilla nodded as if she could hardly believe the truth herself. "But I had nothing to do with it. I wasn't even here when they filmed the music video or the home visit." Concern crossed her features. "Did you think I had something to do with Brett's death?"

"No," I said, because I didn't. Not really. I didn't want to think badly of Savilla, but despite my personal desires, she had made her way onto my suspect list—even if it was in such a low spot that I hadn't even named her to Charlie.

"Good. Because I was as shocked as you," Savilla said. She bit at her lip, thinking. "I hate to say it because he's always seemed like a good guy, but Joe had the most beef with Brett. And he seems strangely close to Presley, don't you think?"

I did think that.

"How did your chat with him go last night?" she asked, stretching as if working out the tension of the last hour.

"Okay. Something's definitely happening between him and Presley, which means something likely happened between him and Brett—even beyond Brett sabotaging his college experience and ultimately his career."

I considered mentioning Lacy's dilemma but thought better of it. I had about eleven hours to help her figure out Brett's password, and perhaps Savilla could help me solve that when the time came, but for now, I'd let it rest.

Savilla grabbed her purse and put an arm through mine. "It would be good to actually locate the Rose Diamond," she commented, almost as an afterthought.

I looked at her with a puzzled expression.

"The diamond, the one Brett was supposed to inherit," she explained. "It's been missing since the 2023 pageant."

That was an important detail.

"Honestly, at first I thought Brett had somehow stolen it, but he never seemed to have a huge influx of cash. Then I thought Daddy had sold it to keep the estate afloat, but now... I'm not sure."

There was a lot there to unpack, but Mr. Froble's assistant came to the door, opened it, and politely gestured that we should leave.

"Coffee?" Savilla suggested again, as we exited the building onto Main Street.

I glanced at my watch, considering the best use of my time. I was pretty sure that Savilla knew things that I didn't even know I needed to know.

"Sure," I agreed, sending Lacy a quick text. She didn't respond immediately like she normally did, and I only hoped she wasn't pacing the mansion anxiously.

Savilla grinned at me as she took my arm. "We'll never be apart ever, ever again," she breathed, studying my face like she was memorizing every detail.

My chest tightened, and I reminded myself that I had a new sister, not a new limb. It would be fine. Besides, maybe Savilla knew something she would now share with me, her blood relation, her own kin. Something that could help solve Brett's murder.

TWENTY-FOUR

Mr. Finch had been generous with his finances in Aubergine, which was part of the reason our roads were regularly repaved and our school system had any kind of arts program. In middle and high school, it seemed that Savilla had inherited his mindset, hosting fundraisers for things as trivial as getting disposable makeup brushes in every girls' restroom on campus to noble causes like funding a new building for the town's animal shelter.

Years ago, when we were fifteen, Savilla and I had spent Saturdays at that animal shelter. I'd bathe the puppies while she photographed them for the adoption website. Even then, we'd played to our strengths. One day, as I'd carefully cleaned around a Lab mix's injured paw, Savilla had circled us with her camera.

"Oh my goodness, he's adorable," she'd said, cooing at the six-month-old puppy as she made cutesy faces. "His whiskers and sad eyes make him look like a little seal."

But when I'd asked if she wanted to pet him, she'd wrinkled her nose. "I don't touch things that poop themselves."

That was Savilla—happy to capture beauty from a safe distance, while I dealt with the mess. Just like now with Brett's murder. She wanted to help solve it, but could she handle getting her hands dirty?

Savilla's words came back to me now as I followed behind her, thinking about the literal and figurative mess of this weekend. We stepped inside the Morning Brew, which was covered in autumnal décor. From the jack-o'-lanterns lining the pastry case to the giant purple spiders hanging from the ceiling, Halloween was written all over this place.

"Hey, Savilla," a lady behind the counter called as soon as we entered.

Preferring to drink my cheap coffee at home, I hadn't been there since well before Momma died, but I recognized the fifty-something woman as Gladys Liplich, longtime proprietor of the only bookstore/café/crystal shop in town.

"It's nearly two o'clock. You're a few hours later than normal," Gladys called, but her tone was friendly. "You want your usual?"

Savilla studied the menu for a minute. "I think I'll do the Maple Moonlit Macchiato today," she said with a grin. "I'm celebrating."

Gladys walked behind the till. "Good for you, darling."

She didn't ask a follow-up question, but Savilla didn't need prompting to introduce me. "You remember DeeDee's niece?"

Gladys turned to me for the first time. "I sure do, but my goodness, I didn't hardly recognize you." Her face pinched in the concerned look most of the townsfolk still gave me almost a year and a half after Momma's death. "I'm sorry about your momma. She was a good lady. Took real good care of my Milton before he passed three years ago."

This was what I expected when people mentioned my mother—that they would also reference a person that she'd nursed. It was Momma's legacy.

"Thank you," I said simply.

"What can I get for you today?" Gladys now asked, waiting for me to place my order.

I scanned the menu, confused by most of the offerings. The Magician's Morning Mocha, the Tarot-fic Cortado, the Lucky Latte. "I'll just have a cup of coffee."

Gladys gave me a look that I was fairly certain she reserved for people not from around here. "What's that, hon?"

"Just a coffee. Black."

"Oh, we don't sell that," Gladys said easily, letting loose a little laugh.

I glanced at the coffee pot behind her. "Isn't that a coffee maker?"

"Well, yes, but I only sell specialty drinks right now." Gladys leaned forward and whispered as if anyone else was actually in the establishment to overhear. "Joe Larson roasted the last batch of beans, a big one, and he nearly burned it to ashes. I redid the menu with a bunch of sugar to compensate, and I gave everything a seasonal flare." Gladys lifted her arms and gestured to the menu above her, on which she, presumably, had drawn ghosts and witches in various corners.

"Joe roasted your coffee?"

"Sure, he's been our house roaster for a year or so now while he tries to find his sea legs." Gladys seemed to recall something. "Didn't he cater the class reunion last night?"

Savilla nodded. "He did, but—"

"I already heard," Gladys said, with a long shake of her head. "That poor boy. He always wanted to make something of himself."

At first I thought she meant Brett, but then I reconsidered. "Wait, sorry. Do you mean Brett? Or Joe?"

"Joe," Gladys said, taking two pieces of pumpkin loaf out of the case, placing them on plates, and sliding both of them across the counter. "On the house." She leaned on her elbows. "Joe's a good boy, but he keeps getting knocked down before he can get back up again. He's been doing odd jobs around here ever since he got kicked out of that fancy college and came home like a pup with its tail between its legs. And just when he gets an investor in his catering business"—Gladys gestured toward me, which I assumed meant my aunt was the unspoken investor in addition to being some kind of mentor—"a man dies at his first gig." Gladys's eyes widened. "And not just any man! The town sweetheart."

I thought about that definition of Brett. Was he the town sweetheart? Perhaps. He'd at least helped people outside of the pageant world hear of Aubergine, but in my estimation, he hadn't done anything more remarkable than recording a half-decent song and landing a spot on a ridiculous reality show.

"You got any idea who did it?" Gladys asked, eyeing us.

Savilla shook her head. "Not yet, but if there was something omniferous, then Dakota and her man are on the case."

I tried to parse out that one. *Omnipotently nefarious?* That guess was as good as any.

Gladys gave me a half-grin, ignoring Savilla's word choice. "That's right. You and the new sheriff are an item, aren't you?"

I gave a slight shrug and assumed a blank expression as I scanned the menu again. "Actually, I think I'll have the Eerie Espresso."

"Great choice," Gladys said, thankfully not asking any follow-up questions as she moved to a large metal machine to start our drinks.

As soon as we had our pumpkin loaf and I'd sipped my surprisingly tasty drink, Savilla gave me the most intense look I'd ever seen from her, making me nearly choke. "What? Do I have something on my face?"

Savilla bit the inside of her cheek and dropped her eyes to the table for a second before looking back up at me. "I need to tell you something."

Despite the treats, my mouth went dry. *Oh God. Here comes*

the confession. She's the one who killed Brett, and she's confiding in me as her brand-new sibling. My heart practically jumped into my neck.

"I couldn't bear to tell StepMommy and Nanny Kate, but we are hemoragitically losing money at The Rose."

"Okay?" I said, knowing a thing or two about money flowing out faster than it was coming in. I also had not yet wrapped my mind around the idea of owning half the estate, so if she told me it was worth pennies, it wouldn't actually change my life much.

"All of our pageant sponsors pulled their funding after Daddy's death and I don't think I even want to do the pageant anymore, so I've—we've—got no income to keep the lights on past Christmas." She took a deep breath. "At least, that's what Daddy's financial guy told me."

I noticed her use of *we*, and I wasn't sure I liked it.

"I was already thinking about getting help to turn the estate into something amazing," Savilla continued. "And I think the universe has totally provided an answer."

"And by answer, you mean..."

"You!" Savilla grinned widely as if proud of both the universe and herself. "Now that we're co-owners, I'm sure of it. We are totally in this together."

Her expression was a combination of relief and longing, and though I understood both of those impulses after finding my own need for community this summer, I was certain that I couldn't be her only solution.

"So, the first thing we need to do," Savilla continued, "is to find money to do some renovations, bring The Rose into the twenty-first century, you know?"

I did not know, but she took a sip of her drink and kept talking.

"To do that, we definitely need a cash infusion."

That caught my attention. "You don't have cash?"

"Not much." Savilla shrugged with the carefree attitude of

the permanently wealthy. I reminded myself that someone would always loan her money if she didn't have her own. "If we could find the Rose Diamond, that would be more than enough to give us a fresh start."

Us. There was that plural pronoun again.

"Yeah," she said, relaxing into her chair as if settling in for a long chat, "apparently Daddy was losing the family money faster than ever."

I thought of what I'd discovered this summer at the pageant: that Mr. Finch was an investor in Dr. Bellingham's plastic surgery business, that he and Mr. Finch were close, that Dr. Bellingham had helped plan Mr. Finch's murder. This must have been an investment that had soured in more ways than one for Mr. Finch.

Savilla took a sip of her drink. "Daddy was never really a great businessman."

"Then why didn't he sell the diamond?" I asked. "Before it disappeared?"

"The finance guy said that he had arranged to sell it, but then one day it was missing from the display case."

It was reminiscent of Miss 2001's missing crown.

"And you're sure Brett didn't steal it?" I asked.

"No. Definitely not. Otherwise, Brett wouldn't have demanded the diamond be passed to him in the will." Savilla caught herself as if she'd misspoken but then her shoulders relaxed as she realized something. "I guess it's not a secret anymore."

"What do you mean?"

Savilla hovered over her steaming cup, warming her hands. "At first I thought Daddy was weirdly fixated on helping Brett, specifically by starting a production company that first recorded his song and later funded the *Small Town, Big Romance* show."

My eyes widened. "So your father was a producer on the show?"

"Yep. *The* producer. I mean, he hired professionals who knew what they were doing, but yeah, from day one. I think he liked the control, especially after he started losing so much money in other investments. Daddy was a bit of a... a narcissist." Savilla's brow furrowed as if she hated to admit the fact – one that didn't surprise me in the least. Anyone who'd spent five minutes with the man could assume as much. He could be charming and charismatic, but he also wanted to control any narrative. He wanted to preserve his family's image. He wanted power, and he would do almost anything to be the one calling the shots. "At first, I thought Daddy was being helpful to Brett because he saw him as a kind of son he never had, but that never sat quite right."

The image of Brett walking side by side in the gardens with Mr. Finch came to mind. Mr. Finch's smile was there, but it had seemed forced, their conversation staged. I'd figured that was because of the numerous cameras on them, but Savilla seemed to be suggesting something else.

"Then I found out..." Savilla's expression almost exactly mirrored the one I'd seen on Lacy's face last night, when she'd told me how Brett had threatened her.

I waited a few beats as Savilla put both hands on the table in front of her as if to steady herself. She closed her eyes briefly before opening them and looking straight at me.

"I found out that he blackmailed Daddy with footage... of me and Brett. Together."

My heart stuttered. "This may be a strange question, but do you know how Brett threatened your dad?"

"He said he would send out the footage via email," she said, making the same exasperated face that Lacy had made.

My mouth went dry. Brett was a predictable scumbag, using the same methods on more than one victim. It was sickening. "Did it come from an account with the name allmy-ladies@mail.com?"

"Yes, how did you...?" Savilla's voice lowered to a whisper as she read me.

I shook my head—I couldn't even begin to answer that question right now. "Did you and Brett... Were you together at some point?"

"For, like, half a second." Savilla waved a hand, tossing aside this part of the past. "It was a fling about a year or two after I graduated from college, and I was in between relationships. Brett was in New York for a week, and I showed him the sites and we just, I don't know, clicked. It was nothing, more than nothing, but apparently, he'd filmed that *more than nothing* and held on to it in order to squeeze money out of my father."

Understanding dawned. "That's why Mr. Finch—your, our..." I was struggling to find what to call Mr. Finch. "That's why he started the production company?"

"And why he made an entire production company to launch Brett's music career, which actually made money at first. The problem is that the TV show siphoned off all the profits and then some. I had no idea until after the show aired when I found Daddy's email open and saw a message from Brett, reminding him of what he had on me. I'm not saying that Daddy had ever been great with money, having had his entire inheritance handed to him, but he got so much worse after that. Eventually he lost so much that by summer he'd started making deals with museums to sell off a bunch of our gems."

That would explain the empty cases in the Color Gallery at The Rose.

"Why wouldn't Brett just ask for the diamond then and there? Why have it written into Mr. Finch's will?"

"He was getting what he wanted from Daddy with the production company, and he didn't want to have to pay a dime on it. If it came as property in part of an inheritance, he could find a way to work around paying taxes, but if it was given to him as a gift... well, someone would have to pay, and Daddy was running out of money too fast. Brett didn't want to totally bank-rupt him. He just wanted the diamond. Putting it in the will was a kind of insurance against Brett leaking the video of the two of us." Savilla let out a heavy breath. "Daddy was of the mind that it's good to keep your friends close and enemies closer."

In this case, the old adage hadn't served Mr. Finch well. Any friends he'd had seemed to turn to enemies, and keeping them close had gotten him killed.

I took another sip of my drink, considering the most signifi-cant things I'd learned in the past two hours, besides the fact that I might or might not be very rich.

1. Brett had blackmailed Mr. Finch in almost the very same way that he'd threatened Lacy, who only had until midnight to stop his awful email from making their way into the world.
2. Mr. Finch's most precious gem, the Rose Diamond, had disappeared after the 2023 pageant and shortly before Brett's homestay visit on *Small Town, Big Romance*.
3. Brett was somehow even more of an asshole than I'd imagined.

As we cleared off the table and placed our dirty dishes in a wash basin, I considered what came next. Hopefully, that after-noon, Charlie would be able to tell me what the forensics lab and the coroner had found out about Brett's death. The infor-mation should help point us in a direction that steered far from Lacy.

As we were saying goodbye to Gladys, a bell above the door tinkled, and when I turned around to see who was entering the Morning Brew, there stood Deputy Wright, her hand wrapped possessively around Charlie's bicep.

TWENTY-FIVE

As soon as Charlie saw me, he shook off the deputy's hand and stepped toward me.

"Dakota," he said, the single word laden with uncertainty. "Did you get my note?"

I thought of the simple sentence he'd scrawled: *Meeting with Wright this morning to discuss case.*

"Yep," I said. "It was very informative."

He stood awkwardly between me and Deputy Wright, whose face had assumed a more professional expression, the flirtatious grin she'd been beaming at him wiped away for now.

In that moment, I despised my insecurity. Momma had taught me to be a strong, independent woman in so many ways, and I was proud that despite losing her, I'd forged ahead. I was about to graduate from one of the most challenging veterinary programs in the country with full honors and a fellowship recommendation. But when it came to romance, I'd never had an example of relationships, good or bad. Maybe that's why I couldn't quite get a grip when it came to Charlie.

He nodded in greeting to Savilla. "I'm not sure you had the

chance to meet my new deputy last night during the questioning."

"I haven't had the pleasure," Savilla said, though her voice wasn't raised in that high pitch she reserved for those she was actually pleased to meet. "Charlie did my interview, which was much too short. I was almost offended not to be more of a suspect." She laughed, but the deputy didn't seem to get the joke.

"Jill Wright, this is Savilla Finch, owner of The Rose," Charlie said, motioning between the two of them.

Savilla reached out a hand even though her smile didn't quite reach her eyes and her lips were tight. I could tell that she was also disturbed by the visual of the pair of them entering the café. She seemed to be taking her newly discovered role as my sister seriously. "I assume you're both at the Morning Brew as part of the investigation?" she asked.

It startled me to hear the edge to her voice, one that said she wasn't about to stand for any shenanigans.

"We wanted to drop by the station to run a background check on a couple of people staying at The Rose, so we decided to grab a coffee," Charlie answered, before turning to me. "I actually heard from the lab this morning. Do you have a few minutes?"

I wasn't sure that I wanted to talk to Charlie, especially not if I was going to be sitting across from him and his deputy, staring at the two of them side by side, being reminded what a nice matching pair they made in uniform. I'd seen obvious desire in the deputy's eyes, but Charlie was more difficult to read. Still, how could he not respond to the advances of such a woman like Jill Wright?

I nodded curtly, telling myself that I would time my stay just as I'd hoped to do last night at the reunion. They could order their coffee, and I would sit across from them for ten minutes, max.

"Why don't I ride with Jill back to The Rose?" Savilla asked, interrupting my plan and improvising her own. "That way the two of you"—she waved a hand from me to Charlie—"can discuss whatever you need to discuss for as long as you need to discuss it?"

"Actually, Charlie and I were planning to—" Deputy Wright began.

"No," Charlie interrupted, his eyes still on me. "That's a good idea. You should go with Savilla and check on things at The Rose. We'll be behind shortly."

The deputy's eyes flitted toward me, her expression annoyed. "Fine," she said. "Let me get a coffee to go and we can head out."

"Goody," Savilla said with a facetiousness I'd never heard her use. "We can get to know each other on the way home."

Savilla shot me a look as if to say she would take things from here, and I almost felt a smile forming on my lips before I glanced back at Charlie and saw his sheepish frown. Was he embarrassed that I'd caught him flirting with another woman? Or did he actually have something to discuss with me? Perhaps it was both.

A group of tourists, antiquers it looked like, stepped into the coffee shop, so it took several minutes for Gladys to ring up the new orders and make their drinks. While we waited, Deputy Wright actually tried to make conversation with me.

"Charlie says you're in a veterinary program?"

Even though it might be unreasonable, I hated hearing his name on her lips—and anyway, he was her boss. She shouldn't have been using his first name.

"Fourth year," I answered.

"How many years does it take?"

"This is my last year, and next semester is almost entirely clinical."

Charlie listened in, probably hoping we didn't start talking about him.

"How long have you been an officer?" I asked her.

"Nine years," she said. "College wasn't really my thing, so I dropped out after a year. I thought it might be fun to do target practice for my job."

I checked her expression to see if she was kidding.

Deputy Wright touched the taser at her belt and swished her ponytail. "How long have you known Charlie?"

"Four months."

"We've been working together for six years," she said. "We were paired together for a theft case in Mount Cedar. Some creep was stealing money—and anything else he could get his hands on—from his own mother. We put him behind bars and decided we worked well together."

I hated what I saw as her smug expression, particularly because I couldn't help but compare the length of our relationships, which, based on pure longevity, meant I was obviously the loser here.

"When he got the sheriff gig, he asked if I would join him, but it took me a while to finish things up where I was stationed."

In the face of Jill's prior claim, my lack was almost staggering. We didn't even have a friendship to fall back on, and what we did have might not be made to last.

Mercifully, Gladys called Charlie and Jill to the bar to pick up their drinks.

"It was nice to finally meet you outside of an interview," the deputy said in a tone I couldn't read as she mixed a pack of artificial sweetener into her coffee.

Savilla started peppering her with questions and steering her toward the door so Charlie and I would be left alone. Gladys's chatter and the grinding of the espresso machine sounded above the Halloween music coming through the overhead speakers.

Charlie looked around for a corner table where we could talk while "Monster Mash" rang out, but the few chairs were taken now. He raised his chin toward the ceiling. "You want to go upstairs to my place?"

"You live above the Morning Brew?" I was surprised by the fact, but more surprised that I somehow hadn't known the location of my... Charlie's apartment.

"Yeah, I thought I told you." Charlie narrowed his eyes as if he couldn't have forgotten to mention it.

I remembered him saying how much he loved the smell of coffee when he woke up in his new place, but I could have sworn he'd never mentioned he was literally living above a coffee shop.

"Maybe you did," I said vaguely, following him out the door. We rounded the corner to a narrow alley and up a set of stairs to a second-floor entrance that spurred off into two different apartments.

"My neighbor is Gladys—she's actually been letting Kitty out this weekend while I've been at The Rose. Our walls are so thin that I wake up when her alarm goes off at four in the morning. I'm always relieved when she's not the first one on duty." He pulled out his keys, opened the door, and flipped on the lights as he continued talking. "Gladys gives me free coffee though, and Joe's batches aren't usually as bad as this last one. She told you he burned the beans while roasting them?"

"Do you know Joe?" I asked, ignoring his question. "Like, are you two friendly?"

"I've seen him around. He's a real hustler, a hard worker— and he's at every town meeting."

Charlie was the second person close to me who'd had something quasi-nice to say about Joe, but I couldn't let go of the idea of him as a prime suspect. Largely because if I removed him from my list, it would make Lacy's name rise higher.

As soon as I stepped into the apartment, Kitty crawled from

the spot where he'd been lying on Charlie's leather couch and stretched before meandering over to me, sniffing at my feet then looking up for an ear rub. Kitty had traveled up to New York with Charlie several times, so we'd become best buds.

With Kitty at my side, I allowed myself a second to check out Charlie's apartment, which was distinctly *him*. A dog bed, rarely used since Kitty preferred one worn couch cushion, was in the corner. On the wall hung a black-and-white Ansel Adams photograph of a winding river with majestic mountains. On the end table was a dog-eared copy of a John Scalzi novel, and next to a speaker system was a Lowden guitar with a scarred spot on the body. Sometimes, Charlie would play me and Kitty a bedtime tune over Zoom. He wasn't the most accomplished musician, but I enjoyed his faltering notes. More than that, though, I liked to watch how his face would change, relaxing into the melody as he let go of the day's stress.

Now Charlie sat down on a loveseat, and I debated whether to remain standing. I didn't want him to think I wanted to be here.

He watched me with curiosity, as if I were a scared foal about to bolt. Kitty nudged at the back of my legs, practically moving me to the edge of an upholstered chair, where I sat and he decided to lay his head on my knee. *He thinks he's a lap dog,* Charlie had often said as Kitty tried to wedge himself between us while we watched a movie.

"Joe is actually part of what—or who—I wanted to talk about," Charlie said. "I heard from the lab this morning, and there were no signs of poisoning in Brett's system, which confirms that whatever he was drinking wasn't the cause of death."

"So he just choked?"

"No," Charlie said. "It's much worse and definitely foul play."

"Meaning?" I leaned forward, my elbows on my knees. I

was no longer concerned about the status of my relationship with Charlie or the question of whether or not Deputy Jill Wright might be encroaching on my territory.

"Brett had an esophageal perforation."

From my training, I knew this term. Mammals, but particularly dogs, swallow inedible material all the time: bones, sticks, or even kids' toys. If an object slices the esophagus on the way down, there's a decent chance it will slice parts of the colon, although Brett's death had been so sudden, that likely wouldn't have been the case.

"Was anything in his small intestines?" I asked.

"No, but there was something inside of him." Charlie's eyes narrowed as if he couldn't quite figure out how to explain what he'd learned. "It was an object, a jagged-edged diamond about this big." He used his thumb and forefinger to make the shape of a circle about an inch in diameter.

After the revelations in Mr. Froble's office about Brett and the Rose Diamond, the detail landed hard. "What color was it?"

"Here," he said, opening up his phone and passing it to me. On the screen was a light pink gem in what I guessed was the outstretched, gloved hand of the coroner. The stone was far less polished than the version of it I'd seen on Savilla's phone that morning, but I recognized it immediately.

"That's..." I bit my lip.

Charlie read my expression. "What?"

"It's the Rose Diamond," I said, tilting the phone so he could see the demarcations that were supposed to be like petals on a rose. "See how it's cut?"

I pictured Brett again, regularly practicing intermittent fasting, according to Presley. He'd ordered a drink from the bar, and she'd carried it to where he'd stood talking with Lacy in hushed tones at the edge of the Primrose Ballroom dance floor.

I filled Charlie in on my thinking, including what Savilla had told me less than an hour ago about the stone being missing since the summer of 2023, but I didn't yet mention the black-mail scheme. I wasn't ready to give up Lacy's secret quite yet. "But how would this stone go from being at the estate in 2023 to Brett's stomach last night?" I mused.

"It wasn't in his stomach," Charlie said. "They found it lodged in his trachea."

Charlie pulled out the report from the coroner and handed it to me.

At the top read *Office of the Medical Examiner* and under-neath was a sketch of a generic man's outline with one single mark over the left side of the chest where the diamond had been found. Underneath was an explanation of the means of death, as well as additional observations. Inflammation in the trachea and lungs, facial edema, swollen tongue, and neck abrasions.

I read the smallest print in the bottom of the page aloud. "Means of death: obstruction of airway, causing asphyxiation. Signs of strangulation."

"That's what bothers me. Presley insists that Brett was strangled, even though he was obviously clawing at his own throat," Charlie said.

I remembered well her strange intrusion upon our examina-tion of the body shortly after Brett's death. "By her great-grand-mother's magical curse," I reminded him. "If she was guilty of trying to kill him and make it look like an accident, I would think that she would either keep her mouth shut or just attribute it to choking."

"Right, but criminals sometimes overdo their lies as a kind of compensation for the truth." Charlie sucked his teeth for a long moment. "Even if she did go to all that trouble, seems like it would've involved a lot of chance."

"And why take a chance on murder? Why not ensure it?" I finished, trying to think like a killer but coming up short. Another concern came to mind, perhaps just as important. "How did Brett not notice the stone?"

"He was drunk," Charlie said, pointing at the blood alcohol level. It was startlingly high. He'd obviously had even more alcohol than Presley had realized.

"You think maybe he assumed the diamond was an ice cube?" I asked, forming a theory. "Maybe he was drinking so fast that he somehow swallowed it."

"Inhaled it, more like," Charlie said.

"I suppose." I tried to reason it out. "He hadn't eaten all day, and according to Presley, he drank like a fish. Her cliché, not mine."

"They didn't find any food in his stomach," Charlie mused. "And I guess he chugged it."

"Presley would know how he took his drink. On the rocks, for example."

"Do you think she could've found the diamond and slipped it into his drink in the hopes that it would get lodged in his throat?"

This seemed like a stretch to me, but we were brainstorming, which was what mattered. The Rose Diamond had been missing for more than two years, but even so, Mr. Finch had included it in his updated will, which meant that he must've expected it to reappear at some point.

These were the kinds of moments when Charlie and I meshed well, completing one another's sentences, our thoughts an extension of the other's. I loved it.

"If we assume that Presley was trying to kill him—then why?" Charlie asked. "Why would she want her boyfriend dead?"

"She doesn't need money," I said, before correcting myself. "At least, I don't think so." I would've assumed the same about the Finch estate until a couple of hours ago.

"Presley could've killed him out of jealousy," Charlie suggested.

Heat rose to my cheeks as I considered my own jealous

thoughts about Charlie's deputy, but I tamped them back down. This was different. "That's a good point. Brett had been wanting to start drama—literally, for his show—by having Presley catch him in the act with another girl."

Charlie fixed his eyes on me, trying to see beneath the words I was saying. "How do you know that?"

I could lie, tell him that one of Brett's camera crew had let it slip. I could say that Presley had pulled me aside to say she was in on the idea. Neither of those was true and would only lead to more questions. Besides, if Charlie could read me, which he often could, then he would be able to tell if I was making up a story.

"Lacy told me." I exhaled. "Brett wanted her to be the other girl because they'd dated in high school."

Charlie's brow furrowed, and he reached into his pocket and pulled out a notebook and pen.

I put my head in my hands. "God, please. Don't write that down."

"Why not?"

"Because it's, I don't know, private information."

"Dakota, nothing is private in a murder investigation—or if it is, it shouldn't be."

TWENTY-SIX

The drive back to The Rose was a quiet one, both Charlie and I lost in our own thoughts. Dusk was setting in, and the day had passed too quickly for the weight of it. As we pulled up the long drive and rounded the circle that led to the main entrance of the house, I wasn't surprised to see Deputy Wright waiting outside, under the lit lamp at the front of the house, as if she'd been tracking Charlie's movements.

I scoffed as soon as I spotted her.

"What?" Charlie asked, obviously unaware.

"Nothing," I muttered, just before we were about to pull up in front of the steps.

Charlie slammed on the brakes, startling me.

I turned to him. "What was that for?"

"You won't talk to me." Charlie's tone was elevated ever so slightly, enough to get my attention since he wasn't the kind of man who raised his voice in any situation.

I met his eyes, those inlets into his soul, and I saw confusion and frustration and perhaps even a feeling of betrayal.

"You're quiet and moody," Charlie continued. "And I have no idea what's going on in your mind."

I was the moody one? What about him? The one who couldn't seem to separate his work self from his personal life, the one who could be delightful and endearing one day and reserved and repressed the next.

"I get that the circumstances this weekend, they're... extreme." He huffed out a breath. "But you've just... You're acting so... not normal." His brow furrowed as he struggled to find the words. "Talk to me. Let me in."

Frustration heated my cheeks. Charlie had no idea of the load I'd carried into this weekend—even before a man had died right in front of me. Sure, I could've told him about Savilla or the worries about my career plans, but I'd been waiting to talk in person this weekend. Then Brett had died and Charlie had been so... so infuriatingly distant. It was almost enough to make me explode.

"You want me to talk?" I started, my voice already a pitch higher. "Fine. In the next forty-eight hours I need to decide whether I'll start a practice here in Aubergine or take a fellowship in San Diego, a decision that will impact the next four years at a minimum. On top of that I found out that I've inherited half of a freaking palace that may be a financial money pit if my new half-sister, Savilla Finch, is to be believed."

He startled. "Your half-sister?"

"Mr. Finch is—was—my father," I said, almost like a confession.

"Okay. Wow. That's a lot." He stared at the steering wheel as if trying to sort through the list of things I'd just thrown at him. "And San Diego?"

"It's a program my professor wants me to consider." I clenched my jaw and released it, trying to let go of tension that wouldn't abate. "Then on my first night back home, one of my former classmates, who also happened to be a total asshat, was murdered." I took a deep breath, deciding to try trusting him with everything. "Did you know that Brett blackmailed Mr.

Finch so he could inherit one of the most valuable diamonds in the world?"

"I had no idea," Charlie said evenly. He studied me, waiting for me to get all my words out.

"Yeah, he has some awful video of Savilla, and he threatened to leak it unless Mr. Finch gave him what he wanted. Which is actually really similar to what he did to Lacy..." I trailed off, running out of steam as I thought about the few remaining hours until her business and her life might be turned upside down by Brett's email from the dead.

"Honestly, I'm having trouble keeping up." Charlie put a gentle hand to my face. "Could you, maybe, start at the beginning? I promise I'll listen."

At his touch, something in me loosened, and my eyes met his. He was asking me to trust him with what I knew, to lay it all out on the table. So I did.

Over the next few minutes, I caught him up on everything I knew, which was a kind of trust fall for me.

He listened without jotting down notes, keeping his gaze fixed on mine the entire time.

"And the two people on the case are a gorgeous deputy and my boyfriend who—" I stopped mid-sentence, realizing that I'd used a word for Charlie that I'd never used before. I tried to recover. "And now I have to decide what to do with you," I finished, putting my elbow on the window.

Out the window, the deputy was staring at our car, likely trying to see why it had stalled.

Charlie's lips turned up on the right side and he narrowed his eyes. "What do you mean that you have to decide what to do with me?" Despite all of the information I'd just spewed, his expression was actually amused.

"I don't know," I breathed out. "Like, what if we break up? Or what if we aren't even a... an item."

"An item?" He cocked his head. "Is this the 1950s?"

I frowned at him. "I mean, despite the fact that I just humiliatingly called you my boyfriend, we haven't actually defined anything."

Charlie tapped a hand against the steering wheel. "I thought we were too old and wise to need to put a label on things, but, sure, I can do that if you want."

A label? If I want? Who didn't want to define a relationship at some point? Although, I guess I hadn't been in a hurry until this weekend had threatened to topple us.

"I do want," I said simply, straightening my shoulders as if about to enter an official meeting.

He lifted a shoulder. "Okay."

This sounded too easy, and it made me suspicious, especially after how hard life had been for the last two years. But before I had time to think about it for long, he wrapped his palm around my fingers until the back of my hand was smothered by his own.

"I'm only interested in dating *you*. In fact, I've only been dating you for the past four months because I thought we were exclusive," Charlie said. "I guess I'm old-fashioned like that, but since you'd like to be officially asked, Dakota Green, would you go steady with me?"

Despite my swirling mind and the fact that him asking this question didn't actually fix any of my real problems, I let out a soft laugh for the first time. "Do I get your class ring?"

"You can have anything you want from me," he said, his voice husky with intent. Almost like he loved me.

I shook off the intensity of his stare. Calling him my boyfriend was enough for now.

I nodded toward the deputy, who appeared to have given up on figuring out what was happening inside the car and was opening the front door to go back inside. "What about her?"

"Jill?"

"The very one," I said. "And please don't tell me that you have no idea she's interested in you."

He made an expression that said he'd been avoiding thinking about that very thing. "Lately, I've been wondering, but we've worked together for so long that I didn't want to assume—and, to be clear, I don't feel the same way about her." He stole a glance at me to make sure I believed him. "Jill was a great partner and she's doing well as a second-in-command, but I swear, that's it for me."

I wanted to believe him.

He took a second to figure out what to say next. I was afraid that he was about to backtrack, to tell me that actually he wasn't sure about her, about me, about any of this. Instead, he surprised me with his next few words.

"She doesn't like dogs," he said, as if that should be explanation enough.

It was not.

So he continued. "Jill's parents take her on a two-week vacation to the Swiss Alps every winter to ski, and she doesn't like to read anything except *People* magazine. She won't try new foods —it's always buttered pasta and grilled chicken when she eats out—and she only listens to classical music. She became a police officer because she didn't like college and she said she wanted to find out what it's like to be a 'working person.' She's good at her job, and she's a great person... for someone else, who will fall madly in love with her someday." His look begged me to believe him. "As for me and you, I guess I think of you as my girlfriend even though we've never said that out loud. I can't do anything about what you decide to do next with your career, but as for me, I'm..." Here, a smile crept into his intense focus, and I knew he was about to say something cheesy. "I'm in it to win it."

I couldn't help but laugh out loud that time. After a moment, I lifted my hand so that our fingers were entwined.

He lifted my hand and kissed the back of it. "I'm open to

figuring out a way to make this work, Dakota Green, but you've got to figure out what makes you happy—not what other people think looks like success. Remember what you told me when I was trying so hard to get the good people of Aubergine to like me?"

I bit my lip, remembering all too well because it was the same thing Momma always said to me when I was on the precipice of making decisions.

"'Don't do things to impress the kind of people who don't give a fig about you.'"

Hearing my mother's words on Charlie's lips was like an anchor for my unmoored soul. I stared at the view out of the windshield, the blue haze over the mountains reminding me of their permanence in the middle of life's uncertainties.

"I don't like working with you," I said, as I kept my eyes on the peaks and ridges in the distance.

Charlie let out a breath. "I see we've come to the brutally honest part of the conversation."

"I'm not trying to be mean, but you're kind of..." *Jerky? Stubborn? No, I probably shouldn't go there.* "Except for a few minutes up there in your apartment... well, and last night... you've been kind of cold," I said. "It's, like, it's not even *you*."

"I've heard that before," he admitted. "I can flip the work switch on really easily, but then it's kind of hard for me to flip it back off."

I thought of our months of long-distance chats and realized something for the first time. "When you call me at night, you always wait at least an hour or two until your shift has ended. Is that why?"

"I guess so. It takes me time to decompress. This job is pretty stressful. Even when we don't have a murder on our hands, someone is upset about something: a parking ticket or a domestic dispute. It varies day to day, but I'm not good at going in and out of work mode." His eyes found mine. "I promise I'll try to be better. But, Dakota, you're good at this work. You found Mr. Finch's murderer."

It was true, and I'd enjoyed the problem-solving, especially the way it had let me use my medical knowledge.

"How about this? We can figure out the work part later, but for now..."—Charlie restarted the engine, putting the car back into gear—"you ready to finish this thing?"

I knew he meant the investigation, but the question resonated more deeply than that.

"Ready," I said, as he pulled around the circular drive and let me out of the car.

TWENTY-SEVEN

When I entered the vestibule, Savilla was speaking with Mina —or perhaps comforting her.

"Everything all right?" I asked, as I approached them.

"Lee tried to leave, and the police wouldn't let him. And then..." Mina wiped at her nose and tried to compose herself.

"He became violent, swung at one of the officers. They've put an ankle monitor on him and told him he absolutely cannot leave the estate," Savilla continued.

"Do they actually think he's a threat?" I asked, wondering if this was the reason that the deputy had been stalking our car. Charlie must've turned off his walkie-talkie, trusting her to handle things.

"I don't think so," Mina said, sniffling one last time. "He's just a belligerent jerk who doesn't know how to cooperate." She looked between the two of us. "I swear, though, he is harmless."

I wasn't sure that was the right word for what I'd seen of him with her in the gardens in the early hours, and hearing about his behavior now with an officer of the law wasn't helping his case.

"I get it," Mina said, sliding into a wingback chair. "He wants to go home and see his family. Our flight was supposed to leave tonight."

"How long does the sheriff want everyone to stay near Aubergine?"

"No idea." Mina looked up at me and shrugged. "Thankfully, I can go stay with Gram. I told Lee he was welcome too, but he wasn't hearing it." She let her head fall in her hands. "Nothing is... right."

I knew the sentiment, one I'd felt often when Momma had been in the later stages of her illness. Whether it was a long line at the pharmacy, traffic on the way to the hospital, the lack of a parking spot—it all felt too hard when already anticipating the coming loss staring me in the face every second of every day.

I touched her shoulder, and Savilla put a hand on her other side.

Mina attempted a smile. "At least Gram is getting out of the hospital. The car is bringing her here."

"To the estate?" I asked, hopeful. "That's good, right?"

"She does seem happy when she's here, always reminisces about the year she won. Even though she complained about how much had changed, every time I saw her on that judges' dais, I could tell she was in her element. She taught me so much." Mina stared out the window at the mountain peaks. "Aubergine, this house – it's comforting to her."

I could tell that Mina was seeing the past, present, and future colliding. The shadow of imminent loss hung over her.

"What did you learn from her?" I asked, gently nudging her to recall better memories.

Mina kept her gaze steady. "I learned how to really see people, for better or worse." Her voice took on a different timbre, almost as if she was slipping into a different persona, her voice sounding more like Miss 1962's raspy one. It sounded so familiar, and at first I figured it was merely because I'd gotten to know her grandmother this past summer. But no, that wasn't it —or it wasn't the only reason.

I spoke slowly as my thoughts coalesced. "Mina?"

She shifted toward me.

"You said that you worked on *Small Town, Big Romance*, right?"

"Yeah."

"What exactly did you do?"

"I told you. I was a gopher before I was pulled into work off-screen."

"And off-screen, you were...?" I waited for her to finish the statement.

"The interviewer," Mina answered, her eyes narrowing as if she wasn't sure where I was going with these questions.

I closed my eyes. That's why I'd recognized Mina's voice. It wasn't just that she sounded so like the grandmother she resembled. I knew her voice from the clips of the show. Mina had been there all along.

"Why are you asking?" Mina wondered, hesitant at my inquisitiveness—and perhaps a bit defensive. "You don't think that I have anything to do with this weekend, do you? Because I wasn't hiding anything."

"No, no, it's not that," I tried to reassure her. "I'm just trying to find all the links. This helps."

Mina nodded, accepting my explanation and then seemed to remember something. "Lee didn't like that they'd pulled me into the show that way, said it distracted me from 'being behind the camera.'" She put the last few words in air quotes and lowered her voice to better match his. "He thought that Brett had something to do with me getting on the show."

I noticed the purple rings lining her eyes. She was exhausted.

Mina heaved out a deep breath before standing and facing

me, and I was reminded that the concerns about Brett, though important, weren't the first thing on her mind. She was thinking about her grandmother too.

She sniffled as she spoke. "It's gonna be hard, isn't it?"

I knew exactly what she meant, and there was nothing I could tell her to make it less painful.

Savilla leaned her head against my shoulder, reminding me that she was there with us. "I told Mina about my father. And about your mother, about losing her."

I didn't mind that she'd shared this experience, not really. But I still wasn't sure what to say about the coming days. It would be hard beyond her wildest imaginings, and then it would slowly start to seal over, like a fine layer of balm, the balm of time. The wound would always be there, at least in the form of a scar, but that's how I wanted it. I didn't want to forget.

Mina hesitated a second longer before reaching out to pull both me and Savilla into a hug, the three of us bonded by loss. Then, without another word, she walked away.

Savilla and I watched her go, and then I tried to collect myself and bring some semblance of normalcy back to the moment. Regardless of our personal feelings, we also had a job to do.

"I think we should check out your dad's office," I decided. "Maybe he had information about the estate, the Rose Diamond, the password." I was forming a plan of action as I spoke, but it felt right. I recalled the layout of the dollhouse. "It's on the fourth floor, right?"

"Good memory," Savilla said. "Let me grab my keys from behind the front desk."

As she went to find them, my mind created a new pathway as to how we might solve this case. If we could find any clues about the password or if we could figure out how the Rose Diamond had disappeared before making its way into Brett's throat one day ago, then perhaps we could find the murderer.

I checked my watch, counting the hours until midnight when the emails would be released. About five to go. The dominoes were ready to fall, and I felt in my gut that it started with the most treasured Finch jewel.

"All right. You ready to visit the Diamond Mine?" Savilla asked, coming back with her key ring.

I scrunched my nose. "Is that what he called his office?"

Savilla smiled. "I named it that when I was a kid because it sounded more interesting than his boring old office. I would make treasure maps and force Nanny Kate to go on adventures all around the grounds. I had new names for every room."

Nostalgia passed over her face, which reminded me of the fact that whether or not she showed it, she'd lost so much in such a short time.

Savilla possessively tucked an arm in mine and led the way, taking us to the west wing of the estate with its vining wallpaper and yellow lighting reminiscent of the Gilded Age.

We didn't pass a single person as we went, and Savilla must've noticed me looking around because she said, "The deputy told me that she and Charlie let almost everyone head home after lunch, just told them to not venture too far from town until the case was solved. Of course, the main suspects have to stay."

"They must think the killer is in Brett's inner circle," I mused. "So, who's still here?"

"Me, you, Presley, Joe, Mina, Lee, Lacy, and... her boyfriend, what's-his-name."

"Anton," I reminded her.

"Right. Jemma is sticking around because she's in between shows, and Will and Valerie Hurt stayed because she wants to see the drama." Savilla lifted one brow. "So, there are ten people, not counting me."

Joe and Presley were still firmly situated at the top of my

list, and I hoped against hope that Lacy wasn't at the top of anyone else's.

"How is our sheriff?" Savilla asked, studying me. "Your face tells me you talked about more than Brett's death."

I didn't say anything, so she prodded me, reminding me that her newly discovered role as my sister was making her feel more connected and perhaps more entitled to intrude on my personal life. I didn't mind it as much as I thought I would.

"Did he take you in his arms and beg you to marry him as soon as this case is closed?" Savilla clenched a hand over her heart. "Ooo... did you tell him that you're an heiress?"

"Am I an heiress if there's not an inheritance?"

"Great question. Worse comes to worst, we sell the place and *Thelma & Louise* our way to freedom," Savilla teased as we reached the fourth floor.

I squinted. It wasn't a malapropism, but it was a misguided goal. "Have you ever actually watched that movie?"

"Sure, years ago with Nanny Kate, but I fell asleep before it was over. Why?"

"No reason." I couldn't help but chuckle.

Savilla led me down a long corridor past her former nursery, where my aunt had been staying when she'd been accused of murder four months ago. At the last room on the right, Savilla inserted a key into the lock and put her fingerprint against an electronic reader that had been installed on the door, but she didn't need to do either. It swung open on its hinges, opening even before the scanner lit up.

Someone had already been here.

"What the...?" Savilla mumbled, as she stepped inside.

Other than the scanner and the door having somehow been broken, there were no other indications that anyone had trespassed. A large cherry wood desk and an even larger worksta-tion were spotless, no mess or overturned drawers. If someone had entered Mr. Finch's former office, they'd left without seeming to bother anything in there.

"Maybe the police were in here?"

"I doubt it," Savilla said. "Why would they be? And I can't imagine who else might've known to look here."

Despite its spaciousness, the room was cozy. The wallpaper only came to the wainscotting midway up the wall, and it was gray, almost silver, with tiny stalks of lavender interspersed across it. In addition to the desk and work station, there was a grated fireplace, one wide single window that looked onto the front lawn, and a set of chairs facing one another.

"This used to be the quarters for the head lady's maid," Savilla said, studying her father's workstation without touching anything on it. An assortment of empty brooches, bracelets, earrings, and even a couple of crowns, lined the otherwise empty table. It looked as if he'd been preparing to set stones into various pieces. "He converted it when I was four or five, around the time Nanny Kate came to live here with us. I think it was the only place he could find peace and quiet with her and Step-Mommy roaming the halls. But then, a few years ago, after I graduated, he and StepMommy started living in New York most of the time, so we were only here once or twice a year. Anytime we came back to visit, though, he always spent time in his office. I think it gave him something to do, especially when he started losing so much money." Savilla inhaled deeply as she surveyed the room. "He must've been in such distress, knowing things were getting bad."

"And Glenda and Katie had no idea?"

"I don't think so. I didn't know either until he said I should take out a life insurance policy on him. He always said things were fine, just fine."

"That must've also been when he started selling off gemstones," I added, as I spotted a large rectangular leather volume with *Accounts* engraved on the front. I picked it up and turned through the pages to find rows of numbers dating back to the fall of 2023. It was a much more in-depth version of the accounting that I'd found in a pocket-sized ledger in his apartment this past summer.

"The financial guy told me that Daddy was a bit paranoid, kept all of his accounts by hand, said he didn't trust anything online," Savilla told me as she ran a finger down a page of numbers. "He obviously wasn't fully in his right mind, he couldn't have been."

I sat down and tracked the depleting numbers while Savilla followed my hand. There were eight accounts across three different banks, labeled by acronyms that I could guess—based on the couple of finance classes I'd taken in college—meant things like checking, savings, money market, index fund, and bonds.

The accounts were much too small for an estate of this size, and the withdrawal rate from them had been massive. With a quick estimation, it appeared that Savilla—and I—had less than a hundred grand in all the accounts combined. This was still a sizable amount for someone who'd been raised by a mother who was a small-town nurse and an aunt who designed fashion for a living, but even I knew it wasn't enough to sustain a place like The Rose long term. As soon as one of the dozen or so industrial-sized boilers, heaters, or air conditioning units failed, The Rose would be sunk.

Savilla's eyes began to well, though I wasn't sure if it was because she missed her father or because she had no idea what she would do next with a property this size—and only enough money to keep it going for another few months without money coming in to maintain it. These were certainly rich-people problems, but it was still a decision Savilla had to make on her own, unless I agreed to somehow help her.

I hesitated only a moment before putting an arm around her, and Savilla rested her head against me. I pictured Momma's face buried in Aunt DeeDee's shoulder when we'd gotten the news that the treatment was no longer working. She hadn't wanted me to take the burden; though back then, I'd resented what I'd viewed as Momma pulling away from me. In my brief time of having an actual sister, I thought I might better understand now.

While I hadn't been raised in the same household as Savilla, I'd come of age in the same community at the same time as her. We'd had very different socioeconomic upbringings, but we'd both had two strong women—who had been sisters in fact—directing our lives and soothing our heartaches.

I squeezed Savilla tighter, and after a few moments, she lifted her head, wiped her eyes, and looked at me with gratitude.

"I just remembered... The last time I was up here, Daddy actually talked about Brett while he was removing stones from that piece there..." Savilla gestured to a necklace with one very large center setting and a row of smaller prongs running up both sides of the gold, all the way to the clasp. It was like a version of the Hope Diamond necklace that I remembered seeing on display in Washington, D.C., when our class had taken an overnight field trip there in seventh grade.

Other kids hadn't been interested in that part of the Museum of Natural History, and to be fair, I'd liked the exhibit of the stuffed prehistoric animals more. Still, I'd appreciated the low lighting and the soothing classical music of the gem exhibit amid the overstimulating chatter of my peers. I recalled pressing my face to the glass, marveling at the sparkling blue center and the stories the curator told of the many people who'd owned it and come to unfortunate ends.

"Are you thinking of the time we saw the Hope Diamond?" Savilla asked, almost as if she could read my mind. "You and I were the only two interested in it."

"Were we?" I tried to recall Savilla's middle school face

pressed to the other side of the glass box as we stood in the rounded corridor in the museum, a domed ceiling rising above us. She'd been in my life for all of it, and for that, I was grateful, especially now that I knew of our actual connection.

Savilla was family, and she was also invested in this case for more than one reason: It was her father who'd been killed four months ago and her home where Brett had died.

I could take a chance and fully include her in the investigation, or I could keep trying to manage pieces of it on my own. I glanced at her again, and I practically heard Momma's voice: *Sometimes you gotta take a chance and trust people.*

I had no time to make a pro/con list, so I studied Savilla's eyes, which seemed guileless enough.

"Listen." I held her arm. "What I'm about to tell you is privileged information. It could help us figure out who killed Brett, but you have to keep it to yourself, understand?"

Savilla nodded and crossed her heart. "Hope to die," she said, before catching her word choice. "You know what I mean."

After allowing myself one more second's hesitation, I told her everything: from the items I'd found in Joe's locker, to the video of Brett's death, to him blackmailing Lacy, to the coroner's report.

Savilla's face was a study in concentration as she fingered one of the necklace settings. "The Rose Diamond killed Brett Brinkley?"

I nodded. "Someone stole the diamond—or at least found where it was located—and dropped it in his drink, knowing that Brett was the kind of guy to down his glass of whiskey on the rocks in a single gulp."

"Okay," Savilla said, thinking out loud. "The killer knew Brett well, and they knew our house well too. They'd mostly likely been to the estate, likely at the 2023 pageant, when the stone went missing."

I ran through the list of suspects still at the house. Who had been here during the pageant two years ago? My mind stumbled over the obvious—Savilla, Lacy, Aunt DeeDee—but I refused to believe any of them had taken the diamond. That left Brett himself.

Or someone hiding in plain sight. Someone who knew The Rose's secrets better than any of us realized.

Someone who might be watching me piece it all together right now.

TWENTY-EIGHT

Savilla's financial planner called, and since it had to do with the future of the estate, she took it. I wanted to check in with Lacy and see if she'd made any progress on the email password front, so we decided to split up for a bit.

Savilla headed downstairs and toward her room, and I started down the hall in the opposite direction toward the elevator, passing the guest rooms. I paused in front of one because I recognized two familiar voices coming from inside.

Aunt DeeDee and Joe.

I stopped in my tracks, knowing that Aunt DeeDee would not want me listening to her through a closed door. She would tell me that if I had questions, then I should come right out and ask them. Still, what if Joe said something to her that he wouldn't say to anyone else, especially Charlie or his officers? If my sneaking around helped the case, the allowance would have to be made.

I decided to stay, and pressed my ear to the door just like I'd done outside of the Media Room when I'd heard Lacy and Anton's conversation last night.

Joe's voice was muffled, as if he'd been crying. "I may have wanted him dead, but I had nothing to do with his death."

The words froze me in place.

"I know, dear," Aunt DeeDee responded, her tone sympathetic. I could almost see the gentle expression that she always gave me when I was in distress. "From my vantage point, I can see a list of folks who may have wanted to put Brett Brinkley in his place a time or two."

"But the sheriff isn't questioning them about dropping a diamond in his drink."

Okay, word had gotten out about how Brett had died.

"That doesn't mean a thing," Aunt DeeDee crooned empathetically. "Remember that four months ago the sheriff had me behind bars at the local jail even though he knew I was innocent. I just had to be patient until he had enough evidence to clear me."

I thought that was a pretty generous interpretation of Charlie's actions, but I also knew she wasn't wrong. The sheriff was nothing if not meticulous in his investigations, so if he'd let the information about the diamond slip, then he had a reason for not holding those cards close to his chest. Besides, there wasn't any particular reason to keep people from knowing Brett's cause of death, and perhaps it would put the killer on alert that Charlie was hot on their tail. Maybe it would even pressure them into coming forward with a confession.

"What I can't figure out is how the diamond would get inside his drink. I made it. I used the ice from the bucket, and I would've noticed just by the weight of the tongs if I was accidentally slipping something heavier into a glass."

I closed my eyes, trying to recall both my memory of the order of events as well as the video I'd watched multiple times. Frustratingly, I kept getting stuck on one central image: that of Lacy's hand hovering over his drink as she whispered in Brett's ear. But no, that was a mere distraction. It had to be.

"Was anyone else behind the bar with you?" Aunt DeeDee asked.

"No, and I handed the glass directly to…"

"To Brett?" Aunt DeeDee asked, after a few seconds of silence.

I knew that was wrong. I could picture exactly who he'd handed it to.

"No, no, that's what I thought, but maybe it was to…" He took a long pause. "I handed the glass to Presley, and she took it over to Brett at the edge of the dance floor." Joe finally breathed out.

I tried to remember exactly where Presley had been in Brett's death tableau. She'd handed the drink to Brett and then her figure had disappeared off-screen for a moment. Jenna's microphone had fed back, and I thought I'd caught a glimpse of Presley heading toward the sound board. Had she been going for the back door of the ballroom instead? Had Presley been deciding whether or not to flee the scene of her crime?

But no, that didn't make sense, right? Because as soon as I was on the ground, starting CPR, Presley was next to me. But what had she been doing? Crying, yes, but what else? I couldn't remember, and she'd been out of the view of the camera's angle. I knew this, though: Presley had not been helping me try to save Brett. However she'd appeared or acted, she'd been the closest one to me, but I hadn't even asked her to call 911.

Presley. My mind circled the name. She and Brett weren't engaged, but surely he'd been planning to propose, especially after Mr. Finch died and he knew he would inherit the Rose Diamond. If nothing else, he would want to bask in the publicity the engagement would bring both of them.

My mind began to merge clips of the past twenty-four hours together as it also stretched to include the longer history of Brett and the women he'd known—and exploited. Lacy and Savilla had both, directly or not, been victims of his blackmailing tactics, his attempt to exploit their intimacy with him. Lacy had been emotionally and physically close to him, but Savilla's relationship with him had been a brief, mostly physical fling. Still, Brett had kept tangible pieces of their moments together—in photographs and on camera—and later used these to threaten both women.

Brett seemed to have a pattern, but certainly it hadn't extended to another one of his victims, had it?

Presley's rise to fame following *Small Town, Big Romance* had come right after she and Brett had won the show, but it just so happened that within a month of winning, Presley had supposedly also released a sex tape of her and Brett together. She'd then used the momentum to start her own empire, which included fast-fashion for women with curves, and a beauty line specifically marketed to the middle-class woman.

Paris Hilton and Kim Kardashian were part of her day-to-day world, and though I much preferred the *American Veterinary Journal* to *US Weekly*, even I'd heard infamous stories of Presley: How she'd rented an island and invited Beyoncé to perform for the weekend, how she'd appeared before Congress to argue for women's rights, how she'd met the pope and told him that birth control should be provided for free to women across the globe. Presley was not only gorgeous; she was strategic and smart.

In the media, the assumption had always been that Presley was the one to leak the video online, particularly since afterward she hadn't filed a lawsuit or chided anyone publicly for the indiscretion. Instead, she had figuratively leaned into the moment, going on late-night shows where she led the hosts in yoga poses as she joked about her sexual flexibility. I'd barely watched all of this, of course, but it had been so commonplace to see her on magazine covers next to my former classmate that I'd noticed.

I had no problem with a woman choosing to do whatever

she wanted with her body, but after discovering Brett's way of using women, I suddenly wondered if Presley might have been one of Brett's unwitting victims. Perhaps he'd been the one to release the video, and instead of hiding, Presley had found a way to use it to her advantage? If that was true, it would certainly have sown seeds of animosity in her relationship with Brett early on.

"It couldn't have been her," Joe said quickly, even though Aunt DeeDee wasn't accusing Presley of anything. "I know her. We've become... friends. She didn't do it."

This seemed as good a time as any to make an entrance. I knocked, and after a few seconds of silence, Aunt DeeDee came to the door, her eyes lighting as I entered the room.

"I couldn't help but overhear you talking about Presley," I said, trying not to indicate how long I'd actually been listening outside the door.

Aunt DeeDee stood between Joe and me, looking back and forth a couple of times before her eyes landed on Joe. "You should tell her," Aunt DeeDee prodded.

I raised an eyebrow as I studied this man in the same black slacks and white shirt he'd worn last night, but now they were crumpled and stained.

Joe hesitated before speaking. "I know you took the CD I made of Brett on the show," he said, surprising me. It was embarrassing to be caught, yes, but more than that, I wasn't sure that my filching of a CD warranted the accusatory tone. "I mentioned it going missing to DeeDee, and she told me that you think I had something to do with Brett's death."

I glanced at my aunt, frowning. She could read me, knew that I didn't appreciate her sharing anything with Joe, much less that I'd borrowed something that belonged to him. But her lifted chin said it all—she trusted people, and maybe I should learn to do the same.

"I know it looks like I'm obsessed with Brett," Joe said. "But the CD was something I was hoping to surprise him with this weekend, though I'm not proud of it."

"Why wouldn't you be proud of surprising Brett?" I asked.

Joe's eyes darted to Aunt DeeDee, and she signaled for him to continue.

"I was planning to do a little viewing party of Presley and Brett's best moments on the show, and then we were going to tell him in front of everyone, including his cameras, that Presley and I..." He cleared his throat. "That the two of us are in love."

The news wasn't exactly shocking, but I realized that the plan smacked of what Brett had been planning to do to Presley by being caught on camera with another woman—Lacy—in order to boost the drama in his show. Except in this version, Brett would've been the lovelorn boyfriend cast aside so Presley could be with a man less rich, less famous, less everything. A huge embarrassment, and one that might've doomed his show before it had even aired.

I wondered suddenly if Brett had recently gotten wind of Presley and Joe's plan and decided to take matters into his own hands by embarrassing her before she could embarrass him.

"I was going to get even with him for everything he did to me in our first semester of college, planting steroids in my locker, getting me kicked out." Joe stood behind the one chair in the room, his knuckles white as he gripped the back of it. "Brett changed the course of my life, totally for the worse, but then Presley and I happened to meet when *Big Romance* came to The Rose for the home visit. Brett was talking strategy that morning with Mr. Finch, so Presley stopped by the Morning Brew where I was dropping off a batch of coffee I'd roasted. It was like love at first sight, but Presley... she was afraid to leave him."

She was afraid for two entire years? I wasn't an expert on relationships, but to me, that sounded more like Presley leading Joe on rather than actual fear.

"Why would she be afraid?" I didn't ask the real question, which in my mind was, *How could Brett have anything worse on her than a sex tape?*

"Brett was manipulative, threatening, vindictive. Presley thought that if she left him, then she would lose her public persona, her business, and..." He hesitated as if trying to believe the words coming out of his mouth, "... opportunities."

"Opportunities?" I asked, still suspicious of this reasoning. I caught Aunt DeeDee's eye and saw the skepticism on her face as well. Presley Lombardi may have been a victim but she was also very much playing two lovers against one another.

"Advertising deals, future reality TV gigs, product partnerships," Joe answered, losing momentum as he spoke. He hung his head as he realized how he sounded – like a classic case of a cuckold. All three of us could see it.

"And you're still sure that Presley didn't have anything to do with Brett's death?" I asked, trying to tread gently so as to not overwhelm him with the realization that seemed to be settling across his brow. Surely, we could all see that Presley had more than one motive—feeling threatened by her own boyfriend, the potential publicity that could come from a TMZ-worthy announcement of her tragic loss, and perhaps even secretly wanting to be with Joe. For the cherry on top, Joe had just confirmed that Presley had had opportunity to slip the diamond in his drink by taking Brett's glass to him.

The question remained, though, of how the diamond might have ended up in Presley's possession.

Joe shook his head, but he didn't defend Presley this time. Instead, he let his eyes fall to the floor for several beats.

I knew well the struggle of whether or not to trust your own perception in a relationship, so I felt for him. Fortunately for me, I never expected Charlie to be on the wrong side of a murder investigation.

Joe looked straight at me. "Presley is a very spiritual

person," he said, seemingly apropos of nothing. "That's why I really don't think... oh God, have I gotten this all wrong?"

I glanced from Joe to Aunt DeeDee as I tried to parse out his meaning: Presley was a good person, a spiritual person, so surely she couldn't also be a killer.

"Listen, this is the real reason that I don't think Presley killed him." Joe stopped, seeming to carefully consider his next words. "She said she... she wants to contact Brett."

"Contact him?" I repeated.

Next to me, Aunt DeeDee went rigid. She was a fairly liturgical kind of Baptist, but she believed enough in the woo-woo supernatural that she'd forbidden me from playing with Ouija boards at sleepovers. She wouldn't even let me go to the palm reading booth at the county fair when I was thirteen. Contacting a dead man was certainly not on Aunt DeeDee's bucket list.

Joe swallowed hard. "Presley told me that she wants to do a séance. Tonight. She wants to ask Brett who killed him."

I laughed out loud before I could stop myself, but then I realized that he was dead serious.

TWENTY-NINE

"You'll obviously need to conduct it or lead it—or whatever you call running a séance," Aunt DeeDee said matter-of-factly, sounding less like my aunt than I'd ever heard her.

"This from the woman who made me burn a pack of tarot cards someone gave me in sixth grade?"

Aunt DeeDee gave me a look that said this ask was completely different. "You know this isn't the same."

Do I though?

"It's exactly because you know it's a load of hogwash that you have to do it," she explained. "Maybe Presley—or whoever the murderer is—will reveal themselves."

I blinked at my aunt, the woman who hadn't wanted me to trick or treat when I was five years old because Halloween was "the devil's holiday." She and Momma had gotten in a disagreement that was less a fight and more a bemused discussion before they'd compromised. Aunt DeeDee would take me to the church's fall festival, where sweet old ladies handed out lollipops taped to a book of Psalms, and then I would trick or treat with Lacy around town. Momma had indulged Aunt DeeDee, figuring that any child would like double candy.

"You do realize that I have no idea how to conduct a séance," I said.

Aunt DeeDee waved away that excuse. "Fiddlesticks. You sit in a circle, light some candles, and wave your hands around while mumbling to summon the dead. I would do it, but no one would believe me." Her eyes lit with an idea. "You can use the Vampire Room."

"Oh, Lord," I breathed, wondering if it was some kind of twisted fate that I'd discussed this very room with Savilla last night in front of her to-scale dollhouse.

"Language, dear," said my aunt.

The irony was almost too rich.

"How do you know about the Vampire Room?"

"There's very little I don't know about this pageant, darlin'."

"It's not the worst idea," Joe said, speaking up for the first time. "Not that I think Presley had anything to do with Brett's death, but if someone else did, then maybe they'll out themselves."

The two of them were right. It struck me once again that Aunt DeeDee believed in Joe, that she basically lived her life trusting people until they proved she shouldn't.

Before I could respond, my phone rang, startling me more than it should have. It was Lacy.

"Hello?" I answered.

"Where are you?" Lacy's voice was tear-filled.

I didn't know how to answer. If I told her I was in Joe's room discussing a possible séance with my aunt, there would be too many questions. "On the fourth floor," I said instead. "Why? What's wrong?"

"Can you meet me in the back garden?"

"Sure."

"Near the rose hedge maze."

"Be right there." I hung up. "I've got to go check on Lacy. I guess, spread the word about the... the séance?" I could hardly believe I was saying those words.

"We'll do it in a couple of hours," Aunt DeeDee decided. "When the moon is high in the sky. That sounds like a thing people would do."

I screwed up my mouth as I studied this woman who seemed nothing like my aunt. Still, this might give me enough time to help Lacy. That email was supposed to go out to her clients at midnight, but perhaps if we got Presley—or whomever —to confess, they would suddenly remember useful information to help us break into Brett's account.

Between searching for an email password, where the diamond might have been hidden, and a murderer, my night was packed.

Aunt DeeDee gave me a knowing look. "You can figure this out, Dakota. You can."

I was grateful for her confidence because in that moment, knowing that both my friend and half-sister needed me as much as the investigation did, I certainly felt less than.

When I reached the back garden, the stars were blaring through the indigo haze of the Blue Ridge Mountains.

Anton was pacing in front of the maze, staring at his phone and fuming. As I drew nearer, I spotted Lacy on the bench, leaning forward, her eyes down. She looked up as she heard me approach.

"What happened?" I asked, glancing between the two of them.

He stopped and held up the screen of his phone so I could see words that were too tiny to read from that distance. "Brett Brinkley's email," he said, through clenched teeth. His face was a deep red and he was practically spitting.

"He set it up to send early to Anton, along with a threat," Lacy said, trying not to cry.

"If this man weren't already dead, I would kill him myself."
There was venom in Anton's words.

I read the screen as Lacy came to my side.

Anton,

*Please enjoy the photos Lacy shared with me. To me, she's like a
rare jewel, an irreplaceable gem, though not the one that got
away. Encourage her to behave before these are shared with her
clients. I know TMZ would love to get their hands on these.
Sincerely,*

BB

TMZ, huh? That very same supposedly-news outlet had
likely already spread the word of his death. If Brett had actually
auto-timed the images to go to them tonight at midnight, they'd
be very confused—and likely very excited. An anonymous
missive was always fascinating, especially if it carried the hint of
sex and murder. These images would be not only visible to
Lacy's clients. They would be everywhere by tomorrow morning, and Lacy's name would become a household term for the
kind of woman who didn't meet society's puritanical expectations.

I cringed as I once again read Brett's formal-sounding words
filled with such malicious meaning and scrolled down to see
three attachments that I didn't open.

"Two are photos." Lacy sniffed. "The third one is a one-
minute video of us in the act. I had no idea he had... something
like that."

Brett had done it again, recording an intimate moment for
future use. Bile rose in the back of my throat.

I didn't need to look at the attachments to know how
harmful they were. Lacy's emotions blanketed her face.

"You know I'm not angry with you," Anton said, moving to the other side of Lacy and pulling her into his arms. "I'm furious with him, with his sick, twisted..." He clenched his hands like he'd gotten Brett's neck in his grip and was ready to squeeze. He looked at me as if I had some kind of answer. "Brett dated Lacy a decade ago and he was still obsessed with her?"

"I don't think he was obsessed with me," Lacy said, staring at the ground. "He just wanted views for his show, and he thought I was an easy target."

"Why couldn't he have hired an actress if he was so intent on having the content for his show?" Anton asked. "Or found some other girl who wanted fifteen minutes of fame?"

My stomach turned over. I thought I might know. Brett was a man with power, a man who wanted to see if he could actually get away with threatening a vulnerable person. He likely got some sort of jolt of machismo out of wielding his control, but ultimately, he'd arranged all of this—as well as the blackmailing of Mr. Finch and perhaps at one time even his own girlfriend— because he could.

"It's after eight," Lacy said, checking her phone. "I have less than four hours until these photos go to my clients, to *TMZ*. Until they're everywhere."

Anton locked eyes with Lacy, and in that moment I could see how much he loved, even adored, her.

"Okay," I said. "We have how many more tries with the password?"

"Two, maybe one?" Lacy answered. "I tried it twice last night, and I'm not sure if the count resets after a certain amount of time."

I read the message to Anton one more time, pointing to the middle phrase: *though not the one that got away.*

"This is just like in the password hint," I suggested. "We still need to find the name of this person."

"Does it matter at this point?" Anton asked. "This email

seems less like a clue with some hidden message and more like it was intended to threaten Lacy and make me want to kill him."

Before I could respond, my phone dinged with messages from Savilla.

> Talked to financial guy. He had these images
> from when Daddy got the diamond appraised a
> few years ago when he was going to sell it.

My phone dinged again, and an image came through, this one a close-up of the edge of the Rose Diamond, a series of tiny numbers, reading 1434.7.

"What are those?" I mumbled. "A serial number?"

Anton began to pace again, still fuming, while Lacy peered over my shoulder. "No. It's a code,' she clarified. 'It means, *I love you more. Forever.*"

"How do you know that?"

"The numbers correspond to the number of letters in the words," Lacy answered. "It's something Brett used to do. Write me little notes with codes."

"Is this a thing?" I asked.

Anton, who was listening, seemed as baffled as me.

"Yeah, Katy Perry released an album called 143 last year." Lacy looked at the two of us as if we were aliens from another planet. "And it's a line in Brett's song, in the bridge at the end." She started humming and then sang the words, "I love you more. Forever."

I wasn't convinced, but Lacy certainly was. "It has to be a code from him," she insisted.

One last message from Savilla confirmed Lacy's theory.

> I asked finance guy to see records. The
> numbers were added to the stone in 2022 when
> it was appraised—and before it disappeared.

Which meant Brett must've requested the numbers be

added around the time he blackmailed Mr. Finch with the video of Savilla, a kind of extra guarantee that Mr. Finch was serious about leaving him the stone.

I considered Brett's message as well as this new intel, that maybe wasn't so new. "In the Music Room, what did you say the password hint on Brett's email was?"

Lacy had memorized it by now. "It said, 'Diamond numbers, hashtag, lowercase, name of the one that got away.'"

"What did you try?"

"I put in 4#lacy, because he gave me a ring with four tiny diamonds when we were dating." Realization dawned on Lacy's face. "But maybe this is the number he was talking about."

"Since you're not the one who got away, that part is wrong too."

We were one step closer to the answer, one step closer to rebalancing the scales of justice.

"I think everything may be connected. Give me a couple more hours, and we'll figure this out. I promise." I looked into her eyes, willing her to trust me, willing myself to be right.

Lacy started to tear up as she kept my gaze. "And if we run out of time?"

"Then I'll make a video of myself riding bareback in the nude and send them to all of your clients to distract them from two silly pictures and a video from before your brain was finished cooking. Deal?"

Lacy didn't quite laugh but she did give me the edge of a smile. I would take it.

THIRTY

Lacy sent Anton to call his friend who knew someone who knew someone who was a hacker, which was a long shot but worth trying. Then, she joined me in the Finches' family room, where Aunt DeeDee said we could scavenge for supplies for our fake séance. In a little over an hour we would meet Savilla on the main floor before venturing into the bowels of the estate to the Vampire Room.

Like most families, even the Finches had a bin filled with soft blankets and a closet full of games they may have never played.

"What does someone even take to a séance?" I asked as Lacy, Aunt DeeDee, and I started looking through cupboards.

Aunt DeeDee pulled out her phone and entered my question into a new AI chat she'd downloaded a couple of months ago. She'd named it Alistair, and often referred to the software as if it was less of a search engine and more of a smart boyfriend.

She read from the screen. "Alistair says we need low lighting..."

I spotted a scented candle and a giant decorative one and

put them in a box. From the other side of the room Lacy grabbed several votives.

"Next is... incense and/or herbs."

"Any ideas?" I asked.

"I'll get some oregano and basil from the kitchen."

"I don't think that's what Alistair means," Lacy said, sounding uncertain.

"It's fine." Aunt DeeDee was unbothered. "We also need an item that belonged to the person we want to contact."

"We'll see if Presley can contribute that," I said.

"Oh my." Aunt DeeDee continued to read Alistair's list. "This says we should have a Ouija board or tarot cards." She looked at both of us. "The Finches wouldn't have anything like that, would they?"

I glanced at the neat rows of games and spotted playing cards. "What about UNO?"

Lacy lifted an eyebrow as I tossed them in the box.

It took another half hour to find everything else on the list and then some. Instead of crystals, we decided to take a moment at the beginning of the ordeal to remind everyone that The Rose was—or used to be—full of sparkly rocks. For an altar, we grabbed the squatty potty that Aunt DeeDee remembered was in her bathroom.

"Here's a shawl," Aunt DeeDee said, placing her cozy fleece wraparound on top of the blankets we'd also added to the box. "It wasn't on the list, but I've always imagined that someone leading a séance must be wearing a shawl."

That sounded accurate for our ragtag attempt at a quasi-spiritual experience.

Lacy patted the stuffed box. "I think we've done well for throwing it together so fast."

"And Savilla is inviting Presley, Joe, Valerie and Will Hurt, and the film crew, so we should have a good-sized crowd."

"And Doris," Aunt DeeDee added. "Miss 1962 herself."

That's right. Mina's grandmother would be there as well. I thought of the cranky eighty-something-year-old with renewed affection, and the investigator side in me wondered what insights she might be able to add. "What kind of roles has Doris held at the pageant since she won?"

"Most recently, a judge. She did that for a couple of decades or so," Aunt DeeDee said. "Back when I competed in the nineties, she was a liaison, reaching out to the contestants in the weeks running up to the pageant to give advice. Afterward, she would act as a mentor to the winner. That's how I originally got to know her."

"Did she know Brett?"

"I would think so. Though she lives in Richmond, she was in Aubergine every summer, and we aren't exactly a burgeoning metropolis." Aunt DeeDee considered and then snapped a finger. "In fact, Brett worked the show a few times during his high school and college days. They'd have certainly run into each other then."

I tried to recall if I'd seen Brett at the pageant this past summer. Surely I would remember if he'd been in attendance, although my view of Brett until this weekend had been the less of him, the better.

Aunt DeeDee must've read my mind. "He wasn't here this year, but I'm sure I've seen him in the audience at other pageants. He liked to come home and show off his accomplishments, talk about whatever new thing he was planning. None of them were really successful until that dreadful song and the TV show."

"You mentioned the film crew. Are you going to record tonight?" Lacy asked me.

"We'll set up a camera in the corner. Just so we can catch any possible confession on film."

"From your mouth to God's ears." Aunt DeeDee lifted her eyes to the heavens. "I'm just ready for all this to be over.

Savilla and you two and The Rose have seen enough tragedy."

She wasn't wrong. I looked to Aunt DeeDee. "Are you joining us in the Vampire Room?"

"I'll watch from the wings, as they say. But, honestly, that space has always creeped me out."

"Because of the murals?" I recalled what Savilla had told me about her great-grandmother's décor choices.

"No, not that," Aunt DeeDee answered. "Though how anyone could think that a painting of a little boy being chased by a giant bat with fangs is a good idea for wall art is beyond me."

I was intrigued.

"No," Aunt DeeDee continued, "it's the true story that disturbs me. Years ago, when Mr. Finch was a kid, his father employed a butler who had terrible sleep issues." The mention of the butler reminded me of Savilla's story about how the butler had died here decades earlier. "Insomnia and sleepwalking. It grew so bad in fact that every night around two a.m., Frederick would awaken to hear the poor man climbing up and down the sub-basement stairs."

"But aren't all the family bedrooms on the third and fourth floors?" Lacy asked.

"That's what was so strange. Mr. Finch swore that he could hear the squeaking all the way from the bottom floor of the house to the top." Aunt DeeDee ran a hand along the wall of the family room, covered in simple blue paint. "I've heard strange sounds myself during pageant week. I think it's something to do with the construction."

Lacy and I caught one another's eye, the memory of that locked room with no exit still on both of our minds. The Rose had more mysteries and hidden spaces than I'd ever imagined.

"One night, sometime in the nineteen fifties, I can't quite remember the year, the butler was sleepwalking, and he fell headfirst down the stairs," Aunt DeeDee continued. "Mr. Finch heard the noise and ran down six flights of stairs to find the butler's body lying across the threshold of the Vampire Room. It looked like he'd somehow crawled there after breaking his neck."

"Or the room had pulled him inside," Lacy said in a mock-spooky voice, as she wiggled her fingers in the air.

"Child, no. The good Lord has a plan for those he calls home," Aunt DeeDee protested. "Still, some say that the butler's footsteps can still be heard tromping back and forth, up and down the stairs. Not that I put any credence in that kind of nonsense."

I shivered, despite the fact that I also refused to believe in such things.

"Your momma did some looking into our ancestry years ago and found out that the butler was our third cousin twice removed."

That made me stop.

"We're related to someone who worked at The Rose?" The idea of coming from a lineage on both sides of The Rose's wealth distribution wasn't one I'd considered.

Aunt DeeDee studied me, knowing that I was reckoning with my past in all sorts of ways this weekend.

I could suddenly see a family tree branching in two very different directions, one side providing the green canopy of shade for people to bask in and the other winding toward the forest floor, weighed down by heavy rains.

I now had to navigate both sides.

THIRTY-ONE

It was almost 10:30 p.m. when Savilla, Jemma, Lacy, and I began to descend into the bowels of the Rose Palace.

We reached the basement first. It seemed nearly identical to the main floor in terms of upgrades and upholstery, but when we came to the sub-basement, everything changed.

I wouldn't have known that I was still inside The Rose if I hadn't just come from the opulence above. It wasn't that there was a dirt floor under our feet, but there was a dankness in the air and a feeling, if it can be called that, of enclosure.

I glided a hand along the wall, imagining the butler distantly related to me who'd fallen to his death at the bottom of these stairs.

"I loved playing down here as a kid with Nanny Kate," Savilla said.

"What did the two of you do?" I asked, trying to distract myself from the shadows our figures created as we walked past rooms without doors, most of them filled with boxes.

"We played all sorts of games: hide and seek, tag, Mother May I? But my favorite was pretend," Savilla said. "Nanny Kate and I would stand in a doorway along this hall and take turns deciding what scene we would act out as soon as we stepped across the threshold. She always wanted me to play classroom or archeologist so she could turn it into a learning opportunity, but my favorite was funeral."

"Funeral?" Jemma was appalled. "How old were you?"

"Six? Seven?" Savilla shrugged. "Nanny Kate never let me play the corpse."

What a strange childhood Savilla had led. Morbid games in the maze of her multimillion-dollar estate. Even stranger that this could've been me.

"Here we are," Savilla said. We stood in front of a threshold that actually did have a door, a very sturdy red one from the looks of it.

I knocked softly, and the wood sounded thick and sturdy.

"Completely soundproof," Savilla told us.

"That means that if we get stuck inside, no one will hear us scream," Jemma added, obviously joking to mask her own discomfort.

Savilla opened the door, flipped a panel of knobs that served as the light switches, and stood back. The door creaked on its hinges.

I glanced at Lacy and Jemma to see which of them wanted to go first, but neither volunteered. Hefting the box's weight from one arm to the other, I put a toe across. I could do this. I had to do this. For Lacy, for Charlie, for me.

Just before we came down here, I'd texted Charlie to meet me in our room. Thankfully, Deputy Wright had been otherwise occupied with looking over the footage the film crew had captured to see if we'd missed anything.

He'd listened with a neutral expression as I'd detailed the séance plan, only interrupting me once to ask a question about the order of events.

"You'll call Brett's spirit and then..."

"Go into a trance," I'd finished, knowing how outrageous the idea sounded. "But, you know, a pretend one."

"Got it," he'd said, one eye narrowed. "A fake trance."

I'd read his meaning, and my heart had fallen. "Look, I know it sounds ridiculous. And I realize that you may not have a ticking clock on needing to find out Brett's killer, but if we don't come up with Brett's email password before midnight, then Lacy—"

He'd put a hand on the top of mine. "I do have a ticking clock, and I'm not criticizing your plan. I just want to make sure you're safe. Every minute that we haven't identified the killer, it becomes more unlikely that we'll ever do so because the clues start to vanish the more time that passes. I don't want a case to go cold on my watch." Charlie's hand had moved up to my shoulder and caressed the back of my neck. "But you're more important to me than..." He'd stared into my eyes and blinked several times, trying to find the right words, "... than anything."

Than anything? That had sounded strikingly similar to the three words we had yet to say to one another.

Now, as I made my way to the center of the Vampire Room, I turned to examine the space from various angles.

The glow of the electric lights was shaded by heavy glass casings with ridges, throwing the light in every direction. My eyes roamed from fresco to fresco. Not only was there the little boy being chased by a bat with glinting teeth, but there was also a cluster of vampires in one corner and a coven of witches in another. However, in between these more terrifying murals, there was a pastoral scene of village landscapes and sheep grazing near a shepherd with a crook in hand.

Aside from a few chairs scattered around from a bygone event, there was only one other item in the room: a one-foot statue of a gargoyle nestled in an alcove cut into the wall. That could be a perfect place to hide the camera.

I walked over, inspecting the grimace on the stone figure,

one that made the creature appear half-bored, half-irritated. It was intimidating but not quite evil, with wings outstretched and hands palm-up, as if extending an offering.

There was something about the creature that was off. I bent down so I could better examine it and saw that it was covered in a fine layer of dust everywhere except... the hands. Oddly, those empty palms were dust-free. My eyes trailed down the statue and I spotted something tucked underneath the base. It was black velvet, the kind that was in the display cases in the Color Gallery, and the fabric had an indentation just about the size of a child's palm. I picked it up, fingering the soft surface before placing it in the hands of the creature.

"What's that?" Savilla asked, approaching me from behind.

"I'm not sure," I said vaguely. "Maybe nothing."

Except it felt like something, like a missing piece was falling into place, though I couldn't yet verbalize what I meant.

"Oh God. Is that...?" Savilla toed at something on the ground as she backed away, distracting me from the gargoyle.

I jumped, thinking that she was pointing out a dead mouse, but no... it was a tuft of fuzz. I bent down and plucked out the two-inch-long furry object.

"What is that?" Savilla asked, cringing as I picked it up.

"Fur, but it's not real." I lifted it toward Savilla to touch, but she pulled her hands away.

"How do you know?"

"I guess the same way that you and Lacy can tell a Chanel pump from a knock-off."

That logic she could follow.

"It's definitely not from an animal," I clarified, before studying the area around the statue for more. "But why would it be here?"

"Maybe it's from a jacket," Savilla suggested. "Oooo... or, like, a synthetic mink coat."

I thought of the fuzzy gray jacket Presley had been wearing

on the first night. Had Presley come down here, found the diamond in the paws of the gargoyle statue, and taken it, planning to kill Brett? But how would she know about the Vampire Room, much less that a diamond might be hidden here?

"When's the last time the Vampire Room was actually used?" I asked Savilla.

"Not in my lifetime, as far as I know."

I glanced one more time at the gargoyle holding the velvet and tucked the tuft of fake fur into my pocket to show Charlie. I was getting closer.

THIRTY-TWO

It was almost eleven o'clock when everyone arrived, including Miss 1962, who'd somehow made it down the stairs with a walker, loudly proclaiming that she'd heard we were attempting to contact the dead. I couldn't help but smile at her, an older version of Mina who kept a hand on her gram's shoulder as they took their seat. I lingered on the pair of them, marveling at how alike they appeared despite their fifty-year age difference.

Then, Lacy caught my eye and lifted a finger to remind me we needed to proceed as soon as possible. I reminded myself that Charlie was at the door, ready for whatever might happen in the next few minutes, and I took a deep breath. I'd taken one semester of theater in high school. I could do this.

I rang a bell, stretched out a hand to settle the room, and spoke. "Let's begin, everyone."

I closed my eyes and placed both hands on the table where we'd put all the things that I could pretend to use to contact Brett Brinkley. There was a notebook and pen, a Monopoly board, the UNO deck, and one of Brett's watches that Presley had lent us. Even with the oddities in front of me, no one laughed or said a word. Maybe it was curiosity or maybe it was actual belief, but all fidgeting stopped.

Even though I hadn't personally felt much grief over Brett's death, a somber mood overcame me too. Not that I'd wanted him to die, certainly, and not that I would wish the strange fate of being choked—and, worse, internally torn up and effectively strangled—by a diamond on the worst person I knew, but up until that moment I hadn't felt much in the way of Brett's absence.

I realized, however, that Presley must have felt something as I heard faint crying coming from the direction of where she was seated a few yards away.

I touched the watch and began to speak. "Brett, we are here to listen." I paused, uncertain but trying not to show it. "We want to know you are with us."

Lacy tugged at a thread connected to a card in the center of the UNO deck, and half of the stack tumbled onto its side.

Gasps sounded and a mumbled, *No.*

Okay. This was real to some of them, which meant our plan might actually work.

I picked up the watch and raised it above my head, letting my eyes flutter in a way that I'd seen in movies. "He's here," I said softly. "He's with us now."

Presley, her voice shaky but free of tears, asked, "Are you okay, Brett?"

I stole a glance at her and noticed that she wasn't the one who'd been crying. It was the person next to her. Mina Davis. I supposed that made sense. The two of us had, after all, tried and failed to save his life. When Mina caught my eyes on her, she looked down, and Miss 1962 placed a wrinkled hand on her granddaughter's.

I cleared my throat and did my best Brett impersonation, which had to be all kinds of disrespectful to the dead. But this was where we were at.

"I'm good," I practically growled in an effort to mimic Brett's deeper register.

"Where are you?" Valerie asked, obviously expecting me to say something that fit with her worldview. Heaven or hell, it probably wouldn't matter to her. Because of Aunt DeeDee I was ready for this one.

"At The Rose," I said, in a vague enough way that no one could contradict the statement.

Valerie moved as if to stand, but Will whispered something to her and kept her from leaving.

"Brett," Presley said, as she stood. I could feel the shift in her tone as she spat out the next words: "Don't you have anything to say to me? To Lacy?"

I scrambled for the best response. I needed to say something that sounded like her boyfriend but that would also invite her to confess to killing him—if that was indeed what had happened.

I tried to channel my best narcissist, keeping my eyes closed. "I know you both miss me. Terribly."

When there was no response, I opened my eyes and looked directly at Presley, who had a sad smile on her face. Then, she began to laugh. Or, perhaps *cackle* might be a better word. She pointed a finger at me as the conduit for Brett. "You have no idea how glad I am that you're gone, that I don't have to keep up this silly charade anymore."

My eyes widened, and I wasn't sure I could keep up the Brett pretense in the face of her obvious disdain.

"You trapped me," Presley continued. "You threatened me. You said that if I left you, I would lose everything I'd built. It's the only reason I stayed with you for as long as I did when I have someone who"—Presley looked at Joe, her anger melting—"someone who actually loves me." She sniffled and let Joe pull her close, burying her head in his shoulder before seeming to remember something. "Brett Brinkley, I hope you pay for everything terrible you've done."

Her last words took me by surprise. I'd only glimpsed one layer of Presley, the supposedly grieving girlfriend, and I was now seeing that she, like the rest of us, contained multitudes. She could love and hate Brett at the same time, though it seemed like hate was currently winning.

"Is your killer in the room?" Joe asked, likely wanting to take the attention off Presley. Though he obviously wanted to protect her, to keep her from looking even more guilty, I appreciated that he was getting right to the point.

I took a chance, opened both eyes super wide, and pointed at the *Go to Jail* spot on the Monopoly board. I figured that was a yes if there was one.

Though I was staring straight ahead, I could tell in my periphery that the attendees were looking at one another. Even Lee Frank seemed to be concerned as he squirmed in his seat.

"Tell us who did it," Aunt DeeDee called from the back, just as we'd planned.

"I need to speak with the one who got away," I growled. After all my investigating, I was more and more certain that this would point me in the right direction.

"Is it me?" Lacy asked, right on time.

I took a few beats as if Brett might be considering, and then felt the table for paper and pen, scribbling *NOT YOU* in large letters.

A gasp, or perhaps a hiccup this time.

"Is it me?" Presley asked, briefly lifting her head from Joe's shoulder.

I hadn't expected a question like that from her. Of course she wasn't the one to get away. She'd met him on the show *after* he'd written the song, right? I took a guess and scribbled a giant *NO* on the opposite page.

I let my eyes flit back again in a way that I hoped was frightening enough to a potential lover or killer—or both.

"Is it me?" asked a faint voice, that younger mirror of Miss

1962's, that faceless voice that had traveled into households across America as *Small Town, Big Romance* aired each week in the fall of 2023.

Mina Davis's words left her mouth, swirling and rising above me.

My eyes flew open to see Mina silhouetted by the candles, and that's when I recognized the woman from the video, hidden in shadows. I suddenly knew why that form and figure were so familiar. It wasn't just her voice I knew. It was all of her. She was the woman in the music video, the one that the Rose Diamond may have once been intended for.

Mina Davis was the one that got away.

I took a chance, sensing that a revelation was on the horizon.

YES, I scribbled, staring straight at her.

"I miss you, Brett," Mina mumbled, as she cried into her hands. "I always will."

Her words contained longing and wistfulness and... love? Whatever the mixture, Mina Davis and Brett Brinkley apparently went way, way back.

THIRTY-THREE

Miss 1962 struggled to stand, leaning on her walker and her granddaughter to get back on her feet.

"It's about time you told them," Miss 1962 said to Mina, quietly enough that the hidden camera and those in the back of the room might not be able to catch it. I certainly could hear her, and I was relieved to be in a spot to bear witness to the conversation between them. "You shouldn't be ashamed for loving Brett, even if he was... difficult at times."

Hearing from this older woman made my mind flash to what Presley had said about her own great-grandmother, about her *bisnonna* seeing Brett with another woman. Had that other woman been Mina Davis? It made sense, especially if she'd travelled to Italy with them as part of the film crew. A missing link melded into place.

Mina Davis had worked in L.A. for years. She'd been on—or cut from—a variety of shows before getting behind the camera. She'd been the interviewer on a popular show, which Brett had "won." According to tabloids, even after Presley and Brett had decided to continue their relationship, Brett had kept his place on the West Coast, living separately from Presley most of the time.

Had Brett had a relationship with someone else on the side? Could that someone have been... Mina Davis? Mina had told me that she'd gotten the gig on this new show for her and Lee. Had she asked Brett directly to let her work with him on this new reality show about Brett and Presley? To travel with him to shoot footage?

And if so, what might peering through the lens of a camera at the man you loved for weeks at a time do to someone, especially if that man was acting like he was head over heels for another woman? A woman like Presley Lombardi.

Silence descended on the room as we waited for Mina to speak.

When she didn't, I looked at her directly. "You loved Brett, didn't you?"

Mina, one hand on her gram, looked around at those of us assembled and let loose a heavy sigh. The shadows from the candlelight flickered across her face, and her eyes flitted to the floor for a few seconds before she began.

"I grew up hearing about Gram's pageant adventures each summer, so I already felt like I knew this place. After I graduated college and moved out of my mom's house to get a place of my own, I was struggling to make any headway with auditions, so I came home to visit Gram for a couple of weeks in the summer of 2021. Brett just happened to attend that same pageant." She took her grandmother's hand, and I could see the love pass between them. "Remember, I even wore one of your vintage gowns?"

Miss 1962 patted her, obviously remembering. "The robin-egg-blue taffeta."

"Brett happened to be sitting in the audience next to me. We just..." Mina's eyes welled. "We just clicked."

I thought of the song lyrics, Brett singing about his girl with the frills and lace, his rose, full of love and grace. I'd thought at first that he must have meant Lacy, but that wasn't it. He'd been referring to Mina. At the pageant, in her gram's dress.

"Brett called me his..."

"... his dark lady, his rose," I finished for her.

Mina blinked at me, obviously wondering how I knew those details. "Right. From Shakespeare. Brett wasn't a scholar, but we did perform in a community theater production of *Taming* and we met here, at The Rose."

I vaguely remembered that play from my sophomore year of high school English. The lead was basically an abusive asshole who tamed a woman into adoring him. That sounded about right.

"So the two of you were together?"

Mina nodded. "Officially, for two years—and, sort of, ever since."

Their relationship must not have been a secret... at first. It must've been later that Brett tried to make it look like they'd never been together. But why?

Every eye was on Mina. Even those in the background and those who'd been waiting at the door seemed to lean in to hear that voice that now spoke with the same kind of authority as when she'd been the interviewer on *Small Town, Big Romance*.

"Our relationship was... challenging. We'd break up and then get back together the next day, but I always loved him. Even when we were fighting." A faint smile. "Brett wrote the song for me after one of our biggest fights. He told me he didn't want me to be the one that got away, that he didn't want to lose me."

Mina sniffled. "I loved the song, thought it was the best kind of twist on a traditional love song. It fit our relationship perfectly. I was the one who told him he should record it, so we scraped together all of our savings and he hired musicians and a studio for a full day." Mina put the back of her hand to her nose.

"No one wanted the song at first, but Brett told me he knew a way to get it out there. He spoke to Mr. Finch, who was excited to produce it himself."

I noticed Savilla's face fall. Both of us knew that her father hadn't been excited about being blackmailed by Brett, but we didn't interrupt Mina.

"We had no idea what a hit it would be. Brett got a manager who said that we should keep our relationship a secret, that fans love a good story. We told friends we'd broken up, and we took everything that made us look like a couple off social media. Even in that dumb music video, he made sure that no one could see my face, could see who I really was. He said it was romantic, that only he would know the identity of the one who got away, the one he still had a hold on."

I tried not to show how disturbed I was by that last phrase.

Mina met my eyes. "That summer while we were at The Rose, filming the video right before the pageant, I got to hold the diamond that he—and I—would someday inherit. He said that it would be for me, my engagement ring. I begged him to just give up the charade and marry me then, but he said that he had a plan. Mr. Finch was in his seventies, and when he died, he could get the ring without the tax burdens of being given it now. To prove he was committed to me, he even asked Mr. Finch to write into his will that the diamond would need to be used for Brett's engagement."

That matched what Savilla had told me in his office, and though it seemed strange, I supposed Brett was nothing if not practical in his schemes.

"Brett had said all along that we were playing a long game. I know it sounds silly, but I got swept up in it," Mina continued. "I tried to see it as exciting too, like we were sneaking around and we were the only two who knew we were together." Mina's eyes grew distant for a brief moment. "He would go do a gig and talk about the one who got away and then come back and sleep in bed with me that night."

Mina's face clouded. "He applied to *Small Town, Big Romance* without telling me, though. He thought it would make me happy, God knows why. He said I could get a job on-site and we could sneak away when the cameras weren't rolling. But it was awful watching him with different women each night before he finally ended up with..." Mina pointed at Presley, hissing the final word. "*Her*."

Mina's nostalgia had quickly turned to frustration. "In the end I went along with it, just like I did with anything Brett wanted. The director saw that I had some experience but told me my face was 'better off camera.' It was humiliating." Mina scoffed. "We officially broke up the night before he asked Presley to be his girlfriend, though no one else even knew we were together. If anyone saw us, they probably thought Brett was asking me to grab him a coffee." Mina was crying now, her anger and longing on full display. "That night I told him I was tired of sneaking around and that I couldn't bear to see what came next."

Presley reached toward Mina, who shook off her touch. "I had no idea," Presley said softly.

Mina blinked at Presley as if she couldn't quite register the words, and then she finally let out a long breath. "I know. After Mr. Finch died, I told him it was time to come back to me, but Brett decided that he needed to get ahead just a bit more with you. He swore that it wasn't true love, that after he got the press he needed, he would leave you and come back to me, but then he released that tape of the two of you and..."

Presley put a hand to her stomach and looked as if she might be sick. She turned to Joe. "I knew it was Brett. He told me that some hacker had broken into his computer, but when I asked why he had the video in the first place, he couldn't give me a straight answer."

"Brett had recordings of him with every woman he'd ever slept with." Mina crinkled her nose in disgust. "It was, like, his thing. I told him to delete them, but he wouldn't, and he convinced me..." She swallowed as if she couldn't believe what she was about to say. "Somehow, God knows how, he convinced me that it was funny. Until he finally broke up with me. When I threatened to go to the network, to tell them that Brett was a fraud, he told me that he would send a video of us to *TMZ* and say that *I'd* blackmailed *him* with it. He would claim that I'd told him I wanted to break up him and Presley."

Mina's face fell and she hung her head, obviously ashamed at how far she'd let her relationship with Brett descend. "It was so... twisted."

Twisted was the right word.

Mina lifted her head and stared into her grandmother's eyes, taking a deep breath that shuddered her body. "That last night on set, that's the first time I wanted to kill him."

"But you didn't," Miss 1962 said, seeming frailer than ever. It was as if she were willing the statement to be true.

Out of the corner of my eye, I caught Charlie take a step forward. He hesitated though, listening for more.

"No. Or, at least, not yet. And then when it happened, I... I didn't mean to." Mina's voice was growing louder as she finally told the whole truth. "I didn't know how or when I would do it, but I took this job with every intention of getting Brett to come back to me or..." Mina glanced at the far wall with the gargoyle, where I'd spotted the tuft of fake fur.

"We talked in the parking lot right before the reunion party last night. He said that he'd spoken to Lacy and wanted me to get footage of Presley bursting in on the two of them together. I told him that he could go to hell, but he reminded me that he and Presley were all for show. Told me that he wanted to be with me again. After all of this was over. He reminded me about the diamond from the music video, the one I'd held, the one he'd promised me."

"She's right." Miss 1962 spoke as if I was the confessor in the room. "Mina told me about the diamond and the engagement and how much she loved him, so... I hid the diamond. Two years ago, when I was judging the pageant."

I studied Mina's grandmother, confused. "You did what?"

"I convinced Glenda to show me some of her favorite pieces of family jewelry during the 2023 show—she always loved gloating—and while she was studying a ruby necklace, I swiped the diamond. It was almost too easy." Miss 1962 smiled softly at the memory, as if it'd been nothing more than taking a pack of gum from the grocery store.

"But why would you...?" I couldn't even finish the sentence, so confused was I by Miss 1962's admission.

This time she addressed Mina rather than me, clenching her hand around her granddaughter's as she tried to convey the urgency behind her actions. "That diamond had been promised to you, and I didn't want either of those stupid men—Frederick Finch or Brett Brinkley—to change their minds at the last minute. But if they did, Mina and I would be the only ones who knew where it really was. Besides, it wasn't really stealing."

I raised my eyebrows and Miss 1962 caught my look of disbelief.

"It wasn't," she protested. "I didn't even remove it from the palace. I put it down here. In the gargoyle's hands."

Every eye peered past me to the end of the room where the gargoyle was mostly cloaked in darkness. Without turning around, I could envision the gargoyle's unfurled wings, the empty hands, and the velvet with the indentation the size of a child's palm. The size of the Rose Diamond.

"Brett didn't know the Rose Diamond was missing, but Gram had told me where she'd hidden it. No one ever came down here," Mina admitted. "So, last night I came down here to see if for myself. I lugged my gear with me so I could say I was filming if anyone saw me. After that conversation with Brett in the parking lot, I don't know what came over me, but I knew I had to do something. So, I took it."

Realization spread like a fine mist hanging over the room, and that's when I noticed an object sticking out of one of Mina's bags of gear at her feet. It was a boom mic covered in tufts of fake fur, the same one that she must've been carrying when she came down here and swiped the diamond.

"When I got upstairs to the ballroom and everyone arrived, I pretended to be checking the lighting on Brett when I dropped the diamond in his drink, but I swear, I didn't think..." Mina hung her head and began to cry. "Brett had put me through so much." Her voice hardened. "I thought if he swallowed the stone, the diamond intended for me, he'd understand what it felt like to choke on his own promises. I didn't mean to..." Mina's voice broke. "I just wanted him to hurt like I was hurting."

I took in that last sentence with the heaviness that she meant to convey. Perhaps she hadn't meant for it to happen, but Brett had died.

And Mina Davis was responsible.

The same wave of realization seemed to wash over Mina again as she began crying harder, hunching forward as grief wracked her body for the first time since her lover's death.

THIRTY-FOUR

After Mina had been taken away, I spotted Presley wearing a stricken expression. Joe wrapped his arms around her. Though clearly shaken, she let herself be held.

"It wasn't the curse," she said, pulling back to look into Joe's eyes.

"I told you." Compassion and something else—love, most likely—played about Joe's lips. "You didn't need to stay with him."

"Not for the publicity, not for the money, not for any other reason," Presley said, almost as if she were reminding herself of this truth. She stared into Joe's eyes, saying loudly enough for the room to hear, "*Our* big romance is better than anything I could've ever had with Brett."

Our Big Romance. Those had been the words written on the CD case. Joe had been telling the truth. It had been reminders of Joe and Presley's romance that he'd been carrying around in his backpack, and it must've been her handwriting in his old yearbook. They'd been planning to reveal their relationship this weekend, but they hadn't been planning a murder.

"God rest his bastard soul," Joe said softly.

The two people at the top of my list hadn't been the murderers, and though I'd eventually helped bring the real culprit out of the woodwork, I hadn't discovered the killer as quickly as I would've liked. I'd even felt sympathy for Mina and the impending loss of her grandmother, which was still a reality she would have to face. Perhaps Mina could even use that as part of her defense. Not only had the murder not been premeditated, it had been a decision made during a time of psychological stress. I didn't want Mina to go free, but I wasn't sure that a life in prison was warranted in her case. Thankfully, I wasn't the decider of such things. Now that I'd brought her crime to light, my job was done.

After Charlie had cuffed Mina and sent her with the deputy ahead of him, he came back to me in the Vampire Room, where I sat behind the table, Brett's watch in front of me and Aunt DeeDee's hand on my shoulder as we surveyed the tools of our fake séance – that had actually worked.

"I'm proud of you, baby girl," my aunt said, as she planted a kiss on the top of my head. "Though I hate that it had to be Doris's granddaughter."

"Me too," I told her, meaning it. "They'll take into account that it was an accident, right?"

"The Lord only knows."

"Do you think Doris—Miss 1962—will be all right?"

"She's a tough cookie, might do something to get herself jailed just to be with her granddaughter, but either way, Doris isn't long for this world, and she knows it. But I'm sure she'll do everything she can for Mina until the end."

"I guess that's to be expected."

Aunt DeeDee nodded slowly, studying me. "You are a wonder. I see more and more of your momma in you every day."

This meant more to me than anything else she could say.

"Her way of seeing the world, her way of processing what

life threw at her. The two of you would've made a great investigative team."

I put a hand over hers. "You and I aren't too bad either."

"You did good, Dakota," Charlie said, interrupting us. He gave me an official nod as Aunt DeeDee left the two of us alone. "I'll be at the station for a while, getting Mina booked in."

"I figured."

"What about breakfast tomorrow?" he asked. "Before you head back to school?"

"Are you buying?"

Charlie grinned. "Happily."

"Then, maybe we could go back to your place for a few minutes?" I asked, one eyebrow raised.

"Kitty would love to say goodbye before you leave."

"Goodbye for now," I said firmly. "I'm coming back, one way or another."

"Oh yeah?" Charlie's eyes lightened at the news.

"Someone once told me that I shouldn't make decisions to try to impress people who don't give a fig about me. I've still got to think through what that means, but either way, Aubergine is home."

"Sounds like a wise someone," he mused.

"Well, it was my mother, so, yeah," I said with a slight chuckle.

Charlie leaned forward and gave me a kiss on my forehead and then the tip of my nose. He wanted more, I could feel it, but he showed self-restraint.

"Till the morning," he breathed, before making his way out of the house.

Lacy and Anton had rushed to the door as soon as Mina was in handcuffs, likely trying to find a phone signal. With only a few minutes until midnight, Lacy said the password aloud—a series of numbers, symbols, and letters—as she typed frantically.

"One-four-three-four-seven-hashtag-minadavis,"   Lacy

mumbled. She paused for a second, and then her eyes grew wide in horror. "It didn't work."

"What?" I almost shouted. "It has to work."

I went to her side and took the phone from Lacy. Under the login information, it now said, *One attempt remaining*.

Lacy let out a string of curses. Three minutes to go.

I took a steadying breath to calm my rapid pulse and ran back through the hint that I'd memorized: *diamond numbers, hashtag, lowercase, name of the one that got away*.

It took me almost a full minute of scanning the clues we'd collected, but then I knew what was wrong. "What was the serial number again?"

Lacy repeated the numbers she'd typed in.

"But it had a period in it, right?" Before she could respond, and with less than two minutes remaining, I dared the final attempt: *1434.7#minadavis*.

The account opened, I went directly to send and deleted the email that was about to make its destructive way into the world at large.

"It's done. We stopped it," I said, letting out a heavy sigh as Lacy fell back into her chair, relief washing across her features. She'd been able to undo the terrible work of her first love, Brett Brinkley.

"It's deleted?" Anton asked.

"The email, the images, the video," Lacy listed. "None of it will go out."

Lacy threw her arms around her boyfriend before sinking into his shoulder in a way that melded the two of them together. She was crying, but this time, they were tears of relief. She waved me over and pulled me into their embrace.

"Thank God for both of you," Lacy said, as she squeezed both of us tighter. "I don't know what I would do without..." She continued crying a few more beats before releasing us and sniffling away the tears.

That's when she looked from me to Anton and then back to me. I could almost read her mind, and though this seemed like neither the time nor place, when Lacy wanted something, she wouldn't be stopped.

"Anton," Lacy said, with all the love in her voice, "you're my partner and the love of my life. We've been dating for two years, but I could spend two hundred with you."

Anton smiled at her, but I could tell he had no idea what was coming next. He hadn't yet learned to read Lacy's mind like I could. Maybe I was clairvoyant after all.

To his surprise, but not to mine, Lacy threw both arms around his neck. Then, she leaned back and gazed into his eyes as she asked him, "Anton, will you marry me?"

Anton's face registered his shock. He released her and stepped backward, though his eyes lingered on hers. His body created long shadows in the candlelit room as he turned around and made his way to the door of the Vampire Room, looking back over his shoulder one more time before walking away.

Wide-eyed, Lacy got back to her feet. I took her hand.

"Was it too soon?" Lacy asked, her eyes roaming from the door he'd exited and back to me, trying to understand why he'd run away. "Oh God. I'm too impulsive. I know this, and yet I keep trying to—"

I pulled her close, quieting her like a mother with a child. As I comforted her, the other séance attendees began to leave or mingle, most of them talking about how crazy the night had been.

Anton was gone for several minutes before he returned, breathless and lit up with nerves. In his hand was a ring, and everyone stopped what they were doing and watched him as he fell to one knee in front of Lacy, who had turned to watch him with tears in her eyes. Instead of asking the question though, he gave an answer to the question she'd asked him minutes earlier.

"I thought you'd never ask," Anton said, as he slipped the ring on her finger and pulled Lacy in for a kiss.

EPILOGUE

It was Sunday afternoon. I would be heading back to New York that evening, and I was still debating what to tell my professor.

Aunt DeeDee was making a full spread at Momma's house for our late lunch. Anton and Lacy were set to arrive, making it a sort of celebratory occasion, and Savilla would join us too. Charlie would get here after he checked in one more time at the station. Fried chicken, black-eyed peas, fried green tomatoes, and mashed potatoes. "With margarine to keep our figures intact," Aunt DeeDee claimed, even as she added a thick slab of bacon to the peas.

"What in tarnation are you planning to do with your inheritance?" Aunt DeeDee asked now, for perhaps the fifth time. It had become a kind of singsong statement rather than a question as she cooked.

"Who knows how much I'll actually end up with." I'd already explained Savilla's financial woes, but we had found the Rose Diamond. Presumably that jewel could be sold to remedy some of the Finch money troubles.

Aunt DeeDee waved away my thinking. "When it's all said

and done, however much you're handed, it'll be more than the Greens have ever seen before."

I shook my head in disbelief once again. I no longer really needed the money, after having won the pageant in the summer. I was almost finished paying for school, so what then? Momma had taught me to live frugally, to enjoy the simpler things.

"I'll give some away," I mused. "Probably to that animal sanctuary I've always loved."

Aunt DeeDee nodded, all too familiar with my heart for creatures in need.

"I suppose you could open your own practice here in Aubergine," she suggested, raising one eyebrow as if she wasn't dying for me to move back.

"I suppose I could." I gave her a faint smile, playing it cool.

"The options are endless now." Aunt DeeDee took a sip of iced tea. "And the timing of this inheritance, I'd say, is almost providential, like the good Lord wants you to set up shop right where you belong."

It was the last word that pulled on my heartstrings, because it pointed right at the issue that meant most to me: with Momma gone and with my future before me, where exactly did I belong?

After Lacy arrived to cheers and hugs and had shown off her ring, Anton explained how he'd bought it a year before and had just been waiting for the right time. Then, Aunt DeeDee spilled the news about the will reading and my new sister, detailing everything that I hadn't had the chance to tell Lacy that weekend. Everything from Mr. Froble's stoicism to Savilla's tight embrace to Glenda's fury to my inheritance. Aunt DeeDee was in her element, so I let her have the moment.

"Well, shit," Lacy said, as she sank into a chair. She blinked several times before her eyes landed on me. "So, you're BFFs with Savilla? And you're, what? Rich?"

"First of all, you'll never be replaced, and second, it's just money," I said, shrugging off the word. It wasn't that I wasn't glad to have the money, however much it ended up being, but I wasn't a *rich* kind of person. More of a "mostly doing okay, but barely scraping by at the end of the month" kind of person. Wealth didn't settle comfortably across my shoulders, and I hadn't told anyone that I'd already briefly considered giving it all to Savilla and walking away. But no, I could do good with the money, surely, and it gave me options I hadn't considered: actually having the means to open my own practice here, for one.

"For real, though," Lacy said, setting her chin in her hand that rested on Momma's worn-out dining room table. "Let's plan that trip we've always talked about."

"To the Galapagos?" I asked, perking up.

"To Paris," Lacy corrected. "I am not going to spend my vacation with turtles."

I tried to recall when we'd ever talked about visiting Paris and came up short.

"Remember? On graduation night, you said that we should go to Paris and see some kind of bird?"

I smiled, understanding dawning. "That was Paris, Texas. And it was a cattle egret."

"Aw, disappointing." Lacy poked out her bottom lip before recovering. "Oh, well, we can do both now, maybe even stay with Anton's family."

"They're gonna love you," Anton said, taking a spoonful of banana pudding that Aunt DeeDee had asked him to sample.

"We can do whatever we want," I said with a smile, actually loving that Lacy was inviting herself into my newfound wealth. It was as if she knew I didn't want to do this alone.

"All that money does is give you options, sweetheart," Aunt DeeDee said. "Other than that, nothing's changed."

"Except I have a sister."

"Except for that," Aunt DeeDee admitted, as the front door flung open and the very person let herself inside.

"Are you talking about me?" Savilla asked, hurrying in with a big grin and handing over what was likely the most expensive bottle of wine I'd ever set eyes on.

"Were your ears burning?" Aunt DeeDee asked playfully, as she took the bottle from Savilla's hands.

She didn't answer, but instead grabbed me in one arm and Aunt DeeDee in the other, pulling us close as she squealed, "I can't believe that I finally get to be a Green."

Aunt DeeDee and I wriggled from her tight grip and caught one another's eye.

I don't think that's how it works, I wanted to say, but Aunt DeeDee swatted playfully at me and kissed Savilla on the cheek too.

"Welcome to the family, darling."

A LETTER FROM THE AUTHOR

Thank you for reading *An Heiress's Guide to Death and Diamonds*. I loved diving back into Dakota Green's world at the Rose Palace. If you'd like to hear about my new and upcoming releases, you can sign up for my author newsletter.

www.stormpublishing.co/kristen-bird

If you enjoyed *An Heiress's Guide to Death and Diamonds* and could spare a moment to leave a review, that would be hugely appreciated. Even a short review can make all the difference in encouraging a reader to discover my books for the first time. Thank you so much!

Writing about a ten-year-high-school reunion for the class of 2015 was a fun way to return to the fictional small town of Aubergine, Virginia. Though my high school graduation was more than twenty-five years ago now, I still see how those early friendships formed me. Transporting my characters into this moment made for new relationship dynamics to explore.

The Rose Palace continues to give my cast of characters nooks to explore, and it was entertaining to hint at the spookier aspects of the history of the estate. As a child I travelled with my family to the Winchester Mystery House in San Jose, California, and the memory of standing in a locked room with no exit still gives me the shivers. Perhaps more secret rooms are in Dakota's future.

Finally, female friendships are at the heart of all my stories, and I loved strengthening the bond between Dakota, Lacy, and Savilla. Finding Aunt DeeDee's fearless words of wisdom continued to be a delight, and I so enjoyed guiding Dakota and Charlie through their romance. I'm excited to see what comes next for the two of them—and the rest of the citizens of Aubergine.

Happy reading,

Kristen

www.kristenbird.com

 facebook.com/kristen.bird.writes

 x.com/kbirdwrites

 instagram.com/kristenbirdwrites

www.ingramcontent.com/pod-product-compliance
Lightning Source LLC
Chambersburg PA
CBHW010434170726
48283CB00011B/3205